LOST IN THE RIGHT DIRECTION

A PACIFIC NORTHWEST LOVE STORY
BOOK ONE

MEGAN CARR

LOST IN THE RIGHT DIRECTION

LOST in the RIGHT DIRECTION

Cover design by Renee Barratt, www.thecovercounts.com.

ISBN-13: 978-1-7320694-0-4

Visit:

Megancarrauthor.com

To Brian — my true north.

CHAPTER ONE

MIKE - MAY OF LAST YEAR

WHEN I open my eyes, I'm immediately disoriented. It takes a minute for me to remember where I am — on the couch, in my house in San Diego. I close my eyes and smirk. It is *my* house. Georgia likes to think she owns half of all this but she doesn't. Nothing's in her name, and she's fucking crazy if she thinks that's ever going to change.

I open my eyes again and wince; my ears ringing in pain. The sliver of light coming through the mini blinds feels like a vice grip across my forehead. The taste of stale alcohol fills my mouth, and my teeth feel like they are rattling out of my jaw. I bring my hand up to my face to block the light and try to stop the jackhammer that's going off in my head. I'm already starting to shake. Shit, I need a drink.

"Georgia!" My body recoils against the couch as the sound of my voice bounces off my head and echoes through the house that I now realize is eerily quiet. I attempt to swallow; it feels like glass shards are slowly working their way down my throat. I take a deep breath through my nose, and try and calm the tremors I feel in my fingers. I'm going to need something strong — and quickly — to shake off this blackness that is threatening to overwhelm me.

"Goddammit, Georgia, I need a drink!"

Where is she? If I have to get off this couch, she is going to be sorry.

I lie still and listen for her. I can hear the muffled hum of vehicle engines in the neighborhood outside. What day is it? I try to think about what happened last night, but my mind is hardened cement; the act of recreating memories is causing me actual pain. I think we went out, right? Did we fight? God only knows what she made me do this time. How did I end up on this couch, and why is the thing so damn uncomfortable? More importantly, why isn't she answering me?

I turn my head to the side. Take the largest breath I can physically muster and holler.

"*Georgia!* Where in the *hell* are you?" I can feel vertigo begin to set in, and I force myself to be still. I hold my breath and listen. I hear nothing.

A small prick of panic rises in my chest, and I stamp it out immediately. She wouldn't dare leave me. It's not even possible. She wouldn't survive for one second. Georgia's a lot of things — *bitch* comes to mind right now — but she's no hotshot. She's no adventurer — hell, she can barely go to the store by herself. There's no way she'd ever have the guts to leave me, which is exactly why she'd better have a phenomenal explanation about where she is. The more I think about it, the more pissed I am. How dare she not think to be here when I wake up! She knows I just need a little help getting going again after a big night. After everything I give her, after everything I've provided over the last six years, this is the thanks I get? She'd better show her face in the next five minutes, or I swear...

"*Georgia!*" My head feels like it's going to break in half. My heart is racing now, and I can feel the beginning of a fever. This isn't good. I'm going to have to do some serious damage control before I can head to the station. No way I can show up for duty without a fix.

I rack my brain to visualize where the Vicodin is in the bathroom medicine cabinet while entertaining the idea of smashing my wife's head into that creaky little mirror. I hate it when she makes me feel so angry. No one else causes me to think this way. And I'm so good to her too: providing a home for her, a car to use whenever she wants, a credit card, a cell phone...Jesus, I don't even make her work. She doesn't understand all the sacrifices I make so we can have a good life here. All she does is complain about wanting to get out of the house; always asking if she can go to ridiculous places with her *friends*. I'm pretty sure she's got a boyfriend somewhere. That's probably where she is now. The thought of my beautiful wife in another man's arms is enough to fill me with rage. I will fucking kill them both!

I slowly lower one leg to the ground next to me and gingerly plant my foot on the floor. The vertigo slows, but my stomach is in revolt. A strong wave of nausea passes over me, and I shudder. Okay, c'mon now, Mike, this isn't as bad as it seems. You've been through a hell of a lot worse. Get ahold of yourself and get your ass up off this couch.

I brace my free arm behind me on the couch and slowly prop myself into a semi-seated position. My hand shields me from the light, as my face crumples from the pain in my head. *Kitchen*. I just need to make it to the kitchen. I have the vodka in the freezer and gin in the cupboard. The thought of getting relief from the booze steels my resolve. I sit up completely, take my hand away from my face and swing my other leg over onto the floor. The room swings severely to the left as I attempt to stand. I keep pushing upward, my arms outstretched to grab onto the chair that's a few steps across the room. I stumble forward and throw my body against the chair, clinging to it like a life preserver. My head throbs so hard it feels like my ears are going to bleed, but the only sound I can hear is my own deafening heartbeat. My hands begin to shake hard now. I need to get to the kitchen soon, or I'm going to lose control. The panic in my chest spreads full force through my body, and I feel faint. Pushing away from the chair, I stumble forward, through to the kitchen. I slam into the doorway and look through squinted eyes at the fridge. The door is hanging open, but there's no light on inside. *The fuck?*

I shuffle over to the open door and grab ahold of the freezer handle, ripping it open hard. The light flicks on and blinds me. I have to cover my eyes again as I reach into the top shelf, my fingers tapping for the familiar neck of the bottle. A few plastic wrappers crinkle under the pressure of my fingers, a soft bag of something frozen gives way beneath the movement of my hand. *Where the* — I pull my hand away from my face, my eyes narrowing to slits as I search for the vodka. It's not here. The top shelf, the spot where my bottle always rests, is empty.

Anxiety surges through my nerves as I rake through the freezer, searching. It's not here. At all.

"Georgia! Georgia, please..." I beg, my voice echoing through the house. "C'mon, you've got to help me. I'm so sorry. I know last night was bad. I love —" I don't even finish my sentence because a better thought comes to mind: my beer in the fridge. I slam the freezer shut and begin violently searching the fridge for cans. My arm sweeps each shelf, knocking food and containers over and out onto the floor. Leftover spaghetti and half-empty bottles of salad dressing spill out across my feet and over the cold tile floor. The beer is nowhere to be found. I whip my body around and head to the liquor cabinet across the kitchen like a wolf stalking its prey. As I pass the sink, the light from the window behind it glints and catches my attention. My eyes momentarily flick to the basins, and I come to a sudden halt, mid-step.

My mouth drops open in shock. *No. No! No, no, no, no!* The sink is overflowing with liquor bottles and beer cans — all empties. I dive toward the sink, my stomach folding over the hard edge of the counter, while I pull out empty bottle after empty bottle, putting each one to my lips and tipping the containers straight to the sky. Not a drop touches my tongue — they've all been rinsed clean.

My heart hammers in my chest as real fear surges through me. I rush toward the door that leads to the garage and pull it open hard — barely registering the hole that the handle has left in the wall behind it.

The garage is dark, and the biting smell of alcohol hits me like a wall. I feel my mouth flood with saliva, and I propel myself hurriedly down the stairs to the floor. I can already taste the sweet relief of the booze in my bloodstream, and I thank myself for keeping extra liquor out here.

I misstep down the four stairs and stumble and fall, landing hard on my hip. Pushing my hands against the cold concrete to get back up, I instantly feel pricks of pain in my fingertips and palms. I pull one hand close to my face and run my other hand over my palm. I feel raised, sharp spikes and my fingertips feel sliced open. I haul myself up and feel along the wall for the light switch. The room illuminates, and I realize I am covered in small cuts. Red drops of blood, pool and dot the underside of my hands. As I stare at my hands, I realize that I am covered in glass.

"Georgia?" I say, softly. I'm disconnecting from any sense of urgency, and I know I'm failing quickly.

My eyes slowly rise to take in the rest of the garage, and I stare at the scene before me in absolute horror. My car is gone, and in its place is the smeared outline of a once-present giant pool of liquid. I follow the outline to the center of the floor and try to make sense of what I see: the garage floor is covered in smashed liquor bottles. Shards of glass – light greens and blues, faint grays and dark browns – cover the garage floor like landscaping gravel.

In the center of the pile rests my sledgehammer.

My knees buckle, and I fall hard to the floor. My head bounces off the cool surface, and just before I lose consciousness, I register that the pain feels oddly welcome.

CHAPTER TWO

GEORGIA - MAY OF LAST YEAR

I FIND the first surveillance camera inside our bedroom closet.

It's mid-morning, and Mike is at work. I've already been to the gym and made my weekly stop at the dry cleaners for his uniform shirts. The wire hangers are hooked over my index finger as I walk into our room; the bright San Diego sun already making the air stuffy. I reach up to hang the shirts on my side of the closet first; I need to make room on his rack before I can un-bag the shirts and re-settle them on the smooth wooden hangers he prefers.

As I sweep my clothing across the bar, a heavy, black boat-neck sweater slips off its hanger and crumples; first onto the shelf underneath it, and then slumping into a pile on the carpet at my feet. I bend down to retrieve it, and as I stand, my eye catches something small and black protruding from the shelf in front of me. At first, I think it's just some of Mike's surveillance equipment from work. It's not unusual for him to keep gear scattered throughout the house — I typically just ignore it. But as I step closer to the shelf and lean my body toward the object, I notice a minuscule red blink from the left side. My breath catches as I recoil from the device; my eyes training on the left side, refusing to blink. Two seconds pass and the red light flicks again. This time I feel my eyes narrow as I realize the thing is on. And recording.

It doesn't take long for me to figure out what it is, or that it's probably transmitting to his cell phone. I'm disgusted and furious, and I want to smash the camera into tiny bits and leave them sprinkled all over his perfectly pressed uniforms still hanging in front of me. I wrack my brain trying to remember how many times I've been in here under the false pretense of privacy. I shudder as I see myself in past scenarios; naked after a shower to select clothes to wear, or making sure my bra fits correctly as I dress in front of the mirror. I never once considered a possible violation of my privacy. I feel dirty and embarrassed and immediately wonder who else may have seen the footage. I hold my hand to my mouth in disbelief as I consider the kind of person my husband has become.

I want to call him at work and scream at him. I am blind with rage and without thinking I rush to the telephone and dial. Just before it rings, I slam the phone down hard and realize two things: one — the camera is still probably recording, and two — if I scream at him now and embarrass him at work, I know I won't want to be anywhere near here when he gets home. I have to be careful. I need to be smart.

I calm myself, paste a soft smile on my face, and walk back into the closet. I casually ignore the camera and continue to remove the garment bags from his shirts as if nothing out of the ordinary has happened. I hang each shirt on its appropriate hanger and smooth the crease on each sleeve. When I am finished, I gather the garbage from the floor, turn on my heel, and shut the door quietly behind me.

Over the next few days, I find six more cameras throughout the house. With each discovery, I grow more and more inwardly callous toward my husband. On the exterior, I am the perfect Stepford Wife, and at the end of the week, I even suggest we go out for a romantic dinner. Mike agrees, and he's in a good mood as the evening begins. Before we leave, he makes a cocktail at home for each of us. I have three, maybe four sips in the time it takes him to drain his glass. As we head out to the restaurant, he turns back to the kitchen and makes himself another drink, pouring it into an aluminum water bottle, *for discretion.* I pretend, like usual, not to notice.

We sit at a quiet table near the window, and I constantly boost his ego throughout the night, listening raptly as he complains about his superiors at the station. I lean across the table, my décolletage drawing his eyes downward, and touch his forearm seductively. I remind him how hard he works and how little he is respected. He nods in agreement, his eyes never leaving the hint of black lace I purposefully allow to peek out from my blouse. Our server appears, and Mike immediately orders us drinks. He blatantly rolls his eyes when the young man repeats our order back to us. The server catches Mike's disdain and stammers his apologies. Mike crosses his arms and smirks at the server, signaling a small motion with his index finger and mouthing that the young man *can go now.* I shrink back into my chair, embarrassed. Mike's ego is inflated, and his libido is high. He feels unstoppable.

Instead of quietly discouraging him from drinking, like I normally do, I play up my physical attraction to him and my desire to join in the party. I even order additional drinks for both of us, looking demurely at Mike as a new, older server takes our order. His hand reaches under the tablecloth, and he roughly grabs my knee. I want to recoil from his touch, disgusted and ashamed in front of the employee, but instead, I take a sip of my drink and slowly purse my lips together, letting the tip of my tongue momentarily slide across my lower lip. I notice the server slink away. Mike's pupils dilate, and he strokes his hand along the length of my thigh. I have him exactly where I want him.

Our voices grow louder and louder as the evening wears on. When he stands to use the restroom, he stumbles and nearly falls over. I am only slightly buzzed, having only sipped at my two cocktails, but I play up being just as intoxicated as he is — laughing loudly and encouraging him to continue drinking.

Before long, we are on our way home. I convince him to let me drive by partially unbuttoning my blouse and promising him more as soon as we are home. He's purchased an expensive bottle of Syrah to bring along, and as soon as we slide into the car, he opens it with a wine key he retrieves from the glove box. He takes a long pull from the bottle. When he hands it to me and smiles, I can see his teeth are stained purple, and his eyelids are drooping. I know I need to be careful. His mood could go one of two ways, and for my safety, it's imperative he stay happy — and high.

I playfully laugh at his actions and pretend to take a long drink of wine, too, squeezing my eyes shut in mock distaste and pinching my nose as I pretend to feel the burn down my throat. I say a silent prayer that he will be far enough gone when we get home that he'll pass out cold. The thought of his hands on me brings bile to the back of my throat. I swallow it down and remind myself I need to be prepared to follow this through to the end.

We stumble our way in through the garage of our three-bedroom home that Mike constantly reminds me is his. He pauses as we enter the kitchen and turns to look behind him, pointing to the shelf along the wall that's filled with extra liquor

— his reserves. He attempts to tell me we should make another cocktail, but I laugh too loud and pretend to fall over my own feet in a pitiful attempt to remain standing. Mike ridicules my clumsiness in a jumble of slurred words, and I can tell his anger is rising. I do my best to hold him up, as he seems to inch closer and closer to the ground. I ask him several times if he's all right; each time his answer becomes more and more incomprehensible as his speech thickens.

He hurls repulsive curses at me as he nears unconsciousness, and I remind myself he's come to life in the past and managed to inflict serious wounds while completely drunk, so I know I'm not out of the woods yet. I offer him another drink, as I guide him to the living room and lay him back on the sofa. I soothe him with promises of more booze in hushed tones. This is a lullaby to my husband, and his eyes close almost immediately. His mouth drops open, and his arm dangles over the edge of the cushion. I stare at him, and after a long moment, breathe a huge sigh of relief.

I walk loudly to the kitchen, stopping at the sink to count to fifteen and listen intently for any sound. When I hear nothing, I walk back into the living room and see Mike passed out cold on the couch, snoring. I sit down on the coffee table next to him and begin a conversation with him in a blaring voice.

He doesn't even flinch.

The sour smell of liquor on his breath — on his entire body — overwhelms my senses. It's as if he's bathed in pure alcohol and it's now draining directly from his pores. I stand up and step to the side of the coffee table, holding my hands close together in front of my chest. Every muscle in my body tenses as I prepare to flee from harm. I pull my hands far apart and then quickly clap them together three times as hard as I can, the noise jolting the stillness of the house like a bomb. Mike's body is a concrete block on the sofa. He lies there, completely unmoving. I quickly take off my black heels and pull my hair back into a messy bun, anxious to investigate what he's been up to.

I pull Mike's cell phone with ease out of the jacket he's still wearing, although it takes me some time to crack his password. It finally opens on the fourth try after I enter the date he received his last promotion. Once I have his cell phone unlocked, it's simple to investigate what he's been up to. I find an app that appears to be some sort of tracking device for the car he *lets* me drive. I look through the history, and it reveals exactly where I have been over the last seven days. Red and blue dots ping across a map of downtown San Diego: my gym, the dry cleaners, shops I visited in the mall, a restaurant near Balboa Park, and a residential community off I-8. The dates and times are recorded next to each dot. Business names are outlined in capital letters, and private residences are reflected in neon blue. My mouth drops open in shock.

Continuing through his phone, I find the video feed for the cameras in the house. I click on the app and soon have a checkerboard of screens that show me different areas of our home. I walk to each room and play a literal game of hot and cold, as I look at the phone, and back at the room, seeking out each camera. My hands shake, my stomach feels nauseous, and I run for the kitchen sink and vomit heavily into the porcelain. When the waves pass, I slowly rinse my mouth and wipe my face with a dishtowel as I try to think. I hear the soft hum of the refrigerator, and my eyes draw to its presence in the room. I stare at the fridge for a moment and then deftly drop the dishtowel to the floor as my plan formulates.

It takes some time to open and empty all of the beer in the fridge, his vodka in the freezer, and the dozen or so bottles he keeps in the liquor cabinet. By the time I finish, the sink is piled high with glass and aluminum, and the entire house smells like a distillery. My clothes are wrinkled and stained with splashes of alcohol, but I don't care.

I empty the last bottle and lay it on the mountain that has grown in the sink. I wipe my hands on my skirt as I jog to the garage, flip on the interior light, and head directly to the tool pegboard. Once I find what I need, I slip on Mike's protective eyewear and set to work.

I have to change my clothes after I'm finished in the garage. I'm soaked, and my clothes are covered in small flecks of glass. I notice a few cuts on my legs and hands, but I set that realization aside. I have more important things on my mind.

When I leave the house, I take the security cameras, both of our cell phones, all the cash in his wallet, and all of the jewelry I think will be valuable at a pawn shop. I pack one small suitcase of clothes, my Canon camera, and all the important paperwork I can find: my birth certificate, my social security card, and my passport. I grab our marriage certificate and deliberate a moment before I lower it into the suitcase. I'm unable to actually let it go from my fingers, and after a second, I grab it with both hands and rip it slowly down the center. The paper tears a ragged edge across the carefully crafted calligraphy, the sound incredibly satisfying. I put the two halves together and rip again, faster this time, and repeat the process over and over again. Small pieces of paper begin to fall at my feet and stick at odd angles in the carpet. I grit my teeth as I shred the paper, tears springing to my eyes like tiny needles pricking my corneas. I throw my hands in the air and release the remaining pieces; bits of paper floating down around me like a small, pathetic, snow flurry.

I walk to the front door, and my hand pauses on the brushed nickel doorknob. Turning back, I take a final look at Mike, and at the house I've called home for the last six years. He lies on the couch, motionless. I look him over, repulsed and saddened at the ruin he has become. For a moment I feel a small, fleeting twinge of empathy for what I know will be a painful withdrawal for him when he finally resurfaces. My brain counteracts my compassion, reminding me of the bruises I have learned to cover with expert skill, of the excuses I have conjured with ease, of the life he has stolen from me over the last six years. I remember these things, and I no longer give a damn about the pain *he* might endure.

The dark night is a step away from me as I turn back to the door and open it wide. A shiver slides up my spine as I stand on the threshold. I can taste the thrill of freedom. I can smell the sweet scent of peace. As I walk out of the door, I feel the beginning of a long-absent smile appearing at the corner of my mouth.

By the time the sun comes up over the Interstate, I am just north of the San Fernando Valley. Mike's small Accord hums along the grooved, worn lanes of the massive freeway. I am uneasy, tense with anxiety over what could be happening in my old home. My hands grip the steering wheel as I try to calculate when Mike will regain consciousness.

I keep my speed well within the limit — afraid any police officer that pulls me over will immediately arrest me and call Mike to come and pick me up. I tell myself over and over that as soon as I cross the state line, I will be safe, but in reality, I don't even know if this is true. For a moment I consider a detour into Nevada but decide against it. I am desperate to get to Oregon as quickly as possible. I feel so lost, so destroyed. I just want to go home — and try to start over.

CHAPTER THREE

GEORGIA - MAY THIS YEAR

"TOMORROW? I don't know, Gia, it sounds really dangerous. Are you sure that's a good idea?" Sylvia asks. A fine line appears in the center of her forehead.

My sister's two-year-old German shepherd, Guthrie, lies below me on the hardwood floor. His body curls along the front of the living room sofa that Sylvia and I are lounging on, and I can hear his quiet snores. I uncurl one of my legs and run my bare foot along his soft fur as I consider her question. Maybe she's right. Maybe this *isn't* the smartest decision. I sip my San Pellegrino and turn my head to look out through the living room windows. It's dusk but still warm outside; an evening breeze drifts in, and the natural linen curtains ripple and rise from the open window.

I turn my attention back to Guthrie and lean forward to pet his head. I have to admit, it's my natural instinct to shy away from anything new. It took me a week to convince myself that this trip even sounded like something I could handle, and as I hear the subtle tone of disapproval in Sylvia's voice, I feel my own self-doubts resurface. A year ago, I wouldn't have dreamed of driving two hours before dawn just so I could hike to the top of a butte in the middle of nowhere and take some probably meaningless pictures.

A big part of me wants to agree with her hesitation, and I chew on the inside of my cheek as I search her eyes — she is my older and wiser sister, after all. She's happily married to a successful attorney, and she and Scott have owned this home for the last eight years. She has her own bank account, maintained from her regular income as an insurance claims adjuster, and she makes and spends her own money — without having to ask permission. She's made smart decisions in her life so far, and common sense tells me I should heed her advice and rethink this trip. And yet, when I imagine hiking alone and reaching the top of the butte by myself, butterflies circle and dance excitedly in my stomach. I want to feel *proud* of myself, and this mini-adventure just feels like a good place to start.

"I think it's going to be great, Sylv," I say. "It's not far from Black Butte Ranch, or Sisters, so it's not like I'm going to be completely off-the-grid. Besides," I continue, "it's just for the day, on a Friday for goodness sake. If I leave the butte by late afternoon, I should be home by eight." I tilt my head to the side and smirk at her. "C'mon. You guys could use some time alone. I know I live in the other end of the house, but you've *got* to be sick of having a permanent houseguest."

Sylvia ignores my attempt at distraction.

"What if you get a flat tire, or run into bad weather?" she asks and reaches to the coffee table to pick up her iced tea.

I sigh. "I've thought about that. The weather looks fine. It's the start of summer, remember? And if, for some reason, I should get a flat tire on the highway, I'll stand next to the Jeep and stick my leg out like a true damsel in distress." My attempt at a joke falls flat as Sylvia sips her tea and rolls her eyes at me. I stutter a laugh in response.

"Seriously, sis. I'll just call Les Schwab. They fixed the last flat tire I had — for free, no less. They're better than AAA! And if I don't have service, I'll wait until it's light and then get out the manual and figure it out." I reach over and lay my hand on her bare knee. "People do this kind of thing all the time. Besides, don't you think at thirty-three-years-old I should learn how to change a tire?"

"No, I don't. That's how people end up as murder victims." She tilts her head to gauge how that idea sits with me before continuing. "Seriously though. What if you get hurt up there? What if you run into someone dangerous?"

"Well, it's a non-technical hike. It's not far from a popular resort and a small town," I argue. "Plus, I've been practicing. Remember?" I shrug my shoulders at her. "I'll be fine, sis. Here, listen." I pick up my hiking book from the coffee table, flip to the dog-eared page and begin to skim out loud.

"Okay, so it's 'situated in the midst of the Central Oregon plateau'...um...there's a 'steep but amazing view-packed trail that's 1.9 miles to the summit'...the hike showcases 'ponderosa pine trees, low snowbrush, and lots of wildflowers...'" I leave out the last part, about the trail gaining 1600 feet in elevation and that it's considered moderately difficult.

Sylvia's face is unmoved.

"Okay, but listen. It's more than just a hike. There's cool stuff up there to see." I lean in toward her, a smile growing across my face. "There's an active fire lookout tower, as well as an older lookout apparently built in, like, 1923 or something. And a cabin up there that I guess is the home of the Forest Service worker that mans the place." I sit back against my throw pillow and the ice in my glass clinks together. "See? Sounds fun!"

"Sounds dangerous." Her voice is flat.

"If it's too dangerous, I promise I'll turn around and come back home. I want to take things slow too, Sylv."

Sylvia sighs and stretches her foot to my leg. Her face relaxes, and the hard line of her mouth softens.

"I just worry about you, Gia. That's all. You've been through so much this past year, and I just don't want anything bad to happen." She avoids my eyes. "Sorry. I know I sound like Mom, but jeez, what do you think she'd say about this?"

At the mention of her name, a hard ball forms in my stomach. Mom and dad have been gone for years, and though Sylvia has managed to quietly accept it, I still struggle with the pain of losing them. Especially mom. She always knew how to listen without passing judgment, and how to help me arrive at a decision without injecting her own opinions. She was a vibrant, beautiful presence in my life — our lives — and I miss her every single day.

I swallow hard and stare at my glass. A drop of condensation slowly forms, and slides off the glass, landing weightlessly on my cotton shorts.

"I think mom would encourage me to weigh the pros and cons and then decide if it seems like a smart thing to do." I take a deep breath and continue. "I think she'd tell me that it's time to discover who I am. Who I *really* am, not who an abusive husband —"

"*Ex*-husband."

"—*Ex*-husband, thinks I should be."

I consider how mom would react, how she'd help guide me to a confident choice, and I feel a small smile appear at the corner of my mouth.

"I think she'd want me to do it."

According to my guidebook, I'm almost at the first turnoff for the trailhead. I've come off the summit of Santiam Pass without any trouble, and I'm proud of my little Jeep's first real road trip. I was hesitant to buy a new vehicle after I arrived in Oregon, but after I found a job and sold the Accord, I had enough for a good down payment and a way to meet my monthly obligation. I love the Jeep. I love that I picked it out. I love that it's my responsibility. But most of all, I love that it belongs to me.

I pull over at the summit and send Sylvia a text message to let her know I'm okay. I'm thankful and relieved to have made it this far. I hardly saw any traffic — a few semi-trucks that gave me ample room to pass at each opportunity, and a couple of lone cars and trucks going the opposite direction. In truth, the drive was pretty peaceful. I turned on my favorite '80's music playlist and followed the twists and turns of the highway as I climbed out of the valley and into the mountains.

I think about the hike as I drive, and although I'm not overly worried about it, whenever doubt does creep in, I glance over at my camera bag in the passenger seat and think about the possible photos I'm going to capture. I've been hiking for weeks at Silver Falls Park in preparation; my trail shoes are broken in, and I'm able to walk the eight-mile loop in pretty good time. I remind myself this hike will do me a world of good. The fresh air, the methodical trudging of one foot in front of the other — it will clear my head and hopefully, my heart.

My headlights reflect a sign on the right indicating Green Ridge Road just ahead. I slow down, and when the intersecting road appears to my left, I feel a brief, silly moment of accomplishment as I turn the wheel and head north.

Even though it's the beginning of summer, the sky is still pitch black. I guess it makes sense — it's 3:45 in the morning. Leaving Silverton at 1:30 a.m. was brutal, but adrenalin and my thermos of black coffee kicked in, and I didn't really begin to feel sluggish until about an hour into the drive. Now, I'm too focused on following directions to the trailhead to feel anything but alert.

As I drive along the paved road, pine trees with thick, cracking bark reflect in my headlights, and I catch huge moths and other winged insects on my windshield. In my peripheral vision, I can see the paper-thin wings of a moth fighting against the pressure of the wind. I watch it for a moment and feel a pang of sympathy emerge as it fights to be free of the glass. Eventually, its purposeful movement ceases, and I notice that the moth's wings now flit only in the direction the wind allows. Glancing at it, I consider why it took me so long to leave Mike. Why didn't I fight harder for myself? Why didn't I leave sooner, when things first started going badly? I consider all the excuses I made — all the lies I told myself and convinced myself to believe. I realize now that I just gave in too quickly. I chose to surrender to his abuse instead of fighting against it. Instead of standing up for myself. I gave his existence more value than my own. The cold realization of this fact fills me with the heavy weight of burning shame, and I resolve that I'm never going to let my defenses down again. No relationship is worth the kind of pain I suffered in the warped name of love.

All at once I am perspiring and am impatient to get on the trail. I press the accelerator and speed along the dark road. After a few miles, my lights reflect a mile-marker and a large wooden signpost. I slow down as I approach the sign, squinting through the darkness to read it. My headlights reflect the words *Black Butte* on the sign and a small arrow below points to the intersecting gravel road on my left. I pull onto the road and take a deep breath. Almost there.

The rough gravel beneath the tires cracks and pops as I turn onto Forest Service Road 1110. The pull of the Jeep's steering wheel against the uneven ground reminds me I need to pay close attention to what's in front of me. After only a few hundred feet, the road narrows to barely more than two car widths and steadily slopes upward. The Jeep's transmission automatically downshifts into a lower gear and begins to nose forward. It's a long, slow uphill climb that forces me to hold the wheel with both hands as it rattles and spasms with every washboard I cross. I try to zigzag across the narrow road to avoid them, but it's useless; the whole road is covered with the obnoxious ruts.

The dim outlines of spindly pine trees become visible as I bounce along the road, and I note that the sky seems to have turned just a fraction lighter. My stomach tightens with anxiety as I realize it will be dawn in a short time — I need to get to the trail.

I drive on — faster over the washboards — which seems to lessen their impact — and soon find myself at a fork in the road. I don't remember any details about this from my guidebook, so I throw the Jeep in park and reach over to grab it, skimming over the directions to reach the trailhead, "*...turn left onto Forest Road 1110. Follow this gravel, winding road for 5 miles to the parking area at the Black Butte Trailhead.*" Great. Absolutely nothing about where to go now. I reach for my cell phone to pull up a map and realize I have zero reception. My stomach sinks, and I feel a slight panic begin to spiral through me. I toss the book onto the passenger seat. What now? Looking to my right, I see the road veers off into blackness, and forward? Well, forward is an even narrower road that's covered in exposed, jagged rocks. I take a deep breath, pull the Jeep into drive and accelerate forward; figuring that as long as I'm heading uphill, I must be going in the right direction.

Between navigating the outcroppings of rocks every few feet, and the ruts and potholes in the road, I have serious trouble keeping the Jeep in any kind of straight line as I plod up the side of the mountain. I start to wonder if I'm on some abandoned logging road and try to imagine how I'm ever going to turn around when the road suddenly smooths out and plateaus. I press forward and realize I've reached what appears to be a large, rounded parking area. I pull up and circle the space, my headlights reflecting the trunks of the pine trees that enclose the area. There isn't another vehicle here or evidence of people at all. I swallow hard.

I bring the Jeep to rest in a spot closest to the trailhead sign and turn off the ignition. My cell phone still shows "No Service" and my hands are unsteady as I hold it. I keep my foot on the brake pedal and look behind me. My red taillights illuminate a small space behind me, and I turn back around and lean back against my seat, closing my eyes for a moment.

I can't actually believe I'm here. In a moment of self-doubt, I imagine starting the Jeep back up and heading home. I can already hear Mike's voice in my head: laughing at me and reminding me of what a fool I am to think I could do something like this. I squeeze my eyes hard against the insults that feel so very real and try to remind myself why I wanted to do this. I open my eyes and glance over at my camera sitting stoically next to me, and the corner of my mouth begins to lift.

When I open the door and step outside, I'm met with a wave of fresh, cool air that smells like vanilla cookies and Christmas. The air in the valley seems heavy and thick compared to the lightness I feel here. I take a deep breath and fill my lungs with what seems like the purest oxygen I've ever inhaled. I look up and see the tops of the trees swaying back and forth. I can hear the subtle sound of the breeze as it blows through the pines, and I'm reminded of a muffled ocean tide as it makes its way to and from the shore.

The peacefulness here makes me feel somewhat safe and comforted, but when I look around, it's as if I've just stepped onto a different planet. It's so quiet and dark that even with the half-moon that's still shining brightly above me I can't see more than ten feet in front of where I'm standing. At home, it's never really *dark,* dark. Streetlights, city lights, and traffic keep most of our night sky disguised. But here, when I look up, I see virtual highways of stars stretched out into infinite destinations across the sky. The inky dark is fading, and I know I need to get on the trail. I lean back into the Jeep and grab my guidebook, keys and wallet, my phone, and my camera from the passenger seat. I put all the items into my backpack and pull out my flashlight as I head to the back door to grab my hiking shoes. I wiggle my feet into them and rub my hands together. It's cold, and I'm glad I chose to wear my thicker black leggings rather than my thin, zip-away hiking pants. I shrug my down vest on, over the dri-fit long sleeve shirt and tank top I'm wearing, and zip it all the way to my chin. Inside the vest pocket is my favorite pair of running gloves, and I put those on too. I adjust the interior plastic bladder that holds my gallon of water, and vent the water tube out of the top, swinging the backpack on over one shoulder and then the other. I take a few pulls on the tube until I have water in my mouth and then shut the door securely. I'm out of reasons to dawdle now, so I lock the Jeep, take a deep breath and set off toward the trailhead. My heart thumps with excitement and anxiety, and for a moment I feel almost nauseous.

My flashlight cuts a very limited range of sight in front of me, and as I walk to the trailhead, the motion of my stride causes the light to bounce all around. Of course, every scary movie I've ever seen, every scary story I've ever heard, every possible terrible circumstance surfaces in my mind and replays with unwanted, incredible detail. My chest tightens as a tense wave of adrenalin flows through my body, and I remind myself — out loud — that professional photographers do this kind of thing every day, and many of them do it right here in Oregon. In fact, I reason, I'll probably meet one of them on the trail, or at the top. The weak smile fades from my face as soon as I remember that I didn't see any other vehicles in the parking lot.

All of these thoughts are shoved to the back of my brain as I step foot onto the actual trail. It's steep. Very steep. The ground is packed clay, covered with fallen pine needles and my shoes scrape and slip along the path, trying to find stability as I plod up what seems like a ninety-degree incline. The sound of my heavy, rapid breathing fills the night as my flashlight jerks all over the trail. I remember reading that this part of the trail consists of two very long, very steep switchbacks that continue until you are high enough to begin traversing the east side of the mountain. The altitude, combined with my adrenalin, leaves me winded and gasping for air after only a short distance, and I feel like I am broadcasting my whereabouts to the entire world.

After what feels like an eternity, I come to the end of the first switchback, round the trail and began to push forward again. I'm hot and already sweaty, and I sip some water and unzip my vest. By the time I reach the end of the second switchback, my vest is off, and I'm sweating like a beast. I fold the vest into a puffy square and shove it into my pack. When I take off again, I realize that the sky is now a lighter shade of gray. I can see the light from the moon, although the trees still hide its physical presence, and the stars are no longer as distinct in the sky. Dawn is just around the corner, and I am determined to beat it.

At the end of the last switchback, I climb out of the tree line. The moon is unobstructed now, and the scenery around me illuminates. Just past the edge of the trail on my right, I can see that the mountain sheers off at a sharp angle. How far down it goes, I can't tell — and I don't want to find out.

I turn off the flashlight as the trail is now visible by moonlight, and push on at an increased pace. Now that I'm out of the trees, I feel my fear levels taper off, and I begin to enjoy the quiet solitude. Except for the sound of the soft thump of my feet and the steady exhalation of my breath as I climb, the world around me is silent, and I feel a sense of long-forgotten peace. As I continue up the trail, I can see the sky above the ridge in front of me begin to turn the faintest shade of pink, and I notice a few birds glide across the sky, bank against an unseen barrier and swoop down into the dark valley below.

I stop to take a few unhurried breaths, grab and sip some water and look ahead up the trail as far as light allows. Suddenly an unbidden memory of a hiking trip Mike and I took early on in our marriage floods my mind.

We had set off one Saturday toward the Anza-Borrego desert, just northeast of our home in San Diego. The drive out was easy and fun — we blared the radio and sang along to songs we knew as we entered the gorgeous blooming desert landscape, anxious to begin our adventure together. It was a happy time, and we were so in love with each other. But I should have noticed the warning signs then: his outright insistency on picking our destination, his biting instructions as we unloaded the car, his control over where we hiked, and what equipment we should bring, essentially insinuating I wasn't smart enough to know these things on my own. And his anger. It would unexpectedly erupt out of nowhere. At other drivers on the freeway, at the people we met along the hike that, as he put it, *looked at him in a menacing way*, and at me when I'd accidentally forgotten to pack the extra water he instructed we bring for the trip. Just thinking of it now makes me tense, and I look down and realize I'm clenching my fists. I shake my head to clear the memories from my mind. I had no idea what lay ahead of me then.

I take another sip of water, spit the tube out of my mouth and promise myself I will finish this task. I remind myself of the gorgeous photographs I will soon have as souvenirs from this adventure, and I shut out the memories of Mike Rutherford.

CHAPTER FOUR

GEORGIA

TWO MILES AT A STRAIGHT uphill climb makes me feel like I've just climbed Mt. Everest. By the time I round the north side of the mountain I am down to my tank top and sucking water like I've just crawled out of Death Valley.

As I approach what my guidebook says is the *left turn to the summit*, I am greeted with the most incredible sight I have ever witnessed: a 360-degree view of the last of the night sky against the breaking dawn of a new day.

The horizon begins to light up as if it's on fire; huge deep pinks burst forth and cut across the peacock blue sky, slicing away the remnants of the night. The colors travel across the sky and reach with delicate tendrils until they touch the tips of the mountains to the south. It's breathtaking, and I know this spectacular show will only increase in beauty. I drop my pack on the trail and rip open the zipper to fish inside for my camera and cell phone. Looping the camera strap around my neck, I slide my cell phone under the strap of my sports bra, throw my pack back on, and scramble up the last of the trail to the summit.

The view from the top astounds me, and I feel my mouth

drop open in sheer awe. Captivated by the sunrise and the incomparable views of the mountains all around me, I turn a slow circle to take it all in. Just as the guidebook reports, the lookout tower, and the D-3 cupola building sit perched behind me along the summit like familiar old friends. Jogging up to the base of the gigantic lookout tower, I dump my pack next to a thick galvanized metal beam that's anchored to the ground and tilt my head back to look up, and still farther up, at the enormous structure. I'm intrigued by its design and purpose, but glancing back down at the camera around my neck I decide that sunrise pictures come first.

The lens cap is off in one quick twist, and I slide it into my pocket as I bring the camera up against the right side of my face. The weight of the camera presses against my cheek as I support it with my left hand, the viewfinder centered at my eye, and I twist the lens to adjust the focus. All at once the scenery in front of me slides into focus, and I feel my face crack into a giant smile.

"Yes!" I shout from behind the camera.

The viewfinder is bright with the color of the rising sun. I press the shutter button down and hold. The camera snaps multiple photographs in a continuous stream of activity. I pull it away from my face to look at the LCD screen and immediately see the last of the photos I've captured. I am stunned by what I see. The color on the screen is as vibrant as any of the oil pastel paintings I've visited in the Portland Art Museum. The pinks and reds of the rising sun are a gorgeous, sharp contrast to the bright cornflower blue of the unclouded sky. I am giddy with excitement at this chance to play with my camera and this natural world around me, so full of color and texture.

I turn and hustle south across the top of the summit. My guidebook identifies the mountains in front of me — Three Sisters, Broken Top, and Mt. Bachelor in the far distance. The growing color in the sky reflects off the snow-covered peaks of the mountain ridges, and I raise my camera to shoot an unknown number of pictures in every direction. I play with the aperture – pointing the camera toward the westward horizon and aim for the last stellar holdouts I can barely see in the sky. As I snap the last of the series, I verify in the LCD screen that I've indeed managed to capture the tiny, almost invisible sparkling stars above the mountains. I drop the camera against my chest and clap my hands together like a small, ecstatic child.

After exhausting a good amount of camera battery life on the sunrise, and confirming, yet again, that I still don't have cell service, I spend the next hour or so investigating the structures on the summit. In addition to the lookout tower, I see the boarded up D-3 cupola building and a large pile of discarded concrete and metal. I hike up the small hill and through the low snowbrush to the base of the lookout tower and switch the camera to black and white. I shoot several angles of the metal beams and rivets that hold the top platform so high in the air. The tower has multiple thick cables fastened to it that seem to further anchor the entire structure to the ground. Is it copper they are made from? I can't quite tell.

Taking a seat on the cold ground, I point my camera straight up. Through the lens, I can contrast the shiny metal that's still wet with dew against the rough cables and the matte sky. The images show I've managed to capture not only the craggy metal texture of the structure but also the shadows and the brightness created as the sun rises higher in the morning sky and touches the tower.

Standing up again, I step back and tilt my head up. It's a massive structure. I estimate it stands about 60 feet above the surface of the summit with staircases that crisscross and climb to intermittent platforms that lead to the crow's nest on top. Imagining what the view must look like from the top, I decide to walk around the base of the structure and search for a way to climb up.

I spot the beginning of a metal staircase on the far side of the tower, and my heart stutters with excitement. But as I near the stairs I realize the top of the ladder is blocked at the first platform by a metal gate that's padlocked shut. My shoulders sink as I slowly climb the seven steps and pull on the lock, just in case. As a last ditch effort, I consider trying to climb around the outside of the structure to make my way to the next set of stairs but decide I'd better not tempt fate.

Satisfied with my collection of tower photographs, I take a few steps backward, pick up my backpack and turn away from the lookout, heading across the summit toward the old cupola building. After a few pictures, I catch sight of a roofline in the distance. I'd forgotten about the cabin!

The Forest Service log cabin is perched on the lower north side of the butte, conveniently out of sight from the end of the hiking trail at the summit. As I look at the face of the small log cabin, its rugged construction gleaming with the first touches of sunshine, an involuntary gasp escapes me — my perfect photograph subject is right in front of me.

I give a wide berth to the cupola and walk toward the small home. Soon enough the exposed rocks and low snowbrush give way to a clear narrow path of packed clay, impervious to evidence of travel that winds down to the cabin. Two scattered piles of chopped wood lie to the right of the front porch. An axe is sticking out of a large stump, and the pale blond wooden handle shines in the morning sun. I stand with my back to the sun and shoot photo after photo of this rustic treasure-filled scene.

Through the viewfinder, I see a small narrow shack with a tiny, rusted tin roof. An outhouse maybe? It occurs to me that I should probably use the restroom, but I set that thought aside and decide to explore and photograph the rest of the cabin first.

The roof of the cabin is shingled with small rectangles of thick wood, and I can see a small metal chimney peeking through on the north side. At each end are two thick lightning rods that extend about five feet into the sky. I pull the camera away from my face, look out over the vast expanse of sky around me and speculate about the magnitude of lightning storms up here.

A small, multi-paned window stands guard at the front of the cabin, and to the left is the front door. The sturdy-looking door is scuffed along the bottom and a thick steel padlock latched across the front reflects in the sunshine. The window appears dark, and as I get closer to the porch, I can tell there is a shade or a curtain drawn behind it. A small stool stands like a statue on the open porch. It peaks my curiosity and dares me to come closer. Dropping the camera against my chest, I venture onto the porch. The cabin looks uninhabited, I didn't see any cars in the parking lot, and it's not yet 9:30 a.m....I think a closer look would be okay.

The porch creaks and pops like a piece of dry kindling in a fire as I step onto it, and I immediately freeze and look down, expecting to see the boards break beneath my feet. After bouncing up and down a few times, I decide the porch will hold – it's just old and probably tight from the cold. I lean my face to the window glass and cup my hands around my eyes, trying to peer inside, but it's no use. A shade is drawn tight against the inside of the window, and all I can see is the foggy outline of my breath growing larger on the glass. Turning around, I lean against the ledge of the window. The wood is warm from the sun, and it feels good against my back. I slide my phone out and check my reception, hoping for the best, but it's not to be. With a sigh and a shrug, I zip the phone into my backpack and decide to give up trying.

To my left, I notice some small gray feathers and splotches of white gathered in the corner of the porch near the wall of the house. I walk over, fighting against the loud groans and complaints of the creaking boards beneath me, and look up. My suspicions are confirmed as I see the remnants of a bird's nest settled in the rafters above. The cabin wall provides support as I steady myself against it, aim the camera at the nest and take a few photographs of the twisted wood and small twigs that stick out at odd angles from the small hideaway. The contrast between the dark shadows underneath the roof, and the sunlight beginning to highlight the materials protruding from the nest strikes me as somewhat beautiful. I wonder if anything is inside the tiny hide-away, but a hollow grumble from my stomach reminds me I have more urgent needs.

The sunshine blankets the front of the cabin, and I feel the warmth cover my entire body. It's powerful and bright, and I reach into a small pocket of my backpack and pull out my sunglasses, sliding them on and then grabbing my food. My stomach growls as I pull the stool over to the cabin wall and sit down, using the smooth log wall as a chair back, and begin to eat my flattened turkey and cheese sandwich.

"Oh my God, I'm starving!" I say and then laugh at myself. Who am I even talking to way out here?

I finish my sandwich in four huge bites, and it's only after I eat my apple, a granola bar and part of the salami and cheese I'd allocated for the hike back down the mountain, do my stomach and brain celebrate in unison that I am, in fact, finally full.

Checking my water supply, I realize I am more than halfway through it. After a few more drinks, I close off the tube and decide I'll save the rest for the hike back down. It should be pretty easy — it was uphill the entire way here — and I know I have more water in the back of the Jeep.

I feel happy and content, and if I let myself admit it, I'm proud too. I tilt my head back against the warmth of the cabin wall and close my eyes behind my sunglasses as I relax in the sunshine and enjoy my full stomach and fatigued muscles. All at once I am overcome with exhaustion. I feel my jaw muscles relax and a huge, intruding yawn takes over. My breath slows, becomes shallow, and I whisper to myself that a tiny nap wouldn't hurt anything. I vaguely register folding my hands in my lap before I slip peacefully into unconsciousness.

A noise somewhere near jolts me into a blurred awakening. My eyes spring open, and I feel my mouth simultaneously clamp shut as I attempt to swallow the dryness in my throat. I sit completely frozen on the stool, still somewhat sleep-paralyzed, as my eyes roam the scenery in front of me. I see nothing out of the ordinary amongst the brush, and I scan the top of the summit up ahead of me, making a horizontal pass along the ridgeline, but I don't see anything. I relax a bit and push my heels down into my trail shoes, stretching and flexing my calf muscles and hamstrings, as I stay seated on the stool. Had I imagined the noise?

I begin to lift my leg off the porch to stretch it out in front of me when I notice movement in the snowbrush up ahead of me. Something large is moving; the thick, low bushes gently shake and bend as whatever it is, pushes alongside them, pressing forward toward the cabin — toward me. I narrow my eyes and squint against the sunlight that's almost blinding me. I'm rigid and holding my breath, staring at the movement in the brush.

And then I see it.

CHAPTER FIVE

GEORGIA

WHAT I CAN SEE OF the bear chills me to my core.

His head is immense — it's larger than my Jeep's steering wheel — and his massive shoulders rise and fall in huge, explosive movements as he meanders in and out of the snow-brush. I feel the blood drain from my head and arms, and suddenly I can't breathe. My heart races in my chest, freezing me in fear. For a split second, I wonder if I can sit quietly, and the bear will pass by me unnoticed, or if I can possibly sneak away to the left and hide behind the north side of the cabin, but I am too shocked to move. I'm cemented in place even though my mind is screaming at me to run.

Time seems to stop as erratic thoughts race through my head. I have no weapon. I have no way to protect myself, and I have nowhere to hide. My eyes flash back up the hill to the bear. He's stopped moving. A moment later his head lifts out of the brush as he looks to the southeast. I feel my mouth drop open, and I suck in a small gasp. His face is an enormously powerful design; his nose and mouth protrude at such a distance that I know in the pit of my stomach only huge, long rows of razor sharp teeth wait inside.

I use this moment to look left at the two woodpiles, and I zero in on the axe handle. A small balloon of hope blossoms in me until, a second later, I realize I'll have to be very close to the huge animal for the axe to do me any good, and that, I do not want, under any circumstances.

I look back to the bear and decide I will try to slink away toward the woodpiles. He's moving again; coming closer to the edge of the snowbrush, and it's only seconds before he'll be on the packed clay boundary around the cabin. Leaving my open backpack at my feet, I slide off the stool like a cat hunting its prey. I hold my camera just inches off my chest — the strap loose around my neck. I don't want to make any noticeable movement, and I creep across the porch in a crouched, duck-footed walk toward the woodpiles — toward the *axe* — all the while keeping an eye on the bear. At the moment, he seems to be snuffling on the ground for something, and I feel a trace of possible triumph. I'm going to make it to the axe, and this bear is going to disappear down the side of the butte. I can almost see it playing like a movie in my head.

And then everything goes wrong.

I'm almost to the edge of the porch, my feet balancing on the last few boards, when suddenly they snap and buckle, giving way under my compressed weight. My right foot falls through the wooden planks, landing very hard on something sharp underneath. My ankle rolls on its side over what feels like a concrete block under the porch. I scream out and then immediately suck in my breath and bite my lower lip, trying to keep quiet. But it's too late. The commotion of the breaking boards combined with my scream feels like a sonic boom in the otherwise uninterrupted silence of the morning. I immediately look to the bear only to find his beady black eyes locked with mine, his body frozen in place.

He's at the edge of the snowbrush now, and I can see a paw sticking out of the greenery. Rather, I can see the giant, lethal *claws* of the paw. He is close to the far end of the cabin, and I am literally stuck in the porch, my ankle throbbing in pain. I can feel something wet and warm begin to fill my sock and I imagine the pool of blood that's starting to form there. I have to get off of this porch. I have to get over to the axe as quickly as possible, but I don't know if I can put any weight on my ankle. I try to pull my leg out of the hole and nearly lose consciousness from the pain that shoots up my body. My head drops to my chest as I attempt to stifle another yell, and I start to cry. It feels like a lightning bolt has just touched my foot and electrocuted the entire right side of my body.

"Come on, Georgia!" I whisper to myself through clenched teeth. "You have to do this!"

Tears repeatedly fall from my eyes as the pain and fear intensify, and I know in a moment when I try to move again, the agony will resume.

I look at the bear again. He is still looking at me, his eyes trained on my face, only now he is slowly moving toward me. I am petrified. My body flushes with heat as a wave of pure adrenalin pulses through my veins. I hold my breath, pull my leg up through the splintered opening in the boards, and scream in agony. My bones feel like bits and pieces of broken metal in a useless sack of hot water.

I am out of the boards, and the bear is twenty-five feet away from me. It begins to trot to where I lie at the edge of the porch. I pull myself over the edge and onto the dirt and slide toward the woodpile. I steal a look behind me. The bear is ten feet away, his front paws touch the wood planks, and I can hear his claws clack on the dry boards as he steps into the space I occupied only a moment ago.

A strong wave of putrid odor reaches me, and I realize it's the bear. It reeks of urine and something like decomposed plant material. As I attempt to pull my body up and onto the weight of my left leg to gain movement, the bear reaches my backpack and stops. I can see his large black nostrils flare as he smells the air above the bag and lowers his head to the open pocket. My lunch! Part of my lunch is still inside. *Please let him eat it. Please let him eat it and move on.* I grit my teeth, pull my left knee underneath my body and stand up in slow, tiny increments. The pain is monumental, and as I hop toward the edge of the woodpile, I have no choice but to drag my right leg beside me, using only my toes as support.

The bear is still occupied with the task of reaching the food in my bag. He paws at the bag, his claws ripping the soft material into thin shreds. I head toward the axe and watch as another few passes of his claws puncture my water reservoir and tiny streams of water shoot up simultaneously from the backpack. I know I don't have much time.

I hobble over to the stump that holds the axe and yank on the handle as hard as I can. My hand practically bounces off the thick wood as it stays put, braced in the stump as if it's cast in cement. I bend to my side and pick up a piece of split wood, my eyes catching sight of the outhouse roofline a few yards away. I lift the piece of wood above my head and bring it down with as much force as I can muster against the axe handle...but it doesn't budge. The bear is slashing again and again at the bag, trying unsuccessfully to ferret out more food items, and I know it won't be long before he realizes there's no more food to be found in there, refocusing his attention instead on the larger meal only a few feet away.

He drops the front of his face back into the bag and moves it across the porch with his muzzle. I hit the axe handle again, and it moves about an inch downward. I slam it once more, and the top of the axe releases from the stump, the shiny face of the blade glinting in the sunlight. One more thump on the handle and the axe is in my hand. I look up at the bear once again just as his mouth comes out of the backpack. We lock eyes with each other and then, as if in frustration, he rolls his weight to his back legs, pulls his front legs off the porch and stands up to his full height, letting loose with an enormous roar that freezes my spine. His razor sharp teeth are on full display and thick bands of saliva stretch and snap between his upper and lower jaws. He drops to his feet and begins to move with intent toward me. I feel nothing as I put weight on both of my feet, turn toward the outhouse and try to jog and limp my way there. I can hear the bear behind me; his paws pounding the ground, his breathing loud and fast as he gains momentum. I reach the door, rip it open and slam it behind me. A small wooden latch holds the door closed, and I jam the axe handle across the small opening, wedging it in between a lateral board, just as the bear slams into the door. His body weight against the rickety structure shoves me backward onto the toilet lid, and the thin planks of the door begin to split and stretch. The bear growls again, and the sound is deafening. I scream as loud as I possibly can for as long as the air in my lungs lasts, and for the first time in my life, the possibility of death is suddenly very, very real.

Through the small cracks in between the boards of the door, I can see the shadow of the bear as he stands up again and moves toward me. I back up against the toilet; lean forward and brace myself against the axe handle. All of the sudden the bear's claws pierce through the wood, inches from my face as he rakes downward through the panels; the wood curling into thin ribbons. I focus on the axe. If I remove it from the hatch, the door will completely fail, and I will instantly be faced with defending myself. If I leave it in place, the door may hold a few moments longer before the bear breaks through but then I won't have the ability to defend myself. There's no time. In a panic, I decide to take my chances with the bear. I stand up from the seat, lean forward with shaking hands and reach for the axe. I wait for the bear to slam against the door again, my fingers inches from the axe handle.

Nothing. No noise, no movement, no sound at all. Every fiber in my being is tense as I hold my breath and lean closer to the door, straining to listen for the bear.

Without warning, the bear hits the door again and the wood bows in and slaps hard against my right cheek and forehead. I recoil from the pain and stumble backward, my vision spotty with black dots. My hands and arms flail in front of me as I regain my footing as fast as I can. I grab the axe and throw open the door, screaming a string of indecipherable words as I raise the axe above my head and prepare to come down into the bear's thick fur.

Just then a series of deafening shots ring out nearby. I freeze. My ears register only the high pitched ringing that fills my head, and I look toward the bear in confusion. He's on all fours again and is looking behind him, up toward the summit of the butte. The full sun is shining directly in my face, and I can barely see the shadow of something — no, some*one* — standing on the summit. I keep one eye on the bear and raise my forearm to block the sun's glare. In the distance, I see the outline of the person jogging down the hill toward me, carrying something long — a rifle maybe? The bear turns his attention back to me, lowers his head and begins to sway back and forth, preparing to move toward me again.

"*Help*! Please help me!"

A second later, another deafening shot rings out through the air, and a small cloud of dust pops and rises at the back foot of the bear. I see the outline of the person — a man — about 100 feet away standing in a narrow "v", a rifle held to his shoulder. His head is down and tilted to the side. At the sound of the shot, the bear quickly turns and runs past me, over the side of the butte and toward the tree line below.

I turn back to the direction of the shot, my knees weakening and a tingling sensation running up my spine. My surroundings slip sideways as my vision turns black. Just before I lose consciousness, I think how odd it is that a man is running toward me.

CHAPTER SIX

BEN

THE ECHO OF THE SCREAM rips across the quiet morning and stops me dead in my tracks. I'm still about three hundred feet from the summit of the butte when I hear it, and there's no doubt in my mind that someone is in serious trouble. It sounds like the cry came from just over the top of the butte. As I stand looking up the trail, I make a snap decision and quickly peel out of my heavy backpack; twisting and turning violently against the padded straps, and throwing it down. I unstrap my rifle from the side of the pack, grab an extra ammunition magazine and take off at a run up the trail.

My heart is jackhammering in my chest, and I'm out of breath almost instantly. My steel toe work boots are weighing me down, and it's awkward to try and run quickly with the rifle. It feels like I'm moving in slow motion and all kinds of awful scenarios flash through my head: someone's hurt at the lookout tower, someone's had a heart attack, or encountered a dangerous person. The possibilities are endless, and I really don't want to encounter any of them.

I push myself harder and dig my boots into the trail, trying to ignore the fatigue in my quadriceps. Just a few more feet and I'll be at the top. I'm gasping for air, and my adrenalin is surging as I try to sprint up the trail, forcing myself to go faster. Small clouds of dust rise beside my feet as I tromp up the path and scramble to the summit. My chest is heaving as I stand there catching my breath, feet apart, hands clamped onto the rifle, holding it across my body. I scan the entire upper summit, but I don't see or hear anything. Swallowing hard, I try to fill my mouth with saliva, and then take off across the butte toward my cabin.

Stopping at the top of the narrow trail, I catch my breath again and look down over the cabin— my eyes darting over the entire landscape. I don't understand — I know the scream came from up here, and yet everything still looks locked up tight, just like I left it yesterday afternoon. Nevertheless, something doesn't feel right, and I can't ignore the prickly feeling at the base of my skull.

I take a deep breath and lower my rife, beginning to feel like a real fool. I'm just about to turn around and head back to retrieve my pack when I realize what's wrong with the scene.

The axe I left in the stump yesterday is gone.

I squint to try and bring the woodpile into sharper focus. Where in the heck could —

"Jesus Christ!" The words rush out before I can even think.

I take a half step backward, and I quickly raise my rifle. Looking through the scope, I confirm what I've seen and suck in a quick breath. Sure enough, there's a bear on all fours facing the front of the outhouse. I make out wide claw marks in the panels of the door and from the way the bear is standing, it looks like it's about to attack again.

Just then, the door flies open, and a woman screaming incomprehensible words lurches out, my axe raised above her head. The bear lowers its head, waits a beat and moves quickly toward the woman.

I don't even think.

I zero in on the bear in the scope. My index finger instinctively slides into place as I aim for the hind end and gently squeeze the trigger and hold. Three rounds fire in succession as the rifle kicks back against the hollow of my shoulder, the sound breaking the sky apart. A cloud of dust rises behind the bear's hind foot, and it flinches and freezes, turning its head back toward me.

Through the scope, I can see the woman. She's focused on the bear but quickly looks at the place I'm standing at the top of the summit. She's squinting at me through one eye, still holding the axe above her head, and I can see the glint of its silver face in the sun.

What in the *world* is going on here?

I shift the rifle to my left hand and begin to jog down the hill, my eyes never leaving the bear and the woman.

As I approach them, I see the bear turn his head back toward the woman. It swings like a slow pendulum, and I know before I see him move that he's going for her again.

"*Help*! Please help me!"

I'm still moving down the hill as I bring the rifle to my shoulder again. I plant my feet, find the bear in my scope and fire again. The shot lands just behind it, and this time the bear bolts hard right, past the outhouse and disappears over the side of the butte. I lower the rifle and take off quickly toward the woman.

She's starting to sway. Her weight is shifting in a strange manner, and I can tell she's about to pass out.

"Hang on now," I yell to her, but it's too late. Her arms suddenly drop as her knees buckle. She sinks to the ground in a heap, smacking her head on a large, round rock.

"Ah hell," I mutter as I hustle over to her. I look around quickly for any sign of the bear before I kneel down next to her in the dirt, resting the rifle within hand's reach against the wall of the outhouse.

Looking over her, I don't see any obvious lacerations or open wounds, but the ankle that's twisted up underneath her looks like it's at an odd direction. I kneel down near the top of her head and note the contusion just above her temple. It's swollen and soft, but it's only about the size of a quarter. I turn my attention to her spine and slowly run my fingertips underneath her skull and down alongside each cervical vertebrae, feeling for anything that's obviously out of place. I don't feel any apparent fractures or dislocations, and as I reach the top of her shoulders, I slide my fingers up and alongside her throat, quickly reassured by the shallow thrum of her pulse.

Coming around to the side of her I open each eyelid and examine her pupils. They don't look dilated, and they both seem to be roughly the same size, but she's still unconscious, and I need to get her inside.

"Hang on now. I'm just gonna run over and unlock the door."

I race to the porch and am taken aback as I spot a large, jagged hole in the floorboards; taking note to repair it as I reach into my pocket and fish out the padlock key. I push the door open, shove the key back into my pants and run back to where the woman is lying on the ground.

Reaching down, I gently scoop her arm over my shoulder and cradle her head in the crook of my left elbow. As I lift her torso off the ground, her head lolls in my arm, and I work to balance the dead weight of the rest of her body. Holding her body close to mine, I come up on one knee, raise her body off the ground and simultaneously rise to a full stand. I give her body a quick jostle, settling her, and head toward the cabin. Glancing down at her, I see that her mouth is slightly open, and I notice a small smattering of freckles covering the bridge of her nose and disappearing across her cheekbones. I exhale loudly, frustrated with myself that I've noticed her, and frustrated she's so attractive.

Once inside, I carefully deposit her onto my bed. It's stuffy inside the cabin, so I unlatch and open the window above her head and move across to the windows at the back of the room, pulling open the dark curtains to expose the bright morning outside. I push open the windows and the sliding glass door and feel the beginning of a cross breeze as I walk back to her. Grabbing a throw blanket from the foot of the bed I drape it lightly across her torso and place a hand on her forehead. She feels cool, no fever. I slide my fingers down to her carotid artery and wait for the familiar rise of the pulse beneath her skin, moving to sit down next to her on the bed. She moves her head to the side and groans but her eyes are still closed, and she's still only semi-unconscious.

Great. This is just exactly what I didn't need today.

I turn my attention to her feet and begin unlacing and taking off her shoes. The left comes off easily, and I set it down on the floor next to the bed. The right one I have to carefully work back and forth to get it off the back of her heel. Her ankle is already noticeably swollen, and I don't want to risk damaging it further. Once I get the shoe off, I concentrate on her foot and begin to slowly peel her sock off. At the side of her ankle, the sock suddenly stops because it's adhered to the skin. I lean forward and gently try to pull the sock away, but it's stuck to her ankle, a mixture of dried blood and dirt seems to have formed a sticky paste, and the cotton has meshed with the area as if the sock were actual flesh. I look at her face hesitantly. This is going to hurt, and I'm not thrilled about being the one to do it. She's still out cold though so it's probably better this way. I decide quick is best and yank the sock back from her skin and off the end of her foot. There's a decent gash across the outside of her ankle, and it immediately begins to bleed afresh, the blood slowly pooling near the lower end of the cut. I grab the sock again and hold it over the wound while I visualize where my first aid kit is. My main one is in my pack...on the trail, but that's too far away. I have one in my desk, but that's just basic supplies. It'll have to do for now though, and I quickly grab it, stopping to give my hands a quick scrub at the sink before I sit down next to her again.

Her wound is filthy, and I begin by brushing away the dirt and dried blood and mopping up the fresh blood with a clean gauze pad. The woman groans softly, and her eyebrows furrow together. Working rapidly, I use three large butterfly strips from my kit and press the wound closed, praying it holds. Surprisingly the strips stay put — for the moment anyway — but I can tell the swelling in her ankle has increased and it won't be long before it bursts open. I find two Ace bandages and unroll the start of one, winding it behind her ankle, across the front and diagonally down across the top of her foot, repeating the process until the majority of her ankle is stabilized. She begins to mumble clear words, and I know I need to finish quickly. I make three ziplock bags of ice from my freezer and use the other bandage to wrap them around her ankle and behind her foot.

I stand up again and look down at her. A few curls of auburn hair trail around her swollen temple, and I can see smudges of dirt across her ear and jawline. A thin, gold necklace chain rests in the hollow of her collarbone, and I'm surprised — and then annoyed — to find myself wondering what her name is.

I shake my head to clear my mind and check my watch again. She's been in and out of consciousness for about fifteen minutes. Her heart rate doesn't seem affected, and she doesn't appear to be going into shock, or in any otherwise immediate danger. Still, after retrieving my rifle from the outhouse and giving the area another scan, I radio the ranger station and talk to Dan. I'd rather talk to Annie, but she's working in Bend today, so I briefly explain to Dan what's happened. Dan's a good kid, and for the most part, he does just fine in his job at the station, but Annie...she's getting on in years, but her common sense never seems to amaze me. She's still as sharp as a tack, and she runs that station like a drill sergeant. Over the years, especially these last two, she's sort of taken me under her wing and provided the quiet, patient support I didn't even know I needed. I shake my head at the memories I don't want to acknowledge and sigh. In times like this, I'd just feel better having her advice.

Dan and I discuss bringing the woman down to the Sisters clinic, but I decide against it due to her injuries and her period of unconsciousness, choosing instead to head directly for St. Charles tomorrow. As I'm signing off with Dan, I hear a gargled voice from across the room and turn to glance at her.

Her eyes are closed, but she's moving her head and trying to say something. Her dark eyebrows pull together, and her lips are moving in slow curves. I take a few steps toward her as she opens her eyes and looks around. I can tell she's disoriented, and I'm about to try and reassure her when she suddenly sits up on her forearms and immediately winces.

"Easy now...try not to move."

CHAPTER SEVEN

MIKE - MAY OF LAST YEAR

I STARE at the back of her head on the pillow next to me and try to remember her name. Long black hair trails over the edge of the pillow and disappears under the sheet, her tanned shoulder rising and falling as she sleeps. Kimberly? No that's not right. Kasey? No. I know it ends in a *y*, but I can't remember what the hell it is. Eh, doesn't matter now. I remember what I got from her last night, and that's all that counts. I chuckle to myself; who needs a name?

I turn my head away and look at the bedroom around me. Clothes, empty booze bottles, and crumpled dollar bills cover the dresser that holds an old broken TV. The black mini blinds are pulled down, hanging crooked across the window, and I can see daylight through the corner that's exposed. Jesus. Did it look like this when I got here last night? I notice her bra hanging from the back of the door, and I stare at the huge cups, smirking to myself; definitely implants.

The fact that I can't remember how I got here, or all of what happened last night, doesn't sit on my mind long. I have more important things to do — like getting my ass out of this house without waking this chick up. I need to get to the station and check on Georgia. I chuckle, thinking about how she left last week. I wonder if she really thinks she can hide from me like I don't already see everywhere she goes. But enough is enough already. She's been gone six days now, and I'm starting to really get pissed. Plus, we're out of food, and I miss her cooking.

She's gone to her sister's before, of course, but never for this long and she's sure as shit never dumped all my booze before. That little escapade is going to cost her, and part of her payment is going to be listening to me recount what I did here with — God, what is this girl's name?

Thinking about Georgia spurs me to really get going. I slowly lift my hips up off the bed, the dingy white sheet pulling tight as my body slides to the left. What's-her-name inhales loudly and begins to move. I freeze. If she rolls over, I'm going to have to talk to—

"—Mmm, morning, baby," she murmurs, still facing away from me.

I close my eyes and play dead as I hear her yawn.

"Some night, huh?" Her foot reaches across the mattress and slides seductively up and down my shin. The motion makes me reconsider leaving, at least just yet anyway, and I open my eyes to sneak a peek under the lifted sheet. Her toned, naked ass is pressing dangerously close to me, and I fight the urge to reach down and grab it.

Instead, I begin rehearsing my typical routine: check my phone, pretend there's been an emergency call, give her the bit about an officer needing backup, grab my stuff, give her a last, sexy kiss and promise to call as I smile, shut the door behind me and get on my radio. Works every time.

"Hey, gorgeous." My voice is velvet as I trail my finger down the center of her tan back. I see a thin white line from her bikini string, and I feel my resolve weakening. “I hate to do this, but I just got a call...”

“You gotta go, baby?” she whines and begins to roll onto her back. The sheet slackens and falls away from her chest, revealing a set of perfectly enhanced tits, complete with two, tiny triangle tan lines. I can’t look away.

“It’s the station, there’s been an—”

“—You can’t stay just a little...longer?” She slides her hand across the bed and grabs hold of me.

“—Emergency,” I stutter, losing the track of my speech as my dick hardens in her hand. “Ah screw it, they can wait.” How can I say no? I lean across and flip her onto her stomach. At least I don’t have to look at her fucking face.

I close my eyes and imagine she’s Georgia. Back home. Back in our bed. Where she belongs.

I’m walking out to the cruiser, buckling my belt and sliding the thick leather through the loop when a silver Land Cruiser pulls up quickly behind my car and kills the ignition. A platinum blonde gets out of the driver’s side, and I can hear her heels clicking on the pavement. A moment later she rounds the SUV, and I stop in mid-step.

Her long, tanned legs are a mile long in her cherry red stilettos, and she’s wearing the shortest, tightest fucking dress I’ve ever seen. Her gold, chain-link purse strap is slung diagonally across her body, right between her tits, and the small, attached bag keeps bouncing on her hip as she walks directly toward me. She’s carrying a manila envelope in her hand.

“Well, well, well. What do we have here?” I murmur, pushing my belt through the loop and adjusting my crotch at the same time.

She's staring at the envelope and nearly walks into me.

"Oh! Hello, *Officer*." She purrs. Her cotton candy voice draws my eyes to her glossy lips.

"Ma'am."

I cross my arms in front of my chest and stare at her. This ought to be good.

"I, well, I was just coming to visit my friend Whitney—"

Whitney. Bingo! I knew it ended in a *y*.

"—She's inside, right?" She shifts her eyes. She doesn't know what to do with her hands. Coke, probably. Or Meth.

"She is." I look her up and down and raise my eyebrows. "And *you* are?"

I grin at her. She's definitely got something — probably in her purse — that she doesn't want me to see.

"Oh, I'm just a work friend," she stammers. "Well, have a nice day."

She starts to walk past me, and her heel catches in a crack in the sidewalk. She stumbles, reaching out for me as I lurch forward to catch her, and drops the envelope on the ground.

"Shit!" She bends down to grab the envelope, and I bend down with her, my eyes locked on the massive cleavage that's threatening to bust out of her dress.

"Are you all right?" I ask as we stand up together, my hand still on her thin arm.

"I think so." She twirls an index finger around the end of one of her long curls. "It's just these silly shoes. My boss says they're required," she says, putting her palm on my chest. "Anyway, thank you, Officer—"

She trails a long, painted fake nail down my uniform to the name on my badge, and smiles like a hooker making a sale.

"—Rutherford."

"Yes, ma'am. Are you sure—"

Suddenly she thrusts the envelope into my hand and stands

up straight, shoulders squared, her face serious. Her entire demeanor has changed.

"Mike Rutherford, I'm with San Diego County Process Servers." Her voice is deep, authoritative. What the hell is going on here?

"Consider yourself officially served," she says, taking a pen and pad of paper from her purse and checking her diamond-encrusted watch. "10:47 a.m., Thursday—"

"You gotta be fucking kidding me!"

"Have a nice day. Oh, and Mike?" she says, smiling sweetly and turning on her heel. "Try not to watch my ass as I walk away."

I barely register what she's said as I open the packet of paperwork and read.

Georgia has filed for divorce.

CHAPTER EIGHT

GEORGIA - MAY THIS YEAR

A COLD, HEAVY PAIN PULLS me out of unconsciousness, and I open my eyes in a stranger's bed. The side of my head feels like I've slept on a brick, and the pain causes me to squint my right eye shut. I'm lying on my back, a soft blanket covering my body. Although I'm disoriented and anxious, I plant my forearms on the bed and try to push myself up to look around. A sudden and incredible pain in my ankle takes my breath away, causing me to instantly wince.

"Easy now...try not to move."

I freeze in place and shift my eyes to find the source of the deep voice. At the end of the bed, half hidden in the dim light stands a tall man. I squint to bring him into focus as he steps closer and rests a hand across the thick wooden footboard.

"Just try to relax," he says quietly. "You're safe."

"Where am I?" My voice is raspy and weak. "Who are you?"

My body aches, and I'm suddenly dizzy. I lay my head back onto the pillow and close my eyes as I try to swallow.

"My name is Ben Harrison. I work for the Forest Service.

You're at the top of Black Butte. It's...about 2:00 p.m. on Friday," he says. "Do you remember what happened?"

I can't focus on any one thought. My brain is swimming with anxiety over the memory of the bear, and my chest tightens as the earlier events replay in my mind. I close my eyes and nod. I wish I could forget.

"Do you remember your name?"

I open my eyes again to see if the room is still spinning. I can focus on the patterns outlined in the exposed logs above me, and I answer slowly.

"I'm Georgia Ruther — I mean, Marks. I'm Georgia Marks. I came up here to hike this morning." I pause, realizing where I must be. "Am I in the cabin?"

A wave of pain shoots up the side of my ankle, and I gasp, leaning my head to the right to look toward my foot.

"Yes, you're in my cabin. Your ankle is pretty damaged. I've wrapped it and packed ice around it, but I would imagine it's probably broken. In fact, now that you're awake you need to take some Ibuprofen," he says, walking around to the side of the bed and peering down at me.

I look up at him momentarily and nod as I let out my breath. He stares at me for a moment.

"Do you have any history of substance abuse?"

My face contorts at his question. "What?"

"I said do you have any history of substance abuse?" His voice is louder now as if I hadn't heard him.

"No," I say flatly. "I don't. What are you even talking about?"

"I need to know if you have any history of drug or alcohol abuse. Have you ever misused prescription medication or been treated, in-patient or out, for substance abuse?"

I stare at him, dumbfounded. Who the hell is this guy? He looks like he's older than me but not by much. Is he a doctor? Why should I tell him—

"Georgia. Can you answer the question for me, please?" he says, crossing his arms over his chest.

The pain in my foot screams at me again, and I wince. "No, like I said *already*. I've never abused drugs or alcohol. Not that it's any of your damn business."

He disappears across the room as I stare up at the ceiling. I'm hurting, and now I'm mad, but most of all I'm filled with disbelief at the realization of the predicament I'm in.

"Here." He's back, standing near my left shoulder, his open palm outstretched to me; two pills cradled there. "This one's Vicodin," he says. "Have you ever taken it before?"

I look from his hand to his face. It's hard to see his expression. His mouth and jaw are covered with a short beard, and his eyes are shadowed by the green US Forest Service baseball cap he's wearing.

Is this guy seriously giving me drugs? I quickly decide I don't even care. My ankle hurts so much I'd probably take heroin if he offered it to me.

"Yeah. I've taken it before." I have Mike to thank for that. "But, how do you have Vicodin?"

He sighs and then answers. "Once upon a time I used to be a paramedic."

"So?"

"So, when I took the job here," he says, waving his hand across the inside of the cabin, "they wanted someone that could provide critical care in backcountry rescue situations, someone who could dispense certain medications if needed." He pauses and tilts his head to one side. "Don't worry. I still work closely with St. Charles Medical, as well as the Forest Service. You want to see my certification?"

"No."

I lift my head off the pillow as I take the pills and reach for the blue and gray earthenware mug he's offering. I swallow them both quickly. The water is cool and quenching against my parched throat, and I realize that I am extremely thirsty and quickly empty the rest of the mug.

"Thanks," I say quietly, handing the mug back to him and laying my cheek against the pillow. He checks his watch, walks over to the other side of the room and slowly sinks into a faded leather chair; letting out a deep sigh as he relaxes.

My eyes scan the rest of the space, and I note the large front window at the front of the cabin, now uncovered and allowing the bright sunshine to stream through in rectangular blocks. Underneath the window are a small wooden table and two chairs, with an unlit camping lantern sitting in the center. To the right of the window, I can see the closed front door with a small kitchen area on the opposite wall.

I rotate my head and look over to the other side of the cabin. Along the south wall is a large wood stove; its dark, shiny metal chimney juts out of the back and heads up through the roof. A wooden crate stands next to the stove, and I can see a few pieces of kindling and rolled up newspaper waiting in a corner. In the middle of the room is a round braided rug that's anchored by two legs of the leather chair the man's sitting in. I can see one of his black boots planted firmly on the rug. The other casually resting over his leg.

The distraction from my pain is short-lived, and I abandon any further observation of the room as the ache in my ankle draws my attention back to my feet. My left foot looks fine, and I can wiggle my toes without any problem. My right foot, however, looks horrendous. My ankle is wrapped in a flesh-colored Ace bandage with three ice packs surrounding it. Only the tip of my foot and the chipped violet nail polish on my toes are visible. I attempt to slowly move my foot and immediately regret the decision, sucking in a hard breath as the pain radiates through my body.

"You'll really want to try and keep that ankle still," he says from across the room. I've already forgotten his name. "I radioed Sisters Clinic to get you checked out, but they advised me to take you straight on to St. Charles; they're better equipped to handle serious injury, and like I said, I think it's probably broken."

My heart plummets.

Broken? A hospital? I can barely manage to wrap my head around these concepts. What about my Jeep? What about my job? More importantly, how am I going to get back home? My temple begins to throb, and I feel a wave of anxiety flood through me. I'm scared, and on top of that, I feel like a complete fool. I was so stupid to come up here like this. I thought I was so brave. I thought doing this on my own would give me some sense of accomplishment. I thought I could prove to myself that I'm not the helpless, incompetent fool that Mike branded me as so many times. Tears threaten to overwhelm me, and I immediately will them away; reminding myself that Mike is no longer in my life and no longer a threat to me.

I decide to distract myself and look over my toes toward the leather chair where he's sitting.

"Thank you...uh, I'm sorry, what was your—"

"It's Ben," he says. "How's your pain level now?"

I pause for a moment and realize the pain in my ankle has actually lessened. It is easier for me to concentrate, although I am starting to feel a little lightheaded.

"Maybe a six now, I guess? Mainly it's the throbbing that's the worst," I reply. "I wanted to say thank you for what you did." My voice is barely a whisper. "I'm really not sure what I would have done had you not..." I swallow hard. I can't finish my sentence. I don't want to think about how close I came to a very different ending.

"Don't worry about it. It's nothing," he says. "I'm just glad I got there when I did. We don't get a lot of bears up here — with all the hikers it kind of keeps them away — so I'm pretty surprised by this myself." His voice is deep and gravely.

"I let the Department of Fish and Wildlife know about this," he says, standing up and taking a step toward me. "And I posted an updated bear sighting near the tower. On the way down, I'll put one on the trailhead board, too."

On the way down? How the heck is that going to happen?

He begins to slowly pace across the floor. "And we'll need to figure out what to do with your vehicle. I'm assuming it's the white Jeep at the trailhead? By the way, I looked around outside but couldn't find a cell phone, wallet, or keys...did you bring a pack or anything with you?"

"What? Yes! I had a backpack with my wallet and keys, some food, and I think my phone was in there too. You didn't see the pack outside? The bear was...well, it was dragging it all over the porch."

He shakes his head in reply, and I feel the panic begin to rise in my chest again.

"Oh, God. What about my camera, did you see that out there? And how are you going to get me down this mountain? And what am I going to do about my Jeep?" I know I'm whining, but I don't care.

Ben abruptly stops pacing. He takes a few quick steps over to the end of the bed and leans forward to plant both hands on the footboard; his shoulders hunching around his ears. His eyes bore into me, and he takes a deep breath, letting it out slowly before speaking.

"Listen, Georgia. I don't know yet, okay? It's not like this kind of thing happens a lot out here. I'm taking it one step at a time, just like you. If you've got any ideas, I'm all ears."

My cheeks flush in response to his tone, and I look away in embarrassment.

After a moment he sighs. "Hey, sorry...I'm just not...I mean it's just that...look, this wasn't how I had envisioned opening up my cabin for the season, okay? I was up here yesterday chopping wood all day, and no bears bothered *me*." He stuffs his hands in his pockets and huffs. "This just wasn't what I planned on doing today."

"Oh, like *I* did?"

"Yeah, well...what were you thinking coming up here alone? What if it wasn't a bear? What if there was some crazy guy up here?"

I slap my hand down hard on the bed. "Oh, you mean like *right now*?"

"Hey! That's not fair," he says, stomping around to the side of the bed and standing over me. "I quite possibly saved your life out there. I carried you in here, wrapped that ankle, and tried to take care of you!" His thick eyebrows pull together, and a small vertical crease appears between them.

"Not fair? You think I *wanted* this to happen? Besides that, what's so wrong with hiking alone? People do it all the time!" I cross my arms over my chest. "And where's my damn camera!"

Tears are burning at the corners of my eyes. I want to jump up out of this stupid bed, run down the mountain to my Jeep, and go home. Home! Oh my God — Sylvia! I gasp as I realize I've totally forgotten about Sylvia. I take a deep breath and look at Ben. His face is flushed under his beard, and his mouth is slightly open. He's about to say something, but I cut him off.

"No! My turn! Listen, I have to contact my sister. She's going to be out of her mind with worry." I can tell he's about to protest, but I continue anyway. "The faster I can contact her, the faster you'll be rid of me."

He clamps his mouth shut and raises his eyebrows, backing up a step and putting his palms out in front of him.

"Works for me, lady. Just give me a number, and I'll radio the station right now." A small victorious smile appears at the corner of his mouth, and I narrow my eyes at him. I'm beginning to detest this guy.

When I open my mouth to rattle off Sylvia's number, I am horrified to realize I don't know it. It's saved in my phone. I never actually dial it whenever I call her. I close my eyes and mumble the words I don't want to say.

"I don't know her number."

"*What*?" he laughs. "You don't know her number? Well, that's the one piece of information I kinda—"

"—It's saved in my phone, okay. Who memorizes phone numbers by heart anymore? What is this, 1985? Do *you* remember everyone's numbers?" I point my finger at him. "Don't answer that!" I am so angry that I can feel the heat rising on my face.

He rubs the back of his neck with his hand and steps away from me. His heavy boots pound against the wood floor, and I can hear him cursing under his breath as he walks to the kitchen. He bangs around for a moment, and then he stomps back toward me. I refuse to look at him. He slams a plastic bottle of water down on the side table next to me.

"Here. In case you get thirsty again!"

With that, he marches across the room, throws the door open and slams it behind him.

CHAPTER NINE

GEORGIA

THE CABIN DOOR CRASHES SHUT so hard a plastic bowl falls off the kitchen counter and bounces along the floor before finally coming to a rest. I let out a deep sigh, my breath shuddering as I exhale; glad he's outside. What the hell? What's this guy's problem anyway? One thing's pretty clear: he needs — or more likely, wants — to get out of the cabin and away from me for a while. If I'm honest, I can hardly blame him. I'm sure he has work to do up here and taking care of an injured hiker is probably not on his agenda. It's pretty obvious he lives up here alone, and he probably likes it that way. The cabin is meager. It's enough for a bachelor, but it's clearly lacking any kind of feminine attention. It smells like pine trees, wood, and camping.

A man-cave if I've ever seen one.

I shake my head to clear my muddled thoughts and refocus on just how angry Sylvia is going to be when I finally get in touch with her. In my defense, it's not like I planned to do this. But I know that really doesn't matter. She was right — she's always right, and I should have listened to her. I should have listened to her about a lot of things, namely Mike Rutherford.

She tried to tell me not to marry Mike. She said there was something about him that just wasn't quite right. I cringe at the memory of how in love I was, how blind I was to the little red flags that should have made me run long and hard in the opposite direction. Instead, I felt like his small transgressions made him more human, that his flaws were proof that he wasn't trying to put on a show for me. I envisioned us sharing our lives together, growing and maturing together as we navigated our future.

I was so wrong.

Pushing the memories from my mind, I look over at the water bottle on the table next to me. It's sitting under the shadow of a small lampshade, and two hardcover books are stacked beside it. I crane my neck to read the titles: *The Great Gatsby* and *Listening for Coyote: A Walk Across Oregon's Wilderness.* I blink a few times, surprised by the Gatsby. It's one of my favorites, and I wonder at his reasons for choosing it — he doesn't strike me as the literary type. Maybe the books were gifts, and he's just using them for decoration, or, more likely, they belong to his girlfriend.

She's got good taste.

I reach over for the water, unscrew the cap and drain half the bottle almost immediately, and then prop myself up on my elbows to take a better look around the cabin. There are two large windows and a glass door to my left, and through them, I can see the gorgeous central Oregon blue sky and a few threads of wispy clouds in the distance. A tall wardrobe is placed along the wall next to me, and I can see a pair of binoculars hanging on a leather strap that's hooked over one of the knobs on the front. The cabin walls are made of exposed log; smooth and round, stained dark brown with age and some kind of plaster fills the spaces between each of them. Very little is on display here: a single framed photograph near the window, and a rifle hanging above the leather chair. Seeing the rifle makes me instantly regret how I've just treated Ben. He did save my life, after all. I guess he has a right to be short-tempered.

Reaching across the bed, I grab the other pillow and use it to prop myself up to a semi-seated position; the high headboard behind me creaking as I lean against it. I reach for the bottle again, take a few more drinks and sit with it resting in my lap. I'm starting to feel slightly cold.

Suddenly Ben bursts through the door, and I flinch so hard the water in my bottle slides violently up the side, and threatens to slosh out. I look at him with wide eyes.

"Here's your dang camera," he says. "And here's your backpack." He seems a little less grumpy, and I notice he's not stomping anymore as he walks across the room and unslings the camera from his neck. "It's pretty banged up. I found it near the woodpile." He thrusts his arm out at me, the camera pushing toward my face.

I attempt a thin smile. "Thank you," I say, and reach to take it from his hand, setting it down on the bed beside me. He dumps the mangled pack on the floor and walks over to the window at the back of the cabin, his hands on his hips.

"Still no phone though. I didn't see any trace of it." His voice is softer now. "Did you go anywhere else up here besides the porch?"

"Yes. Before I came over here, I was up near the lookout tower and the cupola, but honestly, I can't remember if I still had it with me when I sat down on the porch. I didn't even use it to take pictures — my camera was working so well."

I am starting to lose track of the events that have occurred today, and am just about to begin an apology when, to my incredible embarrassment, my stomach growls loudly enough for us both to hear. I cover my belly with both hands and feel my cheeks flush.

He turns wide-eyed to look at me, and for the first time, a small grin pulls at the corner of his mouth.

"Hungry?"

I shrug and tug at my lower lip with my teeth. No way I'm asking him for food. No. Way.

Ben checks his watch. "Well, it *is* almost 4 o'clock. You probably haven't eaten since what? Before 10 a.m.?"

"I guess so," I say, even though I'm starving.

He turns to walk toward the kitchen. "But don't think this is going to be any fancy schmancy food, okay? This is a man's cabin. All I've got is man food."

My eyebrows raise, and my mouth drops open as he walks by.

I can't help but turn my head slightly to watch him in the kitchen. He rattles around, pulling a few things out from an area under the sink, and I can hear him talking to himself, something about his only clean plate. I roll my eyes in sarcastic sympathy, and I realize I'm starting to feel more relaxed.

After a moment, he brings me a small plate of several different snack foods. Crackers, pickles, sliced apple and cheese, and thick slices of salami cover the small blue plate. He's even included a napkin on the corner. He sets it down on the bed next to my camera, and I look up at him and smile.

"Thank you. I really appreciate this."

He looks into my eyes for a moment and then nods. "Welcome."

I layer a cracker with a piece of cheese and try not to shove the whole thing in my mouth at once. "Aren't you going to have anything?" I ask.

"Me? No. I'm not really hungry." He's pacing again back and forth across the room. It's making me nervous.

"Everything okay?"

He stops and walks over to the end of the bed again, looking at me for a moment before he answers.

"Yeah. I'm just trying to figure out what to do with you. Do you have any family nearby? Where are you from, anyway?"

"I live in Silverton...it's near Salem. I'm staying with my sister and her husband right now. Other than Sylvia and Scott, no, I don't have any other family."

Ben stares at me, and I stop chewing. "Whapf?" I say, pushing the large bite of apple and cheese to the side of my mouth.

"No husband or boyfriend?"

Wow, the nerve of this guy.

"No." I begin chewing again and raise an eyebrow at him. Let him think about that for a while.

"Hmm. Well, is that just for looks then?"

I frown at him.

He juts his chin toward my left hand, and I follow his gaze. My wedding band. I'm still wearing it.

"Oh." Of course he thinks I'm married. *Apparently,* you *still think you're married.* I can hear my sister's voice in my head as she's asked me a million times why I still wear it.

"No, no boyfriend. And I'm not married anymore," I say, quietly.

"Sorry. I just assumed...with the ring."

He seems embarrassed — as if he's accidentally entered someone's private room. I just shrug and avoid his eyes. Wearing it helps me feel like less of an obvious target in public, and it keeps some of the pickup lines at bay. Usually.

"Anyway." He crosses the room toward the sink. "What about your sister then? What's her last name? I can have the ranger station get in contact with your local police department."

"It's Sorenson. Her husband's an attorney in town. It's probably too late to get a live person at the office, but you could leave a message on the voicemail. The firm is Kloss & Jenkins." I set the empty plate down at my side. I suddenly have an overwhelming desire to giggle, and my muscles feel like putty.

"All right. Let me see what I can—" He starts to turn away and then stops. "Hey, are you feeling okay? How's your pain level now?"

"Me? Oh, I feel great, maybe 1 or 2 now." I actually do giggle, and I cover my mouth with my hand. What is wrong with me?

"Mmhm. Sounds like the Vicodin's kicked in."

I shrug and finish the water in my bottle. He's such a grownup. This makes me giggle again, and I look sheepishly over toward him, but he's already turning away.

He's busy in the kitchen, and I lean forward a bit so I can watch him. He pulls a coffee mug down from the shelf and then bends over as he rummages through a cabinet.

Dear God, why have I never liked cargo pants before?

A moment later I hear hissing and then the *flick, flick* of a propane burner being lit. The strong odor of the gas floats near me and then dissipates. The scent takes me immediately back to cold mornings sitting around a campground picnic table with my sister — my parents lighting our Coleman camp stove and beginning to cook breakfast. It's so funny how smells can trigger memories: good, and bad, so easily.

"I'm making coffee. Would you like some? I'm afraid I don't have any tea."

"No, thank you. Could I have some more water though, please? This bottle is empty."

This time he fills a glass of water from the tap at the sink and glances over at me. He must see the look on my face.

"It's from a cistern; snow melt from winter," he explains. "Don't worry — it's safe. But it may taste a little weird from the filter it passes through." He walks toward me with the water and for the first time, I actually really look at him. He's wearing an unbuttoned forest green shirt with the sleeves rolled at the elbows. I notice a US Forest Service emblem on the side, and a gray V-neck tee underneath that's tucked into his cargo pants. His outer shirt hangs open, and his t-shirt is tucked into tan cargo pants. A dark brown leather belt sits on his hips, and a small hand-held radio hangs from a belt loop.

As he brings me the glass, I can't help but notice a thick band of muscle standing out across his forearm. My eyes slide up to his face; he's taken off his hat, and I can't help but stare at him. He pauses and looks back at me, a look of bewilderment spreading across his face. My painkillers must truly be working because I don't care at all about manners or if I'm offending him — or embarrassing myself — by staring.

His dark hair is neatly cropped, slightly longer in the front, and his sideburns run right into his short beard; flecks of gray glinting near his jaw bone. I notice a small scar near the corner of his right eye and am appalled to discover I find it appealing. I wonder how he got it, and how old he is. I immediately admonish myself for such ridiculous thoughts. *You look like hell, and you just divorced a cheating husband who liked to beat you up. Who cares how old he is?*

Ben hands me the glass and shifts his eyes away awkwardly. "Okay, I'm going to radio the station in Sisters and see if they can contact Silverton police, or the law firm — what was the name again?"

"Kloss, with a *k*, and Jenkins."

He nods and walks over to a desk in the corner of the cabin and pulls a chair roughly across the floor to sit down. He reaches forward and slides what looks like a large microphone toward him. I can hear him flipping switches, and I listen intently as crackling static cuts across the room. The noise is periodically interrupted by words from Ben, followed by a far-off male voice. I hear Ben describe the bear and the information about my injury. He mentions Sylvia and Scott's names and relays the information about the firm. When he's finished, he switches off the radio and pushes it back against the wall. He lingers at the desk and writes something down in a large book. A thick green ribbon hangs from the end of it — some kind of journal?

I lean my head back against the headboard and look up at the ceiling, and the light reflected there. I feel a little drunk, and I snicker to myself as I consider how in the world I'm going to get down off this mountain. And once I *am* down, how I'm going to get to the hospital. And what's going to happen to my Jeep? My thoughts spiral downward, and I can't help but believe I was crazy to think I could handle life on my own, without Mike to tell me what, and how, to do everything, every minute of every day. I glance down at my wedding band and hang my head at the shame that boils up in me. Why do I still wear this? I despise Mike. I despise that I chose someone so wrong. How could I not have seen the warning signs, and more importantly, why didn't I leave sooner? I am torn between hating myself for choosing the wrong person and hating myself for staying as long as I did.

CHAPTER TEN

MIKE - MAY LAST YEAR

I CALL Frank's office from the cruiser as I leave Whitney's house, divorce papers in my hand. His bimbo secretary tries to put me off, but I blow past her and get him on the line right away. We set up a time for me to come in and strategize how to change Georgia's mind, get her to drop the divorce proceedings, and get her sweet ass back home.

Frank's a good ol' boy, and he's seen me through a lot of tricky shit. I don't know what I'd do without him in my corner. Well, actually, I'd probably be doing five to ten if it weren't for his shady morals and slick use of the California Revised Statutes. He's saved my skin many a time, and I know he'll sort this mess out with Georgia too.

Talk about a shit day. Not only did the Chief ream me for incomplete paperwork, but Frank called before I could even get to his office and told me I'm basically shit out of luck. Turns out I don't have anything to coerce Georgia with because she's threatened to produce medical records and photographs from so-called *domestic violence* emergency room visits I didn't even fucking *know* about. On top of that, she promised to send a copy of everything to my Chief — as well as the Union-Tribune — and she even emailed Frank a few samples of her evidence to back it up.

She isn't fucking bluffing.

But there's no proof it was me. Those pictures...well, I'm pretty sure she had someone do her up with makeup to look that bad. She's lying, of course, but faced with the evidence, Frank says there's no way we should fight it.

I have no choice but to agree to her terms: grant her the divorce, let her keep the Honda, and sell the house immediately, with a 50/50 split of the profit. She told Frank that because we used the money from her parents' estate to buy the house, she should be more than entitled to half of the profit. Hearing that tidbit makes my blood boil, but I feel a little better when I hear she doesn't want any spousal support or alimony, thank fuck. Not that she deserves any more of my money anyway. But still.

He wraps it up by telling me she doesn't want to keep my name.

Jesus. That hurts.

As much as I hate it, I sign the paperwork the following week and list the house the next day. Signing my name on the paperwork makes me feel like hell — luckily my favorite bottle of vodka is there to keep me company — but being forced to put my house on the market...well, that really pisses me off. I figure if she's going to make me sell the house, I'm going to sell it for as cheap as possible.

My sledgehammer turns out to be the best fifty bucks I've ever spent.

The realtor can't get any buyer to look past the holes in the walls, the missing doors, or the clothing and trash I scatter all through the house. It's actually perfect because after everything is said and done I end up breaking even on the son of a bitch — with what I still owe on the house, there's no money left over to split. Even Frank is impressed.

I throw all my stuff in garbage bags and move into a run-down condo with a single guy from work. A year ago his wife divorced him for another guy — some young prick that picked her up at the gym — and now he's stuck making a mortgage payment for a house his keys don't fit in anymore. He's out of here soon though. He talks about relocating north and joining a smaller unit somewhere. They don't have kids, and there's nothing keeping him here. Sometimes I think about doing that too but the idea of starting over sounds like something a loser would do, and I'm sure as hell no goddamn loser.

We commiserate most nights over a bottle of vodka or gin, and although he's a lot older than me, he usually passes out before I even feel buzzed. Fucking lightweight. Still, it's nice to have someone to hang out with.

I leave everything of Georgia's in the house for the new owner to deal with. The only thing I do take with me is her San Diego Padres sweatshirt. And some nights, like tonight, I hold it in my hands and bring it to my face, inhaling deeply. It still smells like her — flowery, spicy, and sexy — and it drives me wild. I bought it for her at our first baseball game after moving here, and she wore that thing religiously every weekend. I'm actually surprised she left it.

We'd laughed so much at that game, eaten too much junk food and cheered on our favorite players as they took the field. The Padres ended up losing that day, but we didn't even notice.

I'd thrown my arm around her, run my hands through the soft brown curls that trailed down her back, and kissed her long and hard, right there, in front of everyone. When we came up for air, we saw ourselves on the big screen, and Georgia covered her face with embarrassment. I can still see the pink flush across her cheeks, the way she could look at me from underneath those long eyelashes. Damn. I still get hard just thinking about her.

I bury my face in her sweatshirt and breathe deeply.

That was before Jason though.

That was before everything went to shit.

I toss the sweatshirt aside, reach for my bottle of beer, and turn on the TV. I need to figure out a way to get my wife back before someone else gets hold of her.

CHAPTER ELEVEN

GEORGIA

SOMETHING I'VE BEEN PUSHING TO the back of my mind, now refuses to be silenced: I have to pee. Badly. All three ice packs on my ankle have turned to liquid, and looking at them reminds me of my own bursting bladder. I'm afraid of the pain that's sure to come with trying to walk, and I'm completely humiliated that I even need to ask for help. I don't even *know* this man, and I'm positive he doesn't want to help some strange woman go to the bathroom. Nevertheless, I can't ignore it any longer. I have to say something.

I watch as Ben finishes writing in the book at his desk, pushes out of his chair and stands up to stretch his arms above his head. He glances at his watch and then turns to the kitchen. It's now or never.

"Uh, Ben?"

He stops and glances at me, eyebrows raised.

"So, I'm really embarrassed even to say this, but I really need to use the restroom." I cringe. I absolutely detest being unable to do things for myself.

"Yeah. I was thinking about that earlier too," he says, walking toward me. "So, you'll have to lean on me, which shouldn't be a problem, but..." He stops. The look on my face must betray my worry. "Don't worry about it, that part will be fine. But...I only have the outhouse here." I notice his cheeks flush slightly as he looks around the room. "What I mean is, you'll have to go back to that place. Will that be ok?"

Oh. That's right. I hadn't even thought of that. Back to the place where a crazed bear nearly killed me. I shove this thought aside. It doesn't matter anymore. This need is urgent. At this point, I would squat outside behind a bush if I could put weight on my ankle.

"It's ok. I'll be fine," I say with resolution.

"Ok, then," he says, standing next to me. "Let's start by moving your left leg off the bed. Good. Just let it hang over the edge a bit. Go slowly." He reaches over me, picks up the liquefied ice packs and sets them away from my ankle. He whistles high through his teeth.

"Now that is a mess indeed," he says, jutting his chin out toward my ankle. I follow his stare and am appalled at what I see. My ankle is huge. Even with the bandage, it's still about three times the size of my left ankle and obviously bruised. I can see the discoloration in my toes already.

I shake my head and steel my jaw. Ben reaches over toward my calf and stops before touching my leg. He looks at me for permission, and I reluctantly nod, scared of the pain to come.

He holds my calf, and I can feel the pressure of his fingertips along the sides of my muscle. He begins to slide my leg toward the edge of the bed and my ankle throbs; even the smallest movement hurts.

"Ok, now I'm going to have you put your weight on your left leg and try to stand up. I'll be supporting you, so I want you to put your arm around my neck when you stand, okay?"

I look up from my seated position into his face. I won't lie. I am scared to death. I hate being vulnerable, and I hate pain. My face must reveal my fear because his rigid expression immediately softens.

"Hey, come on now, you're going to be ok. This really isn't that big of a deal. Don't be embarrassed or worried." His eyes travel modestly over me, and he smirks. "You don't look that heavy." I look at him for a moment and decide I really don't have a choice but to trust him. I nod in favor of continuing.

"On the count of three then. One." He sits next to me on the bed. "Two." He puts my arm around his neck, and I take a deep breath and hold it. "Three." We both stand up.

I am instantly dizzy, and the room begins to tilt. I close my eyes and lean into him as my knee starts to give out.

"Easy now. Take a second here. You haven't been upright for several hours. It's normal to feel dizzy."

I stand for a moment and open my eyes again. The room slowly rights itself, and I'm able to lean away from him and take a breath. My right foot dangles above the floor.

"Ok, better. It's not as bad now," I say.

"Let's get you out of here before that changes then. Ready to hop? Here we go, on three each time, okay? And tell me if you need to rest."

Thankfully we are able to cross the cabin in just over a dozen hops. By the time we reach the front door, my left quad is on fire, and I am so focused on the tension in my leg, and my expanding bladder, that I don't even care to consider what happened on the porch outside, or what took place in the outhouse. All I know is that by the time we reach the outhouse my leg is shaking intensely, and I cannot wait to rip down my workout pants and pee. I don't even speak to Ben. I just hop inside. He grabs the door behind me and holds it shut while I balance myself on the bench, strip my pants and underwear down, and throw open the toilet seat lid. I say a silent prayer of thanks to God as I attend to my humanly needs and decide I never want to drink water again.

When I knock to signal I'm finished, Ben lets the door open up and greets me with a small bottle of hand sanitizer, one side of his mouth turned up at the corner.

We hop back toward the cabin, smaller hops now as my leg is thoroughly worn out. I have to stop several times and take short breaks. We are nearing the porch when I start to ask for another break. "Ben, I'm sorry but could we sto—"

My question is cut short when my body is suddenly whisked upward, legs first.

"Lady, I got things to do, and this hopping business is too damn slow," he grizzles.

He walks quickly as he carries me, both of my arms around his neck. I don't know what to do with my head, so I just hold my neck out straight, the muscles alongside my throat flexed to the maximum. We enter the cabin sideways, and I am reminded of a movie scene where the groom brings the bride across the threshold but forgets to turn and knocks her head against the doorframe. I start to giggle.

He glances at me, "What?" he demands, taking short breaths.

"Nothing. It's nothing. Thank you for carrying me. It's so much easier this way," I say with a smile. "I'm heavy, aren't I?"

It's true. At 5'7" and a size six most people are surprised to know I weigh around one hundred and fifty pounds. It's the gym I guess; lifting weights is the only thing that kept me grounded back then — with Mike — and it's the only thing that keeps me sane now; especially over this last year.

The smile fades from my face as I remember once hiding a bruise with makeup so I could go to the gym. I had to act like everything was fine. I used the typical *I walked into a doorframe* excuse, and my friends placated me with thin smiles and no questions. I was living in a house in hell, and for some reason, I just kept renewing my lease.

Ben sets me down softly, this time in the leather chair, and takes a few steps back.

"No. You're not heavy at all. I just didn't want to hurt you any further."

For some reason these words make me smile.

CHAPTER TWELVE

GEORGIA

"WELL, SINCE I CAN'T GET you out of my cabin tonight, looks like I'll be cooking for two."

His back is to me, and I can't tell if he's being sarcastic or not, so I keep quiet and watch as he scuttles around in the small kitchen. It feels extremely awkward sitting in his chair next to the wood stove, my ankle propped up on the now empty firewood crate, watching him cook for us. He'd started a fire after we came back inside and the warmth from the stove is comforting, although the earlier relief I felt from the Vicodin is wearing off, and my ankle is beginning to ache.

I'm not sure whether to watch him, ask him questions, or focus on something else altogether. It's been a very long time since a man prepared a meal for me, and I'm not sure I like feeling so helpless. Mike cooked when we first started dating, but that quickly came to a screeching halt about a year or so after we were married. By that time, his idea of cooking was insulting everything I made that didn't meet his expectations. Many a dinner ended up washed down the disposal, either because he refused to eat it, *you used too much oregano*, or because he simply never showed up for dinner. So sitting here now, watching Ben cook for us, even though I'm definitely not under any romantic pretense, makes me feel very pampered.

I turn to look out of the back windows of the cabin and sit in awe of the twilight. The hues in the sky look like vivid water-colors on wet paper, and once again I'm stunned at the incredible accomplishments of nature. I sit for a moment and realize the day has almost come to an end — I've been up here for an entire day — and the reason for that is even more unbelievable.

"Do you think that bear will come back?" I ask, turning to Ben. "I mean, do you think the trail should be closed?"

Ben looks at me, the commotion in the kitchen ceasing.

"No. I'd be very surprised if that bear showed up here again." The end of one of the carrots he's chopping flies off the cutting board onto the floor, and he reaches down to retrieve it, tossing it into the garbage, and wiping his hands on the dishtowel hanging over his shoulder.

"Are you surprised it showed up here at all?"

"I am. However, you mentioned you came up at dawn, right?"

"Yeah," I say, nodding.

"Well, I think it's possible you might have disturbed that bear on your way up here. Who knows, maybe she had cubs nearby."

"*She?* How do you know it was female?"

"I don't...for certain. But when I was out looking for your phone I saw the bushes the bear came through. They were walked over and marked in a way that would lead me to believe it was female. That, and she wasn't very big," he says, tossing some chopped vegetables into a cast iron pot on the stove.

I nearly choke. "Wasn't very big! That bear was gigantic!"

Ben glances at me as he brings over what looks like a loaf of bread wrapped in tin foil, and sets it on top of the wood stove.

"Have you even seen a bear before, Georgia?"

"Besides on TV? No. But that bear was not small!" I insist.

He stands across from me and pushes a hand into his pocket. His eyebrows raise, and a small smile pulls across his lips.

"Really?" I say. "That wasn't considered big?"

"Not really," he confirms. "A male black bear can weigh between three and six hundred pounds."

I let that sink in.

"I don't ever want to see another bear. Let alone one that size."

I sit in silence as Ben crouches down next to the wood stove. Even though it's officially the start of summer, it's definitely cooler at this elevation compared to the valley. He throws in a piece of wood and stokes the fire a few times before closing the door and turning the damper inward. He lays a forearm across his bent knee and turns to face me.

"Honestly, I don't think you'll see that bear again. I think it was a fluke accident you two crossed paths to begin with. And I think it was the food in your bag that kept her here at all. I don't have any explanation for why she chased you into the outhouse, or why she kept trying to get in there. That may just remain a mystery. Or it could be, if she had cubs nearby, that you were a threat to her babies." He looks off into the distance. "She could also be sick. A bear acting strangely could be a sign something's wrong with its health."

He stands up and dusts his hands off on his pants. "Dinner's almost ready if you want to come over." He motions for me to come and join him at the table. I stare blankly at him for a moment and sit, unmoving.

"Oh, sorry. I must be pretty tired." He drops his chin and walks back to where I'm sitting, leans over to offer his shoulder and helps me out of the chair and over to the table. It feels odd to slide my arm around the neck of a man I've only just met. I try to keep an open mind and remember he's a medically trained professional...that happens to be very attractive. And muscular. But whatever.

"I'm the one who should be sorry," I say. "I'm sure the last thing you wanted to do was take care of an invalid. I feel awful about this inconvenience to you," I say with sincerity as I sit down at the small wooden table. He hauls the wooden crate over and gently sets my ankle on top of it. It's starting to hurt again, but I try to ignore it.

"It's actually nice to have some company again," he says, quietly. He turns back toward the kitchen and begins to bring dishes to the table.

To my amazement, he sets down a dish of wild rice with roasted vegetables and a pot of beef stew. The warm, rich smell of food fills my nose, and I stare at the presentation before me in awe.

"Wow. You made all of this just now? How did you manage on that teeny little stove?"

"Oh, that reminds me, I almost forgot the bread." He sets mismatched plates down at each of our spots and walks over to the wood stove to retrieve the foil-wrapped loaf. "Annie from my station in Sisters made this for me yesterday. I think she enjoys watching out for me." He opens the foil packet, and a current of steam rises between us, the aroma of homemade bread filling the air. My mouth begins to salivate on cue.

We sit across from each other below the front window, the light quickly turning gray and dispersing into the evening. Ben reaches across the table and turns the lantern on, and the sound of the hissing propane fills the quiet.

I hold my fork in my hand, poised over my plate. Everything looks so good, and I can't decide where to begin first. I steal a glance at Ben across the table. He's already started eating, tearing into his food with both arms on the table and a cloth napkin tucked into his t-shirt. I decide to follow suit.

I try not to sprint to finish my food, but after a few minutes, I look down and realize I'm nearly finished. The food is delicious, and I again offer my thanks and appreciation. He brushes off my compliments with a shrug.

"So," I begin, trying to make small talk. "How did you end up as a Forest Service Ranger?"

He stops with his fork midway to his mouth. "My official title is Forestry Technician, but 'ranger' sounds a lot more interesting."

"Ok, *Forestry Technician.* How long have you been doing this?"

"About six years now."

"And before that, you were a paramedic?" I finish my food and set my fork down, ready to listen intently.

"Yeah, and a teacher," he says quietly. His eyebrows pull together, and he finishes his bite and tosses his napkin across his plate. His face seems to have clouded over.

I am about to ask a follow-up question when he stands up from his chair and takes our empty plates to the sink. He turns the water on, grabs a bottle of dish soap and begins to wash the dishes in the small sink. I don't know what to do or say, so I take an absentminded interest in a thread that's come loose from the zipper in my jacket.

I feel bad that I've obviously somehow opened up a sore subject for him, and watching him wash our dishes makes me want to help. I sit up very tall in my seat, reach over the top of my extended right leg and grab my thigh from both sides. I slowly lift my leg off the crate and set it down gently on the floor. Scooting myself to the edge of my seat and pushing off the table with both hands, I'm able to bring myself to an upright position. The noise causes Ben to turn around.

"Hey! What are you doing?" He drops the dish he's cleaning

into the sudsy water, wipes his wet hands on the back of his pants and walks determinedly over to me.

"I just wanted to try and help you clean up," I say, defensively. "I feel very out of my comfort zone letting you cook *and* clean. Besides, my ankle's feeling a little better," I lie. "As long as I don't move it...and look," I say, pointing to my black and blue foot. "The swelling looks like it's gone down."

Ben hesitates — his hands on his hips. "All right, fine. You can put away those dishes." He points to the dishes drying on a towel. "Just dry them off and put them away on the shelf there. Anywhere's fine. But be careful, please, and don't put any pressure on your foot. And after five minutes you sit back down. Deal?"

"Deal." I quickly agree and wiggle my fingers to reach for his neck as he helps me hop to the kitchen.

As I dry and put away dishes, Ben scrapes food into containers and cleans the rest of the pots and pans. I hadn't noticed that he had a compact refrigerator underneath the counter area. He opens it to put away the leftovers, and I can see it contains a small freezer section that sits above two narrow shelves. A half-gallon of milk and the tops of some beer bottles lying on their sides peek up at me.

"How does that run?" I ask, looking down at the refrigerator.

"I have a generator around the back of the cabin; it runs off of that. I wouldn't trust it to keep food for more than a week, but I usually re-stock after six days anyway."

"So is today your Monday?" I ask.

"Yeah. When I came up this morning, I brought groceries and supplies in my backpack. I hadn't planned on two people though."

I bite the side of my lip. "About that...what's the plan for tomorrow? I know I have to get to the hospital for an exam, but how exactly is that going to happen?" I have so many questions, but I don't want to ramble like a lunatic. I'd been accused of that before.

"Well, I've been giving that a lot of thought. I think we really only have one option, which is something you're not gonna like. The biggest hurdle is going to be getting you from here to the trailhead parking lot. Once we're there, I can drive you to St. Charles, and you can contact your family to pick you up." He's standing next to me at the sink, and he pauses and stares at me for a moment.

"Come on, let's go sit down." He motions for me to put my arm around his neck as he stoops down and helps me hop over to the leather chair. Once I'm seated, he returns with the crate, the lantern, and a chair from the table. He props my foot on the crate, sets the chair down and heads back to the fridge. He returns with the refrozen bags of ice and sets them around my ankle and foot. Before he sits in the chair next to mine, he hangs the lantern from a railroad spike sticking out from one of the log walls. I look out of the back windows and notice the sun has set, and the light in the sky is barely visible. I can just see the beginning of stars.

"So, how are we going to get me down the mountain?" I ask quietly.

He takes a deep breath and leans forward; his forearms rest across his knees, and he slowly unrolls his shirtsleeves. "I think we'll have to alternate between me being your human crutch—"

"And?"

" —And the world's longest piggyback ride." He looks up at me from under his eyebrows. "Neither will be comfortable for either of us, but at least it's all downhill after we get up this little climb out here." He juts his thumb behind him, motioning to the small hill outside the cabin leading to the summit.

My shoulders slump. "I was afraid of that," I say. "And what about your job here, Ben. You can't just take an entire day off, well, two days if you count the time you spent taking care of me today."

He drops his head and rubs the back of his neck for a moment before resting his hands across his knees.

"It's okay. Fire season hasn't really started yet. This was my weekend to open the cabin, and to make sure I have everything ready for the summer – make repairs where needed, make sure my water sources are good..." His eyes meet mine, a serious look on his face. "You're actually very lucky. Had you been here last week, I wouldn't have found you. I only came out this season for the first time yesterday." The look on my face must reflect my horror.

"Sorry," he says, "but, it's true."

We sit in silence together for a moment, and I try not to think about how differently this day could have ended. The sound of the fire crackles between us, and the ice in the bags around my ankle begins to melt and shift. I reposition my leg to adjust my ankle, and the pain causes me to wince.

"How's your pain level?" Ben checks his watch and stands up.

I close my eyes. "I don't know...maybe a six or seven now."

"That's what I thought. I'm sorry, I lost track of time," he says, quietly.

He returns with a glass of water and two small pills. I reach for them and sip the water, a thin smile on my lips.

A yawn escapes my mouth as I sink down lower in my chair, my body warm and full. Sitting here, quite literally with a total stranger in the middle of the woods, I'm surprised to realize how comfortable I am. My eyelids begin to feel heavy, and all of the sudden I am overwhelmed with exhaustion.

"I think it's bedtime for you."

My eyes open at the sound of his voice, and I inhale deeply, looking around the cabin. I avoid looking at the bed.

"Um, what are the sleeping arrangements?"

"You'll sleep in my bed." He stands and reaches a hand toward me. "I know that sounds awkward — it's an interesting circumstance we find ourselves in tonight — but you're injured, and you need your rest. You have a very long day ahead of you tomorrow."

"Yes, but you have to help me down the mountain tomorrow. And this is *your* house," I argue. "Where are you going to sleep?"

"Right where you're sitting."

"Ben, you can't. You're least a foot taller than me, and I'm hanging over the edge of this chair as it is. This will be so uncomfortable for you," I protest.

"Well, if it gets too uncomfortable I'll just grab my sleeping bag and crash out on the rug here, next to the fire. I'll be fine. Believe me, I've slept in worse conditions."

"Me too," I mumble. Memories of sleeping in the guest bedroom with a chair against the locked door flood my mind.

"Pardon me?"

I shake my head and quickly agree with him to move the topic along.

"Ok," I say. "But if you change your mind, you let me sleep on the floor, deal?"

"Deal." He wiggles his outstretched fingers toward me, "C'mon."

I stifle a yawn and lean forward in the chair. He takes the ice packs away and bends down so I can reach my arm around his neck. The scent of his warm skin fills my nostrils, and I want to close my eyes.

"Let's put one of these pillows under your ankle." He helps me sit down on the bed. "Go ahead and lie back."

Scooting myself to the headboard, I sink my head into the down pillow with a small sigh. He gently lifts my ankle and sets the pillow underneath, and then pulls the sheet and blanket over my body. I close my eyes and feel the pull of sleep dragging me under.

"Good night," he whispers.

I snuggle down further into the sheets and turn my head to the side. As I drift off, I hear Ben shut off the lantern; the ensuing silence, broken only by the orchestra of crickets outside. My breathing becomes shallow, and I relax into sleep, feeling safer than I have in a very long time.

CHAPTER THIRTEEN

GEORGIA

I WAKE IN TOTAL DARKNESS and sit up straight in bed, my heart pounding fiercely against my chest. Gasping for breath, a feeling of dread washes over me, and without a doubt...I know. Holding my breath, I turn my head to listen, and then I hear it again — the sound that summoned me from sleep — the sound of someone downstairs stumbling around, walking into furniture, falling, and then kicking the obstacles out of the way.

Mike is home. And he's drunk.

I check the clock on the bedside table: 3:36 a.m. The bars closed an hour and a half ago, and I can only imagine where he's been between that time and now. And how many people's lives have almost ended as a result of his inebriated state.

I can hear him growing angrier downstairs as he tries to find his way through the living room, and I silently pray he will give up and pass out on the couch like he has so many nights before.

"Why do you always move the furniture around down here, Georgia!" he yells. It's not a question, it's an accusation, and I'm better off if I remain silent. "Goddammit, Georgia, answer me!"

I throw the covers back and leap out to grab my bathrobe

that's lying across the foot of our bed. I pick up my cell phone from the nightstand and dial 9-1, and then I stop. Is this truly an emergency? Do I want our neighbors to see the police here? I'm mortified that I will draw even more attention to the awful things that happen in this house, here in this quiet little suburban neighborhood than I really want. I shut the phone off, shrug into my bathrobe as quickly as possible, and cross the room toward the door. My hand pauses on the doorknob lock.

"You're such a...conniving little bitch...you think...you're so smart and... so much better...than me." He's climbing the stairs, two at a time, and I hear him slur his words as he pounds his feet closer and closer to our bedroom. "I'm so sick...of this shit...you're gonna pay...for treating me...so badly."

I silently flip the lock on the handle and look around the room for something to block the door with. My eyes freeze on the dresser in the corner of the room, and I quickly run over and brush everything off the top; a hairbrush, a few books and a picture frame crash and scatter across the floor. I hurry around to the side of the dresser and begin to push with all my strength across the carpeted room. It's heavy and filled with clothing, and it barely moves. *I should have called the police!*

I hear him grab hold of the door handle and I see it turn a fraction to the right, and then quickly back to the left. A moment passes as the realization that the door is locked sinks into his compromised brain. He begins to shout obscenities and pounds on the door. I push the dresser closer and pray the lock will hold until I can get this piece of furniture in front of it. As I push, I yell that the police are on their way.

The pounding stops and all is silent for a moment, and I'm relieved to know that the threat of the police has finally knocked some sense into him. After all, it would be his friends that show up.

Suddenly, a loud crash against the door causes me to flinch, and crouch down in fear. Mike has thrown his body weight against the door, trying to break it open against the lock. I catch my breath again and yell at him through the door to leave me alone, that he's drunk and not thinking, that his friends are on the way. I scream anything and everything I can think of to get him to stop.

He slams himself against the door again. I'm almost there with the dresser, the corner of it barely crossing in front of the entrance. Mike barrels into the door again, and the panel around the handle splits in vertical strips. He thrusts his fist through the narrow opening, his mangled fingers twitching and bending, as he reaches for the lock. I step back from the dresser in slow motion as he yells, his voice inches from the door.

"I'm going to fucking kill you!"

I wake up screaming in pitch black, sitting up in a bed that isn't mine. It's so dark I can't even see my hand in front of my face. I hear movement somewhere in front of me; someone is coming closer, and I hear breathing and shuffling feet.

"Stay back! Stay away from me!" I yell.

I attempt to rip the blankets off my body and jump out of this unfamiliar bed, but as I move my legs and try to push out, a horrible pain rips through my right foot and leg. I gasp in shock and freeze.

I feel the bed sink down at my feet as someone sits.

"Georgia, it's just me, Ben. You're safe. You're here in my cabin. On Black Butte. Remember?" Ben's quiet, calm voice silences my panic as the realization of my surroundings and the events of the last several hours come back to me. I feel Ben's hand on my left foot.

"It's ok. You're ok. No one is going to hurt you here," he reassures, and I swallow back the bile that's climbing up my throat.

"I'm going to get up and turn the lantern on, ok?" he asks and then moves off the bed.

I'm silent. I hear him moving around the inside of the cabin, but I can't see anything. Why is it so dark? How can *he* see?

"I've got the lantern now, hang on a minute."

The sound of propane hisses in the silence of the room, followed by two, loud *click-clicks*.

"There."

A soft glow grows from across the room, and I can see Ben's arm holding the lantern out from his body toward me; the light slowly becoming brighter and brighter. I squint against the light as I watch him walk toward me. Relief floods my body, and I pull my left knee close and wrap my arms around it. I can't help the tears that suddenly fall, and an involuntary sob escapes me in a huge breath. Ben sets the lantern down next to me on the nightstand.

"You wanna talk about it?"

I shake my head and take my hands away from my face, wiping my eyes and sniffing. "I just...I just had a really awful dream," I whisper. "About the bear."

I can't meet his eyes, and he says nothing.

"I was dreaming I couldn't get away from him — I mean, her. I couldn't get away from her, and..." I am stammering. Stammering, and lying through my teeth.

"Who's Mike?" Ben's voice is flat.

My mouth falls open. Had I said his name out loud? What else had I said? Shame and embarrassment take over, and I drop my chin to my chest.

"Mike is my ex-husband," I murmur. "He was a good man that became an abusive alcoholic after a very traumatic work incident." I rattle off the generic description of my marriage that my therapist made me repeat for months after the divorce.

"He *hurt* you?" he growls.

It takes me a minute to answer.

"Yeah, he did. Not in the beginning, but..." I shake my head. I can't finish.

"*Jesus*. How long have you been divorced?" His voice is tense, and I meet his eyes with hesitation.

"Officially? About six months. Since November. But I left him almost a year ago now." I look up at Ben, and I can see his shoulders relax a little. "Divorce takes a long time," I say, mostly to myself.

"Yes. It does." He's looking at me, but I recognize the far away tone of his voice. He's focused somewhere else.

"Were you ever married, Ben?"

He sighs and slowly sits down next to me on the bed. He rests his face in his hands and runs his fingers through his hair before he answers.

"Yeah, once. But that finished a long time ago."

"I'm sorry."

"I used to be too. But I've come to realize it was for the best that it ended."

I nod. I can understand this rationalization, and yet, I'm sad for him. I know the pain. When a marriage ends — when relationships end — it feels like small parts of us end too.

I touch my hand to his knee.

"Thank you. For all that you have done for me. I know," I say, seeing the look on his face. "I know you think it's no big deal, but to me, it's a huge deal," I explain. "I don't really know how to manage when someone is taking care of me. It's a very odd feeling, and to be perfectly honest, I'm not totally sure how to handle it." I pull my hand from his knee suddenly feeling awkward.

Ben sits quietly for a moment and then nods once, solemnly.

"Is your ankle bothering you much now?" he asks, glancing at my foot.

It is. Tremendously. But I don't want to say anything.

"You don't have to answer. I can tell by that look. I'll be right back." He gets up and walks into the kitchen and comes back with a glass of water and another small pill. I take them both with gratitude.

"That should last you through the rest of the night." He checks his watch. "It's just coming up on 1 a.m. now." He takes the glass back to the kitchen, walks over to the wood stove and opens the door to stir the coals. He glances back over his shoulder at me. "You cold?"

"A little. But I can cover up again." I start to adjust the blankets around me and realize, embarrassed, that I need to go to the bathroom again. A heavy sigh escapes my mouth.

"What's wrong?"

"This is so embarrassing. I can't even believe I have to ask you to help me again."

"Oh, you need to use the restroom? No problem. I could use some air anyway."

He opens the tall wardrobe next to the bed and digs around inside. Closing the doors, he steps back and holds up a thick red and black plaid button-up coat, and a dark brown vest. He hands me the coat to put on as he shrugs into the vest and grabs his boots. I'm ready to go and swing my good leg over the side of the bed and wait for him to come over to me.

"You know..." I begin as he helps me stand, my arm naturally winding around his neck, "I'm not going to remember how to do this without help." I see the corner of his mouth turn up as he exhales loudly through his nose. "Hey, it's not every day you get to use facilities as fancy as we have here."

I hop through the cabin, noticing on my way the disheveled

blanket on the rug — his makeshift bed — and I register a pang of guilt.

On the way out of the door we pause so he can grab a headlamp, which he puts over his head and flips the switch. He looks at me, the blaring light piercing my eyes.

"Sexy, eh?"

I shield my face with my free hand. "I'm literally blinded by you," I say, smiling.

I look upward once we are beyond the cabin and am surprised I can't see any stars. The sky is covered, I assume, by clouds, and the air is cold and cuts at my face. I can see the outline of my breath in the headlamp glow as I hop along. This place, on top of this mountain, is so peaceful, so quiet and removed from everything noisy in my life. I can't escape the memories from my past, but being here feels so safe, even including the near-death experience with the bear. I shake my head as I recall the events. What are the odds?

Ben looks over, blinding me again. "What is it? Oh, sorry," he says and points the light straight ahead.

"I was just thinking about my luck, with the bear I mean. Leave it to me to encounter a bear and nearly get eaten alive by it." I can smile about it now. My sister is never going to believe this story.

We reach the outhouse, and as I stand near the door, Ben holds it open for me. He takes the headlamp off and hands it to me. "It just fits right over your head...yeah, just like that," he directs as I slip it around the back of my hair and pull it down over my forehead.

"Like this?" I say and look directly at him. It's his turn to be blinded.

"Okay, okay, fair's fair." He shields himself from the light. "Remember, I could leave you out here," he warns as he shuts the door for me.

"No! I'm sorry, I'm sorry." I say, suddenly anxious for him to stay.

And never leave.

Back inside the cabin, Ben helps me to bed and drapes my coat over the end of the footboard. I work myself under the blankets and lie back against the pillow, slightly propped up. He adds another piece of wood to the fire and turns back to me, pointing to the lantern on the nightstand.

"You want me to turn that off now? The fire's going again, so there will be a little light if that helps?"

"Sure. I'm sorry about waking you up. I just...I don't know. Sorry." I struggle to find the right words, and instead of continuing, I turn to my left and reach for the lantern switch. I can't quite reach it from my position. I sigh, still reaching.

Ben pads over. "Here, I've got it."

He turns the lantern off and stands for a moment next to the bed looking down at me, the soft glow of the fire illuminating the side of his face and body. I am beginning to feel the effects of the Vicodin again, and my eyelids feel heavy. I don't want to fall asleep again. I want to ask him questions about his marriage; how it ended, how he feels living up here all alone...but sleep wins the battle.

A moment later I think I hear Ben's voice, barely a whisper, telling me I'm safe.

And I believe him.

CHAPTER FOURTEEN

GEORGIA

THE MOST GORGEOUS SMELL IN the world drags me from sleep: freshly brewed coffee.

As I lie in bed and stretch my arms over my head, I breathe in deeply through my nose, savoring the intoxicating scent. I remember the events of last night and a small thread of embarrassment weaves through my chest. What must Ben think of me — living with a man that hurt me, both physically *and* emotionally? I frown as I remind myself that I'm none too proud of me either.

Straining my ears, I listen for sounds of Ben in the cabin. Hearing nothing, I slowly sit up and absentmindedly wonder what I must look like from the night. I quickly run my fingers through my tangled hair, the long curls matted from sleep, and twist it up into a messy bun — my usual hair-do. I rub my fingertips under my eyes and smooth out my skin. The realization that I'm distressed about how I look needles me; I'm not ready to acknowledge why it might matter now.

My gaze catches on the rug across the room. Ben's bedding has been cleaned up, and an open book lies on the arm of the leather chair, a pair of dark-rimmed glasses on top. How long has he been awake? And where is he?

I flip the covers back and slide my good leg over the side of the bed. My right leg feels cramped, and I desperately want to flex my foot and stretch, but I know better. I lean over and massage my calf and continue down the sides of my shin just as the front door kicks open, and Ben walks in carrying an armload of firewood, his chin raised above the tall stack in his arms. He heads toward the wood stove and bends down toward the crate. His eyes flick over to me, and the corner of his mouth turns up.

The small flutter in my chest surprises me.

"Morning. How ya feeling?" he asks, dumping the wood into the crate and dusting off the front of his shirt as he stands upright again.

"Hi," I say, shyly. "I'm feeling okay. My leg is a little stiff."

"I bet it is. Let's get you some breakfast and then you can take more Ibuprofen, and Vicodin if you need it."

He walks over to the bed and helps me up and over to the kitchen table. The morning light beams through the front window creating narrow rectangles of light that bounce off the wood table. It's almost blinding.

A moment later he sets a cup of black coffee before me, and I warm my hands around the hot stoneware.

He refuses my offer to help prepare breakfast, so I sit with my coffee and enjoy the view of the sun over the summit, the majestic mountains framing the picture perfectly.

Ben brings over two small bowls of oatmeal topped with bananas, almonds, and diced apple. He sets them on the table along with a French coffee press, half full of fresh java.

"Pretty fancy little coffee maker you've got there," I say, pointing an index finger at the shiny carafe as he pushes it toward the center of the table.

He smiles at me. It's a true smile that reveals a row of

perfectly straight, white teeth, and something in my stomach drops a bit.

"Hey, I may be a hermit up here, but I'll be damned if I can't have good coffee every morning," he says. "*Sisters Coffee* gives me a great deal. I try to stop in there every couple of weeks." He hands me a spoon. "It's a nice place. I'll have to take you in there some—" His eyes flash to mine, and he stutters. "Er, I mean, if you'd like to check it out with your sister, it's a great place to stop." His megawatt smile disappears as he drops his gaze to his bowl.

I think about this quietly for a moment and decide I like the idea of going to coffee with Ben, but then I push the thought to the back of my mind and choose instead to focus on the day that lies ahead.

We both start to speak at the same time.

"So, abou—"

"How are we—"

We both laugh, and I gesture for him to continue.

"I was just going to say we should get going pretty soon. Like I said, it's going to take a while to get down the mountain."

"Yes, I agree." I look around at the cabin. What did I even come up here with? My camera, keys, and wallet; those are still in my backpack. My phone? Well, that's probably a lost cause now. What else?

"I guess I'm pretty ready to go," I say, looking down at my wrinkled, slept-in clothes.

"All right then. Let me clean up these dishes, get you some more painkillers, grab my gear, and we'll try to get you down this mountain."

I start to get up, and Ben holds his hand up to me.

"No, don't try to get up, please. Just relax, and I'll be ready in a minute." He smiles as I take my hands off the table and resume my spot in the chair.

Ben plops what's left of my backpack on the table in front of me. It's a sad sight. The bottom seems to be intact but the top is completely ripped open, thin threads of material hang over the outside, and an entire section near the zipper is missing. I can't help but think what those teeth could have done to flesh – *my* flesh.

He sets my camera next to the pack – the strap is torn but still in good condition – and I lean forward to slip it over my neck. A moment later I switch the strap to cross-body style instead, trying to imagine what will be most comfortable for the hike down. Ben grabs his own pack, puts two water bottles in it, hands me another one and throws some apples, and a few packages of nuts inside.

I turn to look out of the window next to me. The sky is an impossibly brilliant blue with a few pale ribbons of thin, white clouds breaking up the monochromatic palette. I'm suddenly very anxious to get to the hospital and to talk to my sister.

"Do I have an appointment today or it is more of a walk-in thing?"

"Well, I notified my ranger station in Sisters that we would be coming down today," he says. "But because of the trickiness of your condition, we couldn't set an appointment for you. In fact, right before we leave here I need to radio in and let Annie know we're heading down." Ben pauses, his hands resting on top of his tall pack. "I was thinking last night though: I have a first-aid kit here, and I think I can make you a temporary splint to wear. It won't be pretty, and I can't guarantee it will even work, but it might help you put some weight on your foot." He clears his throat and continues. "It's worth a try at least?" His eyebrows rise as he waits for my reply.

"It's fine with me," I quickly agree, "I would really like it if you didn't need to piggyback me down this mountain."

Outside at the woodpile, I can hear him chopping with the axe; a loud smashing sound fills the air followed by soft slicing noises. He returns with two very thin pieces of wood, each about six inches across and about a foot long. He sets them on the table in front of me and walks over to his backpack, digging out his first-aid kit. He produces another Ace bandage, a pair of large socks, and some thick cotton pads. He brings out a t-shirt from the wardrobe and kneels before me. He sets to work, tearing the shirt into wide strips, and I try not to stare as his forearms flex with the motion. When he bends down and reaches for my foot, I can't help but notice the back of his neck and his tan skin thick with muscle. I fight an absurd urge to reach down and run my fingers through his hair and down the nape of his neck. I look away and force myself to think about more important things, like whether or not I have a broken ankle, and how on earth I'm going to get my Jeep home.

Ben carefully guides my right foot into one of the thick socks and slips it up over my swollen ankle. He'd given me another Vicodin at breakfast, so I really don't feel any pain with the movement, but I do begin to feel anxious when he holds one of the wood planks against the inside of my ankle and instructs me to hold the other one along the outside. The pressure produces a small sensation of pain, but nothing compared to how I felt yesterday. He begins to wrap the bandage around the bottom of my foot and up and across my ankle, securing the pieces of wood on either side of my leg. He repeats this process with the strips of t-shirt, and soon my lower right leg resembles that of a small elephant.

"Ok," he says, still kneeling at my feet. "Try to put some weight on it. Oops, hang on a sec." He stands up and retrieves my shoe, loosens the laces until they nearly fall out and helps me put my foot inside. "Ok, now try."

Very carefully I place my foot on the ground and begin to gradually put weight on it. It hurts but it's not unmanageable.

"It's ok...I think."

"Ok, good." He's standing near me with his hands extended as if to catch me, and he begins to take a few steps backward. "Go ahead and stand here for a moment while I gather up the rest of my things." I nod in agreement, feeling a little like a science experiment.

He brings his backpack to the table and sets it down. He slaps the front and back pockets of his cargo pants, mumbling something about keys and wallet, and checks the radio at his hip. He touches the opposite hip and freezes, a frown on his face. He quietly walks over to the desk, opens the drawer and brings out a large knife in a leather sheaf, which he snaps onto his belt. Next, he gathers the coat he let me wear, and his Forest Service cap from the wardrobe, and pauses to retrieve his rifle from above the wood stove. He moves methodically through the cabin, picking up what he needs in an organized way. He's quiet and very focused, and I can tell he's ticking off a mental checklist.

Finally, he stops moving, takes a breath, and looks at me.

"You ready for one more trip to your favorite bathroom?" he asks, adjusting the baseball cap on his head and walking toward me with a grin.

My heart does a small somersault.

"Yep, all set."

When we return to the cabin, we gather our things, and I lean against the kitchen counter as Ben lowers the blind over the front window, pulls thick curtains across the back windows and door, and checks the locks.

Outside the cabin, he padlocks the front door shut and slides his radio from the carrier on his belt. After a quick call to the station, he turns to look at me, eyebrows raised.

"Ready?" He lowers his shoulder to me.

I nod in agreement and reach my arm around his offered neck.

The first few steps are tentative. The majority of my weight is on my left foot, and only the top of my right foot touches the ground. It's a modified hop, really, and after we reach the top of the summit, I am brave enough to put a little more pressure on the ball of my foot.

Although Ben carries both of our packs— mine stuffed inside his large one — I'm still dismayed at how slowly I am forced to travel. My eyes never leave the trail; every step is cautious, every rock an enormous boulder to be avoided, every divot a treacherous canyon. After thirty-five minutes I have already stopped several times for water, and once to sit down and put my ankle up. Each time I feel the need to ask for something, little alarms sound in my head warning me not to be such a bother, not to cause so many problems, to stop asking for so many things. I have to keep reminding myself that Ben is not Mike, that Mike is not here, and that it's perfectly reasonable to ask for a break. Ben's patience seems unending, and each time I ask to rest or mention I need water, he is gracious and polite. I feel like I have all the time in the world, which is both unnerving and extremely welcoming.

The trail is narrow in places — too narrow for us to walk side by side — and Ben has to walk off the trail on the upward side of the mountain so I can stay on the lower, more even ground. The difference in our heights becomes even more pronounced, and soon I have no choice but to put my arm around his waist instead of over his shoulder. This new physical arrangement feels awkward, I think for both of us, however, neither of us mentions anything, and soon it begins to feel very natural to have my arm around his waist, my head leaning into his side. I can feel the warmth of his body, and I try very hard not to think about how that makes me feel.

We make our way down the mountain in relative silence, seemingly lost in our own thoughts. I try not to concentrate on the slow throb in my ankle and foot, and instead, try to figure out how I'm going to get through the next several weeks of recovery and recuperation. If I do have a broken ankle, will that mean surgery? How much time will I be unable to work? Hiking season only just started, and I had really planned to use every weekend for that sole purpose. Now I don't know how long I might have to shelve the idea. All of these thoughts swirl around my brain as we move slowly downward.

Before I can stop myself, I realize I'm thinking about Ben again. I try not to pay too much attention to the new feelings stirring in me about this guy, this guy whose waist I am currently hanging on to. I'm really not sure I'm ready to acknowledge feelings of any kind toward any man. Period. I remind myself just how well I've done on my own, without any interesting people in my life, thank you very much. And despite my sister's best intentions, and several failed blind dates, I admit I'm not ready to open myself up to the dating world anytime soon.

Mike and I lasted nearly seven years together; the last three abusive, and those times left deep wounds in my heart. I've spent the last twelve months getting to know myself again; taking care of myself and discovering what I like and don't like, learning to live semi-alone, and generally making decisions about people I want to keep in my life and people I can do without.

Divorcing Mike was the best decision I'd ever made.

I only wish I'd made it sooner.

CHAPTER FIFTEEN

GEORGIA

THE TREK DOWN THE TRAIL is hard, and I'm in a lot of pain. As we walk down the path, I try to distract myself. How did I end up in this situation, anyway? Why am I here, back in Oregon at the top of this mountain, hanging onto a man I hardly know?

Before I can stop myself, I'm sucked back into the memory of how I met Mike. Part of it makes me smile; after all, I was with Sylvia when I met him, and we were celebrating a happy occasion.

It all seems like a silent movie now. A movie I've seen before, and hated, but still watch because it's familiar.

Officer Michael Rutherford pulled me over on Interstate 5 in Oregon in the early hours of Saturday morning for speeding. I was driving my sister home from her bachelorette party that had just ended in downtown Portland. She'd had a lot to drink and was definitely past the legal limit, while I was stone cold sober, albeit exceedingly tired. I had one focus at 2:30 a.m., get home for immediate sleep. So I really wasn't thinking about my speed when red and blue lights began to flash in my rearview mirror. I signaled and moved my sister's black BMW over to the middle lane and glanced down at my speed: 85 mph. My stomach sank. I knew the lights were for me, but I prayed he would pass me by. The last thing I wanted to deal with was a speeding ticket.

The cruiser moved in behind me in the middle lane and then followed me to the slow lane, staying behind me as I moved to the shoulder. The officer approached my door, shined a flashlight in my face and asked for my license and registration, which I nervously passed to him through the open window. Sylvia was next to me, apparently watching the uniformed cop intently. In her inebriated state, she made no attempt to conceal her thoughts, or keep her voice down.

"Wow, Gia, look how gorgeous this guy is, huh?" Her voice boomed out of the BMW, slurred words and all.

I cringed as I slowly glanced up at him, reading the name 'Rutherford' above his right pocket. He immediately flicked his eyes to meet mine, and for a split-second, he looked familiar to me. A small pull at the back of my brain made me wonder if I somehow knew him, but I raised my eyebrows in surrender — I needed to focus on trying to wiggle my way out of trouble.

After a long conversation about what we were doing out so late, an admonishment about my speeding, and a lecture directed at Sylvia about trying to flirt her way out of a ticket, Officer Rutherford handed me a ticket and told us we could go on one condition: I would need to give him my phone number.

Truth be told, I was incredibly flattered. He *was* gorgeous, Sylvia was right about that. And I had to admit — I was always a sucker for a man in uniform. I smiled and agreed to give him my phone number on one condition: he would need to tear up my speeding ticket.

The rest was history. We dated for about a year, became engaged, I moved into his apartment in Hillsboro, and we married. After two years of extremely hard work and an almost inhuman level of dedication, he was promoted to Detective. After his promotion, we moved to Beaverton where I settled in as an administrative assistant for a small real estate office, and Mike worked long, hard hours with his department. His diligence paid off, and he was offered a terrific position, a higher salary, and better benefits. There was a catch though: the job was in San Diego, roughly eleven hundred miles from where we lived in Northwest Oregon. It also meant he'd need to retake his police academy training in California. On the positive side, the training time would be paid for, and it wouldn't take him long to complete. We both decided it seemed like a great opportunity, and Mike found a buyer for our small condominium practically overnight. Within two weeks we were packed and on the road to San Diego.

I immediately fell in love with the warm California weather. I'd grown up in Oregon and had barely visited anywhere outside the state. My wardrobe at that time consisted of fleece jackets, long pants, and about five or six different raincoats. We put our sunglasses on when we crossed the state line and essentially never took them off.

We house hunted for a week while we lived in a small motel near Interstate 8, and it took me longer than that to quit waking up in the middle of the night from the traffic noise outside. It was louder in California. Everything moved at a different pace; a pace I wasn't used to. But I was young and excited and ready for a new adventure.

We finally found a ranch-style home in an older neighborhood in La Mesa, but it was out of our price range. Despite needing new paint inside, it was in good condition and had what we needed at that time: close proximity to the Interstate, air conditioning, and a new roof. The fact that it came with a small backyard pool and a two-car garage was icing on the cake. Mike and I talked about it and decided it was time to use the money from my parents' estate. They'd want us to have this new start, we agreed, and it made me feel good to contribute to our future. We moved in right away, and Mike jumped into his police academy training.

Almost immediately he befriended Jason, and the two of them were instantly inseparable. Jason had grown up in Mission Beach. His parents were old hippies, and he was basically their exact genetic opposite: conservative, straight-laced, and crew cut. He was the kid that dressed as a police officer every year for Halloween — until he was twelve and decided he was too old for it. He applied for a work permit at age fourteen, received his driver's license on the day of his sixteenth birthday, and had exactly three beers the day he turned twenty-one. He and Mike skated through the academy and quickly became best friends. When it was time for partner assignments, it was only natural the two should work together.

When Jason's father had a heart attack and was rushed to the hospital, Mike was the first person he called. And it was Mike that spent the night on Jason's couch after his dad finally passed, making sure Jason wasn't alone. Jason became a regular at our house after work. He had a spot at the dinner table and a guest room that held a clean uniform and an extra toiletry kit. Mike and Jason ran together every morning before work, pushing each other and holding one another accountable. When Mike's appendix unexpectedly burst, Jason met me at the hospital and visited every day. He was like a protective older brother to me, always quietly joking with me about my unruly hair and inability to hide my emotions, and then he'd laugh, wrap me in a bear hug and help me load the dishwasher. It was an unspoken agreement between Mike and I that our first son would be named Jason, a daughter — Jayden.

Mike and I were always trying to find someone to fix him up with, but the truth was Jason simply wasn't interested in anyone we would introduce him to. He maintained he didn't want to plan how to meet his future wife — he wanted it to happen naturally. He had no interest in casually dating and always told us he'd find whoever he was destined to be with when the time was right.

After his promotion, Mike's job became more stressful and a lot more dangerous. He and Jason worked a lot of late nights and encountered some really intense situations. I would often walk into the kitchen late at night and find Jason and Mike sitting at the table, a half-empty beer in front of each of them and hollow looks on their faces. Mike never talked about the ugly parts of his job with me. He told me he didn't want me to know about that element of the world, about how much evil there really was out there. But with each other, Jason and Mike wouldn't even have to talk. They had a silent understanding of the dangers they faced every day, and they somehow silently supported one another through difficult times.

One late November night, a week before Thanksgiving, Mike and Jason were coming off a 12-hour surveillance detail on a suspected meth house. They were in civilian clothes, driving back to the station in an unmarked Ford Explorer. It was late, and they were both overtired. Mike was still recovering from a bad bout of bronchitis and Jason convinced Mike to let him drive, giving Mike a chance to get some rest on the ride. They merged onto I-8 and headed for the station and Mike fell asleep almost instantly.

That was the last time he saw Jason alive.

Mike never told me all the details, but Jason's mother sat next to me at the funeral, and she shared what she knew about the incident.

Jason and Mike were driving the 8, and they came upon a stranded car on the shoulder. After passing by, Jason realized it was a woman with a flat tire, and he pulled the Explorer over to help. Mike was passed out cold in the passenger seat, and only woke when he heard the screaming brakes and the ear-splitting collision. An inattentive driver had been texting on her phone, and she'd drifted over into the lane next to her. Realizing her mistake, she overreacted and overcorrected her vehicle, losing control and slamming into the back of the disabled car Jason was working on. He was killed instantly. The driver sustained a fractured rib and a dislocated shoulder and was out of the hospital within a week. The woman who owned the stalled vehicle miraculously escaped with only a few minor injuries. Mike, however, was never the same.

He wanted to press charges against the woman for reckless driving and involuntary manslaughter, but it wasn't his place to do so. He had been asleep at the time of the accident. He hadn't witnessed anything except the horrific aftermath. It was Jason's mother's right to file criminal charges, and she refused, stating there was *enough evil in the world already*. Mike went ballistic and began making sexist comments about female drivers, and openly ranting about how stupid this woman — all women — were.

He began working a lot of late nights, later than he had ever worked before, and we barely saw each other. He became increasingly concerned with my well-being, always wanting to know where I was and what I was doing. In a way, I found it comforting that he was suddenly so protective of me, and I chalked it up to his grief process, agreeing to quit my job so I could be home to take care of him, and the house.

Mike was assigned a new partner, and he hated him right

away. The guy could do nothing right, and Mike made no secret of how he felt. In Mike's eyes, he was an incompetent fool with no business being a police officer. He started coming home angry and began drinking a lot. Things between us became tense. As I pulled away, he turned more and more to alcohol. His moods and behavior soon became erratic at home, and when I tried to talk to him about it, things just worsened.

Office events and Christmas parties became tense social engagements for me, and eventually, we stopped attending altogether. Mike acted like the loving, doting husband to everyone around us, while secretly watching my every move, only to berate me and scream at me on the car ride home. He accused me of flirting with every guy in the place and called me terrible names. At home he would holler accusations at me, refusing to listen to anything I said. We stopped trying to have a baby; in fact, we pretty much stopped having sex altogether, which only worsened his paranoia and strengthened the absurd allegations that there was another man in my life.

He began to treat our home and my everyday life like a police investigation — interrogating me after I had been out with friends, or when I came back a little late from shopping. I began making excuses to friends that asked to get together and soon developed a weekly routine that I never deviated from. Sylvia started dropping hints about getting Mike into an AA program, or talking to his supervisor and getting him some help.

The first time Mike struck me was the day I spoke to his supervisor about his drinking. He came home early from work that day, drunk, and in a rage. I was unloading the dishwasher in the kitchen when I heard the garage door slam behind me. I dropped the dish I was holding, and it shattered on the floor in front of me. Mike stormed into the kitchen, picked up a chunk of the plate in one hand and grabbed me by the neck with the other. He held the shard of plate next to my throat and threatened to kill me if I ever talked to anyone at his office about him again, or anything else in our lives. And then he took his hand off my neck and backhanded me across the face. The blow knocked me off my feet, and I fell down onto the broken ceramic pieces, cutting my hands as I tried to catch my fall.

Almost immediately he flipped like a switch and suddenly became the old Mike again: loving and caring and solely focused on my health and happiness. He apologized profusely and told me over and over again how much he loved me, and how he couldn't live without me. I was so completely shocked that I was too afraid to say anything to anyone. And why would I? The weeks that followed were incredibly wonderful times with him. I began to forget the abuse had even occurred, and we talked about trying to have a child again.

But slowly, his obsessive and controlling behaviors returned. He began keeping track of me — monitoring my phone calls and even charting my menstrual period. I was hardly allowed to travel to Oregon to see my sister, and excuses were always made when she would offer to come to me. I wasn't permitted to go out with friends either. Mike would either sulk and give me guilt about wanting to be with my friends more than him, or he would rage and yell about how hard he worked, proclaiming that *he* never went out so why should I? I became the queen of excuses to my family and friends as Mike's drinking problem reached new heights — as did the violence. I secretly visited emergency rooms all over San Diego County for three years of my marriage. The cycle of abuse and control became the only life I knew.

Had it not been for Sylvia and Scott, I would never have escaped from Mike. They arranged the restraining order, they arranged the attorney, and they provided the safety and security of their home in Silverton while I quietly went through divorce proceedings. Thankfully, I never had to use the evidence of abuse against him. As soon as my attorney forwarded a few photographs and medical records, Mike's sleazy lawyer agreed to everything. Scott and Sylvia tried, again and again, to convince me to demand more from the settlement, but I couldn't. A part of me still cared about Mike and wanted him to straighten out his life, and I knew if I took everything I was entitled to, he'd never climb out of the pit he was in. All I wanted was my freedom so I could try and start over again.

For months after I left, Mike would call me and beg for forgiveness, promising he was a changed man and calmly stating he had turned his life around and was ready to prove he could earn my love again. We talked delicately around the subject of Jason, and he admitted his death had wrecked him. I knew the pain he was going through — talking to him about Jason only brought back the hurt I felt after losing my parents — and I wanted to comfort him. It was hard for me to erase the good years, especially when he seemed like such a changed man, and I felt incredibly guilty for breaking his heart. It felt like I was an executioner carrying out a sentence for a man I knew was innocent. And even though I couldn't forget the fear, the pain, or the shame of living in an abusive marriage, all of that somehow seemed lessened by his new calm and accountable demeanor.

We spent late nights talking about our marriage and reminiscing about the early years together; it felt like a high school summer romance, and I secretly considered moving back to California — until I received a call from a woman claiming to be pregnant with Mike's child.

She calmly explained she and Mike had been seeing each other for months, that she wasn't proud of what she was doing — she knew he was married — but she was in love with him and wanted to be able to work things out. She only called me after she discovered Mike had also been unfaithful to *her*. Apparently, a local strip club had become his regular hangout.

After that, I stopped taking Mike's calls and stopped

responding to his emails. I didn't care to investigate as to whether or not the allegations were true. Just the fact that she had called at all was sobering enough for me. I cut him completely out of my life. It was time for me to begin asking some questions about my own life, to begin discovering who Georgia Marks really was, and what I wanted out of life.

And a long hike in the woods seemed like a great way to begin answering those questions.

As Ben and I wind our way down the last switchback of the trail, I can just see the white rooftop of my Jeep through the trees. A huge smile of relief breaks over my face as I lean into Ben and point off to the right.

"There's my Jeep!" I squeal.

Ben squeezes me gently around the shoulder and softly laughs.

We plod down the trail, and I see what I assume is Ben's Forest Service truck parked across the lot, facing the other direction. The truck is white with a green stripe around the sides and rear. A tall antenna stretches upward off the cab, and nubby, all-weather tires with thick traction balance it out. I can feel my excitement build as we near the end of the trail. My heart is pounding in my chest, and an unstoppable smile covers my face. I am going to get off this mountain!

Ben helps me make the final turn from the trail to the parking lot, and we step onto glorious flat ground. I look toward my Jeep and stop dead in my tracks. I feel my smile vanish. All four tires have been slashed, the exterior is covered in red spray paint graffiti, and the windows have been smashed out.

My voice is a whisper.

"Oh my God, Ben."

CHAPTER SIXTEEN

MIKE - EARLY MAY, THIS YEAR

WELL, shit. All those months of sucking up, admitting it was my fault the marriage failed, telling her I was sorry and was making a new start...here it is, May, nearly a year since she left, and it was all for fuckin' nothing. It's a good thing she couldn't see my face when we talked. It was like swallowing rotten food, telling her those lies. The thing is, I know there's a part of me that really does still love her and wants her back. I don't feel the same with her gone. She was my rock, my stability, and her absence doesn't feel right. And worst of all, no woman seems to be able to fill the space she left. It feels almost as bad as when Jason...

Whatever. She's my wife, and her place is here in my house. End of story.

Except now she won't take my calls, and she won't even open the email I send to her trying to explain things. I know she's getting my calls because the spyware I installed on her cell phone shows me everything. I can see her location at all times. I can see calls she makes, calls she receives, text messages, what she searches for on the Internet, and even photographs she takes. It's the best thing I've ever bought, and thinking about it makes me smile.

Ever since Georgia found out about Whitney and the baby — Jesus, I wonder if it's even mine? Doubt it. She's a stripper for fuck's sake. But ever since then she hasn't even looked at my text messages, or opened my damn email. It's like she's cut me out completely.

I can feel my smile turning into a grimace, and my jaw clenches.

I sit at my office desk staring at my computer. Silverton, Oregon is centered on the screen, a small red dot marking its exact location. Of course she'd go to her sister and that lawyer husband of hers. I've never liked that son of a bitch.

Stroking the stubble on my chin, I consider my options.

Hmm. I wonder if my old roomie ever did move up north? And if he did, I wonder how *far* north he went.

CHAPTER SEVENTEEN

MIKE - EARLY MAY, THIS YEAR

TURNS out Bob moved pretty far north after all. All the way to La Pine, Oregon. He joined up with a police department just north of there, in Bend. I'd been close to Bend once on a fishing trip to Madras, but I'd never actually been to the town.

Looking it up on the map, I discover Bend sits about two hours east of Silverton, and there's a small airport about twenty miles away in Redmond.

I can't believe my luck.

Bob is happy to hear from me, a little surprised maybe, but at least he doesn't hang up.

"It's been tough down here, Bob. Shit's been gettin' real old. I've been thinking about taking some time off," I begin.

Bob takes the bait right away.

"Yeah, I know exactly how you feel. That's why I got outta there. Too many memories of Diane. Everywhere I looked there was some reason to think of her. I had to get out. Find someplace new."

"How do you like the new department?" I ask, genuinely interested.

"It's good. A lot smaller, that's for sure. And quieter. Things are pretty basic around here. Mostly low-scale drugs, maybe some domestic issues...it's pretty boring. But I like it that way." He pauses before going on. "San Diego was getting dangerous, you know? I'm actually glad things worked out the way they did, even if my wife, er, *ex*-wife, was a cheating bitch."

I inhale sharply and let it out slowly.

"Yeah, it sounds pretty nice. Maybe I'll come visit you sometime." I laugh off the self-invitation.

Bob responds exactly the way I want him to.

"Hey, why don't you come up and visit at the start of summer? We can go fishing, hang out...I can whoop your ass at cards again," he laughs.

"I appreciate it, Bob, but I don't want to intrude. That's really nice of you though. Maybe sometime, man." I force myself to be silent for a minute. As if on cue, Bob reacts perfectly.

"Hey, Mike, it's no intrusion. It's just me in this run-down trailer. You can come visit anytime. I'd love to see ya."

"I don't know." I sigh. "I think I'd probably be in your way."

"Naw, not at all. You can ride along with me on workdays, and then we'll grab a bite and hang out afterward. Deal?"

I force myself to hesitate for a count of fifteen before answering.

"Well, as long as you're okay with that? I really would like to get away from here," I say, humble as ever.

A moment later a thought occurs to me.

"Hey, Bob? You don't happen to have a computer I could use, do you?"

CHAPTER EIGHTEEN

GEORGIA

BEN AND I STAND SILENTLY looking at the Jeep from across the parking lot.

I have to sit down.

"Would you mind helping me over to that log there?"

"Of course," he says, leading me over. "Georgia, I don't know what to say. I promise you, your Jeep was in perfect condition when I came up here yesterday morning."

I'm speechless. I stare a moment longer at the deflated tires and broken windows before dropping my head into my hands.

"How am I going to get home?" I mumble from under my hands before looking up at him again. "Your truck isn't damaged is it? Can we still get off the mountain?"

Ben walks over to his truck, inspects the tires, walks around the exterior, opens the door and looks inside. He nods his head at me and gives me the thumbs up. He shuts the door, pulls the radio off his belt, and I can hear him talking to the ranger station. He gives a description of the Jeep and the damage sustained as he walks toward me. The radio is held to his mouth, and although I can't hear what's being said from the station, I can tell he's talking about my injury.

"Affirmative, I'm bringing her down. Copy that, the plan is to take her on to St. Charles. Negative, she seems in stable condition — I made her a temporary splint. Copy, Les Schwab. Affirmative, see you soon. Over and out." Ben shuts off the radio and slides it back into the holder at his hip. He holds his hand out to me.

"Ready to go see some doctors?"

I look up into his face, so exhausted and emotionally drained I can barely muster a smile.

"Sure," I sigh.

We begin to hop over to his truck, and I glance over my shoulder at my Jeep.

"Why would someone do this?" I ask as Ben opens the passenger door and helps me inside, closing it behind me.

I can see the Jeep in the rearview mirror, and I sigh and sit back, buckling my seatbelt. The truck has a bench seat across the cab, and a CB radio hangs from the dashboard. Books and paperwork are stacked neatly on the seat with a small bag of unopened almonds on top. The inside of the truck smells warm and earthy, of sweet pine and wood.

Ben slides into the truck and turns the key in the ignition, bringing the truck rumbling to life. He leans forward over the steering wheel, rests his arms across it and takes a long breath.

"Why would someone do this? I don't know. I just don't know." He's looking straight ahead, his eyes locked on something far away. "Sometimes we have vandals come through here. Usually, they only damage the trail or the signs. We did have some cars targeted a few years ago, but nothing like this." Ben turns his head to look at me.

"I've asked the ranger station to send Les Schwab up. They can put some new tires on the Jeep for you, and tow it into Sisters. They've got a good crew there."

I look away, suddenly overcome with emotion. How can I even begin to thank this man for all that he has done for me? I can't help but think about what could have happened to me had he not come to work yesterday morning. What are the odds? I shake my head and my chin drops. I feel Ben's hand over mine, and he gently squeezes my fingers and pats my hand softly before releasing it.

"Let's get you to the doctor. One hurdle at a time, okay?"

I nod in silent agreement and take a deep breath.

The day is well underway as we start down the road from the trailhead. It's warm outside, and the truck is stuffy. Ben rolls both of our windows down and the fresh air breezes through the cab. I smell the pine trees and the soft scent of vanilla in the air. It's crisp and clean; it feels like brand new air, and I can't help but smile. The bun at the back of my head has come undone and small wisps of hair float around my face in the breeze. Pulling my arms up to re-twist my hair into place, I glance over at Ben and notice him looking at me. The corner of his mouth is pulling into a smile.

"What?" I ask, dropping my hands back into my lap.

"Oh, nothing."

The potholes and washboards in the road send us bouncing around inside the truck, and my ankle begins to throb with pain. I try to hold it up off the floor, but it's no use. I grimace with every jar of the cab.

"There's a center seatbelt here if you want to scoot over? Then you can at least put your leg up on the seat."

I shrug and consider the awkwardness of the proximity to him versus the possibility of less pain.

"Okay. I can give it a try I guess." I undo my seatbelt and slide over next to Ben as he drops the paperwork and books to the floor of the truck. I find the seatbelt tucked partially behind the seat, dig it out and buckle myself in. Then I grab my right leg and pull it up onto the seat, bending my knee slightly. This position pushes me backward into Ben, resting firmly against his shoulder, which is jarring up and down with the holes in the road. I lean forward, away from him.

"I don't think this will work either. Your shoulder is digging into my back."

Without a word, Ben extends his arm across the back of the seat and wraps it around my opposite shoulder. He pulls me toward him, securing me against his torso. I can feel the warmth of his body through our shirts, and my heart flip-flops erratically inside my chest.

"Is this better?"

I can tell without even looking at him that he's smiling.

"Yes, actually it is."

As soon as we enter the main highway, Ben offers me his cell phone to call Sylvia, and I immediately sit up straight, excited at the idea of speaking to her. A moment later, I drop my hand against my thigh in exasperation. Oh yeah. I don't know her number. How could I forget that? It doesn't matter anyway as I quickly realize the cellular service through the dense pine tree-lined highway is spotty at best. Instead, Ben agrees to stop at the ranger station in Sisters and check for word from Sylvia there.

The fifteen-minute drive to Sisters is relatively quiet. The ache in my foot keeps my attention, and Ben and I don't really talk much. I realize how nice it feels to just be in someone's presence, not needing to clutter the quiet with unimportant words.

Entering Sisters, we pass a gas station, and behind it, a strip mall filled with a feed store, a bicycle repair/ski and snowboard rental shop, a few fast food places, and a family clinic. The town is replete with wild west themes: wagon wheels skirting walkways, false storefronts sticking up high into the air, American flags blowing in the breeze on shop fronts, and wooden sidewalks bordering boutiques with colorful quilts hanging over the railings. It's like stepping back in time.

Although I had heard about the quaintness of the town, the inimitable beauty of the surrounding Three Sisters mountains after which the town was named, and of course its annual rodeo and quilt show, the truth is I had never actually taken the time to visit the place — a fact I am quickly regretting as I admire the passing scenery.

We round the corner into the main downtown area, and Ben removes his arm from my shoulder, shakes out his hand, and slows the truck to turn left. I sit up straight, peer out through his window, and spot the ranger station. It's a brown, one story, wood building sitting under the shade of several tall pine trees. As we pull into the small parking lot, I notice another truck similar to Ben's sitting near the entrance, and a navy blue Subaru Outback in the adjacent space. Ben parks the truck, shuts off the engine and stretches his arms above his head, his chest expanding with the movement. I can feel my neck begin to flush, and I look away so I don't stare.

"That's Annie's truck over there. I'm glad she's here; I think you'll enjoy meeting her."

Is that sarcasm in his voice? I opt for a silent nod and begin to unbuckle my seatbelt.

Ben comes around and opens the door for me, helping me out of the truck and into our familiar walking position: my arm around his neck as he helps me hop. We start across the parking lot, and I realize what a gorgeous day it is. I can feel the warm sunshine on my shoulders and the back of my exposed neck, and I squint my eyes in the glare of the bright light all around me. As we pass by a tall pine with its wide, splitting bark, a fat grey squirrel runs halfway up the trunk and stops to look at us, his tail twitching madly.

We are just nearing the front of the station when the door bursts open, and a tiny, middle-aged woman in what looks like a light brown drill sergeant hat comes stomping out, her hands firmly planted at the waist of her forest green khakis.

"Benjamin Harrison, what in God's name have you gotten yourself into now?" she barks.

I involuntarily stop hopping and instead, stand perfectly still.

She crosses the small distance between us and does several things all at once: she grabs hold of my free arm, throws it over her shoulder and neck, and helps me walk to the front door, while simultaneously asking and answering her own questions.

"Dear Lord, girl, what in the world happened to you?" she demands, turning her head toward my face, the brim of her hat bumping against my cheek. She is much shorter than I am and she doesn't wait for an answer.

"Well, I'm Annie. I guess if you know Ben, you're in good hands, but by God, what is the matter with your foot? That thing looks awful bad." She leans forward to face Ben, invading my space. I pull my torso backward to accommodate her, and her hat.

"Ben, why in God's name are you not taking her to the ER? What in the world are you two doing here, and what happened to you anyway?" She's pushing the stiff hat brim back in my face now, and I look up at Ben, helpless. He just glances down at me and winks.

"Let's get her inside and then we'll talk, okay, Annie?"

We enter the station and Annie and Ben help me to a small

leather couch situated under two windows, each containing several small square panes framed in thin wood moldings. I sit at one end of the couch, put my foot up and breathe a heavy sigh.

Ben and Annie stand over me; Annie with her hands on her hips and Ben with his hands in his pockets. I'm starting to feel like I'm on display.

"Annie, this is Georgia. She was hiking on the butte early yesterday morning and, well, prepare yourself. She sort of had a run-in with a bear. She—"

Ben is cut off immediately by Annie, who acts as if a firecracker has just gone off in her pants.

"A bear! Good heavens, Benjamin, what in the world? Did she get hurt? Are you hurt, dear?"

I open my mouth to speak but am interrupted by Annie's impatience.

"Did she get hurt, Benjamin? Why in God's name aren't you at the hospital?"

Ben stifles a small laugh and holds up a palm in surrender.

"As I was trying to tell you, Annie, Georgia's alright, but I think she has a broken ankle. We're headed to St. Charles right now. I wanted to stop in here first though and see if her sister had called in." Annie's face relaxes into an expression of confusion.

"I radioed in last night and asked Dan to place a call to her sister in Silverton. Her name is Sylvia."

"Oh, I see," Annie says quietly. She then turns toward the front desk and cups her hands around her mouth.

"*Daniel*! Daniel, come over here, son!"

A tall, thin, balding man with wire-rimmed glasses and thick eyebrows comes trotting around the desk corner and over to Annie. He extends his hand to Ben and the two shake. Ben pats him on the shoulder with his free hand, and Dan's gaze drops down to me, and then over to Annie. The thin smile on Dan's lips disappears immediately as he registers the look on Annie's face. She's staring at him through narrowed eyes, and her arms are locked tight across her chest.

"Daniel. Benjamin here tells me you took a radio call from him last night about a bear up on the butte? Said he asked you to relay a message to this poor woman's sister that lives in Silverville?"

I clear my voice. "Actually, it's Silver*ton* but it—"

Annie turns toward me and narrows her eyes.

" — Uh, never mind." I feel my cheeks flush with embarrassment.

"Yes, that's all true, Mrs. Bayer," Dan says. "I noted it in the log book. I can bring it over to you to take a look if you want?"

Annie nods and Dan scuttles off behind the front desk, reappearing a moment later carrying a thick open book: a twin to the one in the cabin. The same green satin ribbon trails down, hanging in the open space below the spine. Dan runs his finger to the entry in question and lowers the book to Annie.

"Right there, see?" He taps the spot in the book.

Annie scoots her glasses to the end of her nose and looks over the top of them, reading. After a moment, she looks up at Dan.

"Daniel Thomas Mackentire, when you take a radio call from any of our technicians regarding a bear sighting, and *especially* bear-human contact, it is of utmost importance that you let the station manger know about it right away, *by God*!" Her voice booms through the office.

"Yes, Ma'am," Dan says quietly. I avert my eyes to give him some privacy.

"It's my fault, Annie," Ben interjects, touching her arm. "I forgot to tell him to be sure and pass the message on to you. I know how you like to be in the loop. I guess I was just too concerned with taking care of Georgia, and I didn't let him know the way we like to do things here."

I look up at Ben and feel a small stab of admiration.

Annie stares at Ben for a moment and considers what she's just heard. After a minute she drops her arms, and a soft smile appears at the corners of her mouth.

"Well, all right, Benjamin, no harm done I suppose, thank the Lord. Daniel, in the future, I will be apprised of all predatory animal encounters, understood?"

"Yes, Ma'am," Dan says and turns to leave.

"Just a moment please, Daniel. Ms. Georgia has been expecting news from her sister. Could you please check to see if any messages have been received?" She juts her chin toward the desks behind the counter.

I look up at Dan, expectantly, only to find his face drain of color. My stomach sinks as I realize what's coming next.

"Uh, Mrs. Bayer, ma'am, I'm afraid I..." Dan's voice cracks.

Annie's mouth forms a hard line, and she begins to whisper, forcing her clipped words through tight lips.

"Daniel Thomas Mackentire, are you telling me what I think you are telling me? For. The. Love. Of. God. Did you relay the message to the poor girl's sister, or not?"

Dan hesitates and drops his chin, and I see a bald patch at the top of his head.

"No, Ma'am," Dan peeps. And then in a rushed wave, he spits out. "I meant to, honest I did, Mrs. Bayer, but then we had that fire call come in from Redmond, and we had to dispatch back up, and, well..." He looks down at me. "I'm awfully sorry, Miss, it just slipped my mind altogether."

"It's okay, Dan," I reassure him as best as I can. I'm so tired, and I really just want this over with. "I can try her on the way to the hospital...right?" I look to Ben for confirmation, and then say to him directly, "I think we should be going. My ankle is beginning to really hurt."

Ben nods in agreement and claps Dan on the back.

"I'm sorry, Dan. Again, I should have told you to let Annie know right away."

Dan smiles deftly at Ben and nods. He glances at Annie, who's still staring bullets into him, and quickly retreats back to his desk.

"C'mon, young lady, I'll help you two get back to the truck. I will personally place the call to your sister right away, okay?" Annie leans down to help me up and whispers close to my face, "Don't get me wrong, Dan's a good kid, and I'm glad to have him here. He just needs a little more training is all. But, I am sorry, dear." Her watery eyes are filled with honesty.

"Thanks, Annie," I say as we stand and begin to make our way outside and across the parking lot.

"Dan has all the contact info. Will you radio me once you get in touch with Sylvia?" Ben asks.

"It'd be my pleasure, Benjamin. You can count on me." Annie says, straightening her spine. She then turns her attention to me and speaks softly. "Georgia, sweetheart, you take care now. Come back and visit anytime. By God, we'd love to see you again." She gives my shoulder a quick squeeze and shuts the truck door behind me.

She and Ben have a few more words outside the truck, and I watch as Annie draws Ben in for a long hug. Ben shuts his eyes tightly for a moment and pulls away to give her a quick kiss on the cheek before coming around to the truck. A small lump forms in my throat at this raw display, and I have to look away.

"She's sweet, Ben," I say, watching her stomp back across the parking lot.

"She's a mother hen," he counters and then glances over at me and winks. "But I have to admit, I adore that about her."

I hold his gaze for a moment and notice his expression change. The grin at his mouth slowly dies. A soft smile takes its place, and his eyes fall to my lips for a split second before he abruptly turns away and clears his throat.

"Right," he begins in a loud voice. "Let's get you to the hospital, shall we?"

Without waiting for an answer, he checks for traffic and pulls out onto the highway.

CHAPTER NINETEEN

GEORGIA

TRAFFIC IS HEAVY OUTSIDE OF Sisters. A beautiful sunny Saturday in Central Oregon and people are definitely out and about. We soon fall in line behind several SUV's and all-wheel-drive vehicles with Yakima and Thule storage boxes riding shotgun on top of gleaming roof racks. We all gently sway back and forth in our lane, waiting patiently for the next possible spot to pass one another.

I turn to Ben, distracted. "Could I use your cell phone again?"

He glances at me for a moment before reaching inside his shirt pocket and retrieving the phone.

"Of course. Did you remember the number?"

I take the phone and open the display screen, looking for the Internet browsing application.

"Hm? Oh, no. But I'm going to look up the number for the firm and try and leave a message there. No one will get it until Monday, but it'll make me feel better. Good, here it is," I say, tapping my index finger on the website button for Scott's law firm. I press the blue *call* button and bring the phone to my ear.

After a moment I hear the familiar voice of the receptionist; her low, hushed professional tone tells me the firm's office hours and extensions, and I interrupt her and automatically press 5. A moment later I am connected to Scott's voicemail, and the sound of my brother-in-law's recorded voice nearly brings tears to my eyes. I want to be home.

At the sound of the beep, I leave Scott a hurried message, explaining briefly where I am, what's happened, and that I'm currently heading to St. Charles Medical Center in Bend.

From the corner of my eye, I notice Ben reaching for something on the floor.

"...His name is Ben, and he's letting me use this phone. If you get this message, you can try me back at ..." I swing my face toward Ben, my eyes wide. I don't know his phone number, either.

Ben writes quickly on a piece of paper and hands it to me. I take it and see the cell phone number displayed and can't help but look at him and smile, impressed that he anticipated this need. I take the paper and mouth *thank you* to him, and relay the number into the phone. Finally, I explain to Scott that he might be able to reach Ben through the ranger station in Sisters if he needs to get in touch with someone right away. I pause for a moment and then, thinking of nothing else to say, I give my goodbye and hang up.

"Thanks for the number, and for letting me use this," I say.

"Yep. No problem at all."

Ben rolls his window down and the noise of the road and a wave of fresh air fill the truck. He rests his forearm out of the window.

"Do you think the business line of the Silverton police station is open today?" I ask.

He sucks in a shallow breath and considers the question before turning to me and shaking his head.

"No, probably not. But it can't hurt to try."

I open the display again and search for the Silverton Police Department non-emergency number. After a moment I dial and wait. The phone rings three times before a recording blasts in my ear, telling me the business office is currently closed and directing me to hang up and dial 9-1-1 for an emergency.

"No luck?" he asks, his eyebrows raised. I shake my head and switch the phone off, handing it back to him.

"Thanks," I say. He offers me a small smile in return.

We pass a blue sign that says *Viewpoint*, a large white arrow pointing to the right. I automatically turn to look out of my window and am rewarded with an unobstructed view of gorgeous mountains; three grouped together with a fourth not far behind to the south. The snow-capped peaks break out and push into the cloudless, bright blue sky, and I can feel my mouth drop open a bit as I take in the up-close view of the peaks I saw from Black Butte yesterday.

"That's North, Middle and South sister," Ben explains. "And that's Broken Top back behind them."

"Wow," I say, and then laugh. "I'm kind of at a loss for words. I wish I had my camera."

"It's in the back. Do you want me to pull over?"

I shake my head and look over at him.

"No, it's okay. We'd lose our place in this traffic. Besides, I really want to get to the hospital." I turn my head back to the view.

"Maybe on my way out though. So how long have you worked with the Forest Service?"

We are driving close to the speed limit now, and I'm slowly being lulled into relaxation. To keep myself awake and focused, I force myself to make conversation with Ben.

He considers my question for a moment. I can see his eyes flick up and to the right as he thinks.

"Um, this season will be my sixth year," he finally answers.

I sit up straight and stretch my leg out before me. I'm sitting in the center of the cab again, and my back is beginning to hurt.

"What kind of work did you do before?"

"Before this, I taught classes at COCC..." He looks at me in question. I shake my head; I don't know the acronym.

"Central Oregon Community College. I went to school there for my Paramedicine degree and worked as a teaching assistant during my last year. After I graduated, I worked for about a year as a paramedic and quickly decided it was too dark for me — too many unnecessary tragedies. I contacted Annie — I've known her a very long time — and she suggested I interview for this lookout tower job. I took her advice, interviewed, and was offered the position right away. I accepted the job for the summer, and then the college asked if I wouldn't mind teaching a few classes in the fall for the Forest Resource Technology program. I think I taught Wildland Fire Science 1 the first semester." He chuckles to himself. "I think it's safe to say I was a horrible teacher those first few months. Anyway, one class turned into four, and pretty soon I fell into a regular routine: Forest Service tech in the summer and Teacher during the school year." He grows quiet all of the sudden, and I turn to look at him squarely. "I don't teach there anymore." His eyes flit to mine, and for the briefest possible moment, I swear I see a shadow fall across his face. And then, almost as if what I saw a second before was a lie, his familiar smile takes shape across his lips. "Anyway, now here I am," he says, winking at me.

"Here you are," I parrot, "chauffeuring a helpless woman to a hospital, and arranging repair services for her vehicle. Somehow I don't think this was in your job description," I say. I feel terrible for all the problems I've brought upon him.

"Hey." He pushes his shoulder against mine. "Helping

people *is* part of my job description. Besides," he says, "you've been good company for me."

"Do you think you'll stay with this job for a while?" I ask, trying to ignore the goosebumps climbing up my neck.

"I think so, yeah. I enjoyed teaching, but the outdoors is really what I love now. Also," he continues, "the pay is good, the benefits are good, and I get to play Grizzly Adams every summer. I may be lost out there sometimes, but hey," he says, "at least I know I'm headed in the right direction." He laughs, and the corners of his eyes crinkle. I can tell he truly loves his work, even if there is a hint of something sad underneath.

"What about you?" he asks. "What kind of work do you do?"

"Me? Oh, nothing really," I say, waving my hand away.

Ben looks at me. "Nothing?"

"No, not nothing, but it's not really anything important. I just work in an antiques shop in Silverton. It's a simple job that doesn't require me to think much." I turn my head to look out of the window, wanting to be done talking about myself.

"Are you happy doing that?"

"Nope," I mutter, mostly to the window.

"Pardon?"

I turn my head back to look at Ben. He's looking at me with curiosity as if he really *is* interested in what makes me happy.

"Uh, no. It doesn't make me happy anymore..." I hesitate, wondering if I should get into this with him.

"But it used to?"

"Yeah, it did. After I moved back to Silverton. At that time I just wanted something I didn't have to think about, something that I wouldn't have to work very hard at. I just needed a paycheck and something to keep me...I don't know—"

"Distracted?"

"Yes, exactly. Distracted. I wanted to forget about Mike, to forget about the ruins of our marriage, and just work on figuring out who I was without him." I drop my gaze to my lap. I didn't mean to say that much.

"If you don't mind my asking, how did you two meet?"

I snap my head back up to look at him. Is he being sarcastic? No, I don't see any trace of laughter on his face. He seems like he really wants to know.

My stomach balls up a bit as I take a deep breath and tell Ben the whole, long story. When I'm finished, Ben reaches up and turns the soft hum of the radio completely down. There's only silence between us, and at first, it feels awkward, but after a few moments, I realize he's displaying a sort of quiet respectfulness that I've never experienced before.

"Thank you," I say, quietly.

Ben turns his head toward me and reaches his hand toward mine, resting his palm on top of my knuckles and patting his fingers gently before returning it to the steering wheel.

"Absolutely."

I lean my head back against the seat and scrunch down a little. The warm sun on my legs is comforting, and my eyes feel heavy. A huge yawn pulls at my mouth, and I attempt, unsuccessfully, to stifle it. I opt instead to let my eyelids close as the lullaby of the road entices me to sleep. I faintly register the sound of the radio again; a song I recognize begins to play, and my mind crosses into unconsciousness.

CHAPTER TWENTY

GEORGIA

THE SOUND OF BEN TURNING the truck off awakens me from sleep. My head is resting against his shoulder, and my hand has somehow tucked itself into the space between his arm and torso. I slowly untangle myself and sit up, fuzzy with the remnants of sleep.

"We're here," he says quietly.

He stretches his arms out over the wheel, and a yawn escapes his mouth. I rub my eyes and absentmindedly re-tie my bun, unbuckle my seatbelt, and scoot over toward the door. Ben comes around and opens it, but doesn't step aside or move to help me out.

"Stay put for a second, ok?"

I pull my eyebrows together in question but nod anyway. He shuts the door and disappears into the hospital. We're parked at the front of the Emergency Department under the covered, patient drop-off area. The sunny day is an almost blaring brightness against the dark shadows created by the large overhang. I look for Ben but am unable to see anything through the shaded hospital windows.

A moment later the automatic sliding doors reopen, and Ben emerges with a wheelchair and a hospital staff member. I roll my eyes, even though I am so grateful for the respite from hopping.

Ben lets the admittance nurse take the wheelchair, and he turns toward the truck to help me out. I step down and smile weakly at the nurse, quickly glancing at the identification badge that dangles from her neck on a long lariat: Nancy Sherwood, RN. Nancy helps me into the chair and pulls out the right leg extension. She spies my homemade splint and raises her eyes to Ben.

"This your handiwork, hon?" she asks, not waiting for his reply. "It's pretty good."

"It's ugly, but I think it helped," he says with a shrug. "Hey, I'm going to go park this, and I'll meet you inside," he says to me.

Nancy helps place my foot into the chair's leg rest and wheels me into the hospital. We make the typical small talk as she pushes me up to a long row of check-in desks separated by low, upholstered dividers. The room smells acutely of bleach and some kind of weird floral air freshener. My stomach feels slightly sick, and I remember I do not like hospitals.

Nancy rounds the end of the long counter and rejoins me on the other side of the desk, her perfectly manicured fingers poised at her keyboard. My own fingernails are filthy; dark brown clay is packed under the nails, and my cuticles are ripped and torn. I'm embarrassed at how I must look, and smell.

"Ok, hon, let's get some vital information from you."

I respond to each of her questions, wondering how long it will be before I get *the look*. It doesn't take long. After she enters my social security number and birthdate, I watch her eyes scan the information that appears before her on the screen. Her thin lips, covered in a heavy mauve lipstick, separate slightly and she takes a small breath before glancing at me. She can't help herself. None of them can. It's quite the hospital rap sheet she's looking at, and I know what she must be thinking — is Ben the one that caused the injuries, or has he rescued me from them.

She recovers quickly and proceeds with the standard line of questioning about my current injury. Her eyes widen in surprise, and she gasps loudly when I tell her about the bear. I assure her that Ben has made the appropriate notifications about the sighting and that the Sisters' ranger station knows about the incident.

A moment later Ben walks through the sliding doors. He's carrying both of our packs; his own is slung over his shoulder and mine is in his hand. I can't seem to look away as he walks toward me. His gait is confident but not showy — his t-shirt hugs his chest; defining his broad shoulders and thick biceps, and his hips move in a way I wish they wouldn't. He catches my eye, and a perfect smile splits across his face. Suddenly I can't breathe.

He approaches the cubicle I'm parked in front of and motions to the open chair.

"Ok if I sit? Or maybe you would prefer privacy?" He looks over at Nancy, and I follow his gaze. Her fingers are frozen above the keyboard, and she's staring at Ben. She must have been watching him walk, too.

I clear my throat, refocusing.

"No, it's fine. Please, sit." I wave my hand toward the open chair. Nancy snaps out of it, and resumes typing; her long acrylic nails clacking over the keyboard again.

Ben hands my pack to me but remains standing. I pull open the front pocket and fish around inside for my wallet. Retrieving my identification and insurance card, I hand them over to Nancy. While she's photocopying the information, Ben leans in toward me.

"Hey, actually, I'm going to step outside and call the station again, see if they've heard anything," he says, checking his watch.

I look up at him and nod.

He turns and walks outside, and I have to force myself not to watch his backside. I turn toward the desk area to distract myself, only to find that Nancy's gaze is following Ben's rear, and her eyes seem to have glazed over. I can hardly blame her, and I smile at our collective female weakness.

A few moments later Nancy returns to sit in front of me. She has a strange look on her face as she hands me back my driver's license and insurance card. She slowly extends her arms to rest on the desk and folds her hands together neatly in front of her.

"Ms. Marks, I'm afraid your insurance is no longer valid. Have you recently changed carriers?" she asks, her tone hopeful.

I stare at her for a moment, my face frozen.

"I'm sorry, could you say that again? I don't think I follow you."

"It's your insurance, hon. When we enter a patient into our system we verify the insurance information, which I was just trying to do, and..." Her voice is hushed, and a sympathetic look crosses her face. "Well, I'm afraid Providence says this policy has been canceled." She purses her lips together. "Did you recently begin a new policy, maybe with a different carrier?"

I stare at Nancy, expressionless. I can't understand how this could happen. Although we didn't have it written into the divorce decree, Mike promised he would keep me on his insurance, indefinitely, until I could find my own. He said I didn't need to worry about it, that he had it covered, and it was the least he could do since the sale of the house had gone so poorly.

I was such a fool to believe him. What was I thinking? Of course, that was when we were talking almost every day — when I had almost decided to go back to him. How long ago was that? Five months? Six?

"I don't understand," I say, shaking my head at Nancy. "I've had insurance with this carrier for years, almost ten years now.

Surely there must be a mistake." I can feel the panic beginning to flood my system.

"I can let you talk to a customer service rep. Maybe it's a simple fix," she offers.

She removes the receiver from the telephone stationed at her desk and hands it to me. I put it up to my ear, and Nancy pushes a small oval button on the telephone console. A dial tone hums through the line.

"Please wait for just one sec here, and I'll get you an outside line."

Nancy's voice is muffled over the noise in my ear. I watch her push down another button, and a red light illuminates on the console, a louder dial tone sounding in my ear.

"Go ahead now, hon."

Nancy taps her long index fingernail on the insurance card, pointing out the customer service telephone number. I dial it in and wait. After a moment I hear a standard recorded greeting, and I press the "0" to speak to an actual human. A woman who introduces herself as Kelly picks up the line.

I remind myself to stay calm as I speak.

After I provide all of my identifying information, Kelly asks me to please wait while she looks into my policy cancellation. Classical music begins to softly play in the background, and I wonder if I'm in for a long wait. Thankfully, after only a few minutes, Kelly returns to the line.

"Thank you for your patience, Ms. Marks. I am afraid our records do indicate this policy was canceled two months ago. On March 17th, to be exact."

I feel the blood drain from my head. I am equally shocked and indignant.

"But, how can that be?" I demand. "I haven't received any notice, and I didn't cancel the policy! I've regularly made my payments on time." I turn away from Nancy's desk trying to find a small amount of privacy. I glance outside to the parking lot. I can see the back of Ben, but I can't tell what he's doing.

I can hear another keyboard clicking away in the background.

"Well, it looks like you were an insured party, but it was canceled by the policy owner, a Michael Rutherford, on March 17th. A confirmation of cancellation was sent to the address of record on the same date."

I am stunned, and the magnitude of what this means slowly sinks in.

"March? You mean I've been without health insurance for two months? Where has my money been going then?" I clench and unclench my jaw, my words are cut and diced, and I spit them through the phone.

"I am very sorry, Ma'am, but our records show the notice of cancellation was sent to your address of record. If you haven't received notification from your bank yet, I would give them a call right away."

"I know that, but I divorced my hus — okay, let me start over. Mike Rutherford is my ex-husband. When we were married, we lived at the address you have on record. I left him and moved to Oregon, and then we divorced. He promised me that he would keep me on his health insurance as part of our divorce agreement..." I stop talking, suddenly realizing how ridiculous my defense sounds. A man that tormented me for years *promises* to do something nice for me, and I believe him? I take his word? I am disgusted with myself, and how naive I've been. I take a deep breath, drop my forehead into my hands and start over.

"Okay," I say. "Kelly, do you have any alternative plan options you can present to me, as an individual policy? Right now my employer is too small to provide health benefits. And if you do have a policy you can offer, I'll need to know what your company's stance is on pre-existing conditions. I've most likely broken my ankle, and I'm waiting in an ER right now." I am on the verge of tears.

"Let me look into what we can offer you," Kelly says. "What is your email address? I will email you the different plans and prices, and I'll include some information about your pre-existing condition."

It takes me a moment to compose myself. My eyes are stinging, and a large lump has formed in my throat. I want to crawl inside a cave and never come out. I give Kelly my email address and explain it may take some time before I am able to respond, as I no longer have a cell phone.

"You can expect an email from me either later today, or first thing in the morning. I hope you are feeling better soon. Thank you for calling Providence Medical Group. Is there anything else I can do for you today?"

It takes everything in me not to break into a hysterical laugh and give her a list of all the things she *could do for me.*

"No. Thank you."

We hang up, and I slowly replace the receiver. I look up and outside but don't see Ben. I scan what I can see of the parking lot but can't see him anywhere.

Nancy returns to her desk, and I turn to face her.

"So, yeah. It turns out my ex-husband, against our divorce agreement, canceled my health insurance. So, I'm apparently uninsured for this visit today, and anything subsequent, unless Providence can find me a reasonable plan that doesn't disqualify pre-existing conditions," I snarl and feel my face shatter as I start to cry.

Nancy puts her hand on my arm, and I cover my face to hide my breakdown.

"It's okay, hon. We can work this out. I'm sure there is a way to get through this. It may not seem like it right now, but there is always a way. Listen, if your insurance company can't find you something affordable, I can put you in touch with someone here at the hospital that can help you find a state, or a low income, plan, ok?" Nancy pats my arm.

"You don't understand," I complain through my hands. "I can't walk, I can't drive, my Jeep was vandalized, I was attacked by a bear, I'm far away from home, I can't reach my sister, I've lost my phone, and I don't have a place to stay, and now, now I'm *uninsured*!" Huge tears spill down, off my cheeks and onto my wrists.

"Here's some tissue, hon."

I pull my hands away from my face to see Nancy holding several Kleenex in her hand. She gives me the tissues and pushes the box in my direction.

"This day has been pretty awful for you, huh. One step at a time, ok? Now, here comes that handsome fella that brought you in." She smiles at me, and I wipe my eyes with the tissues and quickly blow my nose.

Ben sits in the seat next to me, and I glance over at him and smile weakly. I'm certain my eyes and nose are a nice shade of I've-been-crying-like-a-baby, red.

"Hey, you ok here?" he asks, looking from me to Nancy and back again.

I shrug and then shake my head, about to break into tears again. What in the world is wrong with me? I have been through hell and back in my marriage. Certainly, I can get through this!

I look to Nancy for help, and she nods at me and quickly explains to Ben everything that's just happened. He sighs heavily and shakes his head.

"Man, what a piece of work this guy is."

I wipe away a few stray tears and try to change the subject.

"Did you hear anything from Sylvia?" I am desperate for word from her.

Ben frowns and sits back in his chair.

"No, I'm afraid not. Annie hasn't heard anything more. I did try to look up their last name online, but nothing is listed, other than the law firm, which I called and left another message on the main voicemail. I left my cell phone number and the ranger station's number. I'm not sure what else I can do at this point." His voice seems flat.

"Thanks for trying anyway."

Ben stares at his hands for a long moment. Then he takes his cell phone and pushes it into mine.

"Here."

"What's this for?"

"Well, I've been thinking about it for a while actually. Since my department failed to reach your sister in time, and now that we can't reach her at all, I think it's best if I leave you my phone. I have my radio to communicate with, and besides, there's no reception at the cabin anyway. When you get back on your feet, you can just mail it to me. I *think* I can trust you." Ben smiles weakly and squeezes my hand.

Mail it to him? He's leaving?

I look at Ben and then at Nancy. She must realize what's happening because she winks at me, stands up and quietly walks away.

I turn my attention back to Ben, swallow and look at him sincerely.

"Ben, if you need to get back to work, or whatever, please don't worry about me. I will be completely fine. Especially now that I have this nice new phone." I manage a smile. "I can contact Les Schwab once I get hold of Sylvia, and we can get the rest sorted out. I'm pretty sure I can find a hotel to spend the night in. After all, this town is a giant tourist trap...it shouldn't be too hard." I fake a brave face and smile at him. "Thank you for your incredible amount of help and support. I really don't know how I would have survived without you." I feel a bit weepy in spite of my determination to be completely stoic. "And as soon as I am back home, I will send you your phone in the mail, okay?" I am rambling to avoid the tears I know will spring loose at any minute.

Ben sits back in his chair and sighs. He's staring at me but seems to look right through me, and I have the impression he's weighing something in his mind. He takes a breath to speak just as Nancy returns. She leans over the desk and proceeds to attach a plastic wristband to me. My vital information all concentrated into a few phrases and bright colored symbols.

"There ya go, hon, all set. Now if you wanna go and wait right over there." She points toward a tastefully decorated waiting area behind us. "A nurse should be right out to take you back for x-rays. Don't you worry, you'll be back to new in no time at all."

Ben stands up, takes hold of the back of my wheelchair and pushes me over to the nearest grouping of seats. From what I can tell there are only a few people in the entire room, and for a moment I'm struck by how different this hospital is from all the others I've been in.

He parks the chair at the end of a row and takes a seat next to me. He's looking down at his hands, his forearms resting across the top of his thighs.

He turns to face me. "Can I get you anything? Water?"

I clear my throat. "Oh, no, I'm fine I think. But thank you." Suddenly I feel very awkward.

"Listen, Georgia. I should probably get back to the station. I need to file a formal report about the vandalism and the bear sighting, and check on the cabin to make sure no one is messing around up there." He pauses, a strained look on his face. "Are you going to be okay here on your own?"

A wave of anxiety rolls through me as I realize I don't want him to leave.

"Of course I'll be okay," I lie. "I can handle things from here.

I'm sure I'll hear from Sylvia soon, and she and I can follow up with Les Schwab in the morning. In fact, we'll probably be headed home by tomorrow afternoon."

"Georgia Marks?" a loud male voice calls.

I turn to look behind me and see a young man in green scrubs — a stethoscope tucked into his pocket, clipboard in his hand. I raise my hand to signal him and look back at Ben. He has stood up and is shrugging his pack onto his shoulder. He reaches into a cargo pocket and produces a small, bent pale-white business card, and hands it to me.

"There's the number to the station. If you need to reach me, you can call Annie there, and she'll get in touch with me. My cell number is also listed there, in case you need to give it out to someone." He seems to be making sure he's covered his bases. "So, if you need anything at all, please don't hesitate to let me know."

He takes a step back and shoves his hands in his pockets. I fidget with the card, turning it over and over in my fingers. He seems to be waiting for me to say something.

"Ms. Marks, radiology is waiting." The nurse's tone is unsympathetic.

I look up at Ben, a thin smile across my face. "I can never thank you enough for your help. You've been a terrific friend. A lifesaver." I drop my eyes and then look up at him again. "Hey, maybe I'll see you at the top of a mountain sometime." I offer my hand to shake his.

Ben leans forward and takes my hand in both of his as the backpack slips off his shoulder and falls around his elbow. He squeezes my hand and then quickly brings his face to my cheek, hovering for a moment before leaving a soft kiss. The stubble of his beard tickles my skin, and the scent of him intoxicates me. I close my eyes, paralyzed.

"Take care of yourself," he whispers against my cheekbone. And then he turns and walks out of the hospital. I watch him adjust his baseball cap as the sliding doors open and close behind him.

I stare, unmoving, at the doors. Finally, I wheel myself over to the nurse.

"Let's get that ankle x-rayed, Julia," he says.

I nod, too sad to correct him.

CHAPTER TWENTY-ONE

BEN

"I HAD TO LEAVE HER, Charlie. I had to. I have a whole life to lead here, a job I need to do, and do well. I don't have time to be playing taxicab and nurse. But damn it all if I can't get her off my mind. That adorable laugh and the way she snores in her sleep. 'Course it doesn't hurt that she's absolutely stunning; long, thick, shiny hair, and the way she ties it up in a knot...and her eyes — God, her eyes. I look at her and wonder who in the world would ever dream of doing anything but loving her?

"If you could have seen the way she looked at me when I left though. Man, she looked so helpless, so vulnerable, and yet so brave too. Do you know how hard it was to walk away? But what was I supposed to do? You know I'm in no position to consider any kind of relationship. I know...I know, we would be great friends, that's a given. And I get the feeling there's a mutual attraction between us — I mean, when I kissed her cheek, man it was all I could do to pull away. The truth is, Charlie, I don't know if I trust myself with her — with anyone, for that matter.

"I'm just not ready yet. Right?"

"Right?" I repeat.

Charlie whines and drops his chin onto my lap. He looks at me in sympathy, his brown, glassy eyes unblinking.

"Boy. You're lucky you are a dog," I say, and slide my hand over his smooth head.

CHAPTER TWENTY-TWO

GEORGIA

AFTER AN HOUR IN RADIOLOGY and a long examination by Dr. Flint, the on-call physician, I learn I've sustained a lateral malleolus fracture. Basically, I've broken both the outside and the lower inside of my ankle. Given the nature of my injury, Dr. Flint makes an appointment for me to see a well-known orthopedic surgeon in town tomorrow afternoon, to determine whether or not I need surgery. The news that I do indeed have a broken ankle feels like the mud icing on a cake made entirely of dirt. It's just one more problem I don't need right now.

Thankfully, Dr. Flint helps me adjust by moving quickly through the appointment. He explains what I am likely to encounter with my recovery, and then fits me for an immobilizing brace to wear. It's soft and padded but also very rigid, and strangely enough, it actually makes my ankle feel a lot better right away. Lastly, I'm given a set of crutches to use, which I immediately hate.

"Better than a wheelchair though, right?" Dr. Flint hastily scrawls a signature across his prescription pad. "This one is for the swelling." He rips the paper off the pad with force. "And this one," he finishes hurriedly writing, "is for pain."

Dr. Flint holds the prescriptions in his hand and eyes me carefully. "I see in your chart that you have been taking Vicodin for the last 24 hours. Do you mind if I ask where you got that from?"

I pause momentarily, wondering if I would be getting Ben into trouble, but I decide to just tell the truth. Lying never did anyone any good.

"As I mentioned to the nurse, I was injured at the top of Black Butte while hiking yesterday morning. A Forest Service tech named Ben Harrison found me. He took care of me yesterday and last night. He had the Vicodin. He said he's a Paramedic? I think he had it in a kit or something."

"Do you know what a Vicodin tablet looks like?"

"Uh, I just assumed it was the little, round white pills he gave me that made the pain go away."

Suddenly I feel very naive. Of course I don't know what I've been taking. I could have been taking meth-amphetamines for all I know. You would think after everything I had been through with Mike, I would have been a little more cautious. *Jesus, Georgia!*

Dr. Flint leaves the room momentarily and returns with a double-sided, laminated, color chart displaying different pills.

"Can you tell me if any of these pills match the ones you took?" He hands me the chart, a solemn look on his face.

I scan the pictures on the front; there are four rows and three columns to review. I finally locate the one I think I recognize and put my finger on it.

"This one, I think," I say, hesitantly.

"Ok, good. That is actually Vicodin. I didn't mean to alarm you, Georgia. We just need to make sure that one: you've not been taking an illicit drug or something you shouldn't have been, and two, that the drug you took came from a source that's permitted access. Prescription drug abuse is a rampant problem right now, and we just want to make sure you're safe. Ben Harrison is known to the hospital, and you're right, he was a paramedic — still is, I believe. He's a good man. You couldn't have been helped by anyone better."

The salt of his words sting, and I can only nod in silent agreement.

Dr. Flint takes the drug reference chart and hands me my two prescriptions. I put the appointment card for the surgeon along with my prescriptions in my shredded backpack, sliding it up over my shoulder, and use my new crutches to stand up. I've been holding Ben's cell phone in my hand in case my sister called, and I push the button to check for any updates. Nothing new shows on the screen, so I slide the phone inside my jacket pocket and turn to the doctor.

"Thank you, Dr. Flint, I really appreciate your time."

I lean on my crutches and feel the pressure against my armpits. My backpack slips down to my elbow, and I refasten it across both shoulders before trying to move again — my first lesson with crutches.

"It's my pleasure, Georgia. I'm happy to be of assistance." He turns to hold the door for me and smiles as I crutch past him.

I don't see the familiar face of Nancy anywhere when I arrive back at the check-in area, but I do notice an open desk near the entrance. I head in that direction and find a woman entering information into a computer. As I approach, she looks up at me with an annoyed expression.

"Excuse me," I start, "I'm finished with my exam, but I'm

wondering if Nancy is around? She was going to help me sort out my insurance information."

The woman sighs deeply, and she drops her hands dramatically into her lap.

"Let me see if I can find her. Why don't you have a seat," she says.

I pull my crutches from my armpits, lean them against the chair, pull out Ben's cell phone and sit down. I am hungry, tired, overwhelmed with problems, and ready to get the hell out of this hospital.

I watch as the woman resumes her typing, clicking key after key on the keyboard in rapid-fire succession, the noise echoing through the near-empty room. I stare at her, becoming extremely irritated as I look around the room for a clock. Of course, there isn't one in sight. I feel like I'm in some kind of pseudo-casino; I've been turned around inside this place, and now I've lost track of time. I literally have no idea how long I've been here. I clench my teeth together and take a deep breath in through my nose.

"All right," she says, making her last few keystrokes. "Let me check for Nancy. I'll be right back." She pushes back from her desk, her chair rolling smoothly across the plastic floor mat, and disappears behind a full-length stained glass wall.

Soon she reappears before me and plops down into her chair.

"No. Nancy's gone to lunch. You can have a seat in the waiting area for her to return," she states, matter-of-factly. Her monotone voice and carelessness annoys me.

"You know, I think I really just need to get some food and rest." *And figure out how I'm going to get myself out of this mess.* "Could you point me to a cafe or cafeteria?" I ask, as nicely as possible. I am attempting to kill her with kindness, the golden rule my mother taught me as a child.

"Here's a hospital map." She opens a drawer and hands me a folded booklet. "The cafeteria is through those doors behind you, down the hall to the left and then follow the signs. Okay?" A tight smile appears across her mouth.

"Thank you..." I pause and look at the nametag attached to her lavender scrub top, "...Claire. I appreciate your help. By the way, that color, it looks really nice on you." I smile genuinely; it truly does look good on her.

Claire's thin smile grows, and she softens the look in her eyes. "Why, thank you. That's so nice of you to say. Here." She opens a drawer on the opposite side of her desk and pulls out two small white cards. "These are complimentary dining cards. I think there's about $10 on each one." She presses them into my hands.

I thank her, say a silent prayer of thanks to my mother, grab my crutches and am on my way to discovering what kind of questionable food *this* hospital has to offer.

CHAPTER TWENTY-THREE

GEORGIA

THE CAFETERIA AT ST. CHARLES Medical Center is unlike any I have ever encountered. The room is so tastefully decorated, I have to stop and take it all in. The dozen or so natural wood slab tables remind me more of a trendy gathering spot than a hospital cafeteria, and the walls are framed with artwork so inviting it feels as though I've stepped into a quaint gallery. Situated below the artwork are seating groups of nail-head-trimmed leather chairs and couches, flanked by low coffee tables and modern lamps. I feel as though I have just entered a Restoration Hardware catalog.

The food displays are just as incredible and so numerous I actually feel overwhelmed; a fresh salad bar with every kind of vegetable I can imagine, a homemade soup station with three different choices of freshly baked bread, a gluten-free sandwich bar stand, a barista advertising Stumptown coffee, and a fresh juice and smoothie bar next to that. I stand in awe of the food selections for a good five minutes before I amble over to the smoothie bar and order a cucumber-green apple concoction with protein powder, topped with mandarin orange zest. If I lived in Bend, I would eat at this hospital every day.

After ordering my smoothie, I cross to the sandwich bar and order a grilled porcini mushroom and turkey sandwich with chimichurri sauce and smoked Gouda cheese. I salivate just listening to myself place the order.

I take a sip of my smoothie, and my left eye closes involuntarily, a childhood reaction to very sour tastes that I can't, for the life of me, seem to break. The drink is delicious though, and I sip again, slowly savoring the mix of flavors. I unwrap the sandwich at warp speed, my stomach doing somersaults over itself, and I take huge, unattractive bites. I'm sure my mother would be appalled at my manners, but it's no matter. The food is so good, and I am starving. I haven't eaten since...what time *did* I eat? I can't even remember. Maybe 6:30 a.m.? I look around for a clock and spot one above a doorway; it's 3:35 p.m. No wonder I'm famished.

I finish every bite of my sandwich and drink my entire smoothie in roughly eight minutes. It feels like I've just competed in food Olympics and have taken the gold medal.

Pushing my tray to the edge of my table, I pick up Ben's phone and check again for a message from Sylvia. The screen is blank — no messages. I resolve to call the phone company and re-install a landline again as soon as I get home. This is ridiculous. What were we thinking getting rid of it?

I access the phone keypad and stare at the numbers. I touch the corresponding circles for the standard prefix 5-0-3, and then wait, running possible combinations through my mind. Nothing seems to connect, and I'm just getting frustrated. Instead, I redial the law firm and listen to the sound of the phone ringing back in my ear. I'm just about to push Scott's extension when the phone picks up, mid-ring.

"Kloss and Jenkins..."

I'm almost too stunned to say anything.

"Hello? Kloss and Jenkins, may I help you?"

"Hello! This is Georgia Marks. Who is this please?" I nearly squeal with glee.

"This is Calvin Dorsett. Uh, the offices are closed, ma'am. I just happened to be walking past reception...could I leave a message?" It sounds like he is rummaging through a desk drawer.

"*No*, no message!" I scream to the poor guy. "I'm sorry, I didn't mean to yell in your ear. My brother-in-law is Scott Sorenson. He's an attorney there."

"Oh, hello. I'm Mr. Sorenson's new law clerk. Is there something I can pass along to him? He's not in the office right now."

"Yes, please. Well, actually, I am desperately trying to reach my sister and brother-in-law, but I've lost my cell phone, and I can't remember either of their cell phone numbers. Could you please give me Scott's number, or his wife, Sylvia's?"

There's no response from...crap, what was his name?

I give a tense laugh. "I know this sounds crazy, but this really *is* an emergency. I'm stranded in Bend, and I have a broken ankle. I need them to come pick me up."

"How do I know you're who you say you are?" he asks. "I can't just give out private information like that."

I pause for a moment, considering his question.

"Well, I don't actually know how to prove who I am," I reply. Just then an idea occurs to me. "Tell you what? If you go into his office and sit down at his desk and look to your left, just below the windowsill is a framed photograph of him with Sylvia. They're standing in front of a waterfall, and he's holding his arms around her waist and kissing her forehead. Sylvia's eyes are closed," I say. "I took that picture."

He's silent again for a moment.

"Please hold."

A minute later he picks up the line again.

"All right, I'll give you the number, but I swear, if I get into trouble for this, well, let's just say I *know* people, you follow me?"

I smirk, but scramble in my seat and swivel around to try and find a pen in my bag. I dump the entire thing out on top of my table, and a small black Bic drops out and bounces across the slick wood. I slap my hand down on top of it and grab a stray napkin.

"Gotcha...I'm sorry, what did you say your name was again?"

"It's Calvin. Calvin Dorsett."

"Right, thank you, Calvin. I promise — I'm legitimate. Go ahead. I'm ready when you are," I say, my pen poised above the napkin.

Calvin rattles off Scott's number, and I write and repeat the sequence back to him.

"I can't thank you enough. You're definitely a lifesaver," I say, and take a deep breath. "And now I'm afraid I have to go. Thanks again."

"You're welcome—"

I don't even wait for him to finish his sentence before I end the call, switch screens again and touch the numbers for Scott's cell phone. My heart is skipping excitedly, and I can feel the smile on my face.

The call connects, and I hear it begin to ring. And ring. After five rings, the voicemail picks up, and I hear Scott's voice. I nearly burst into tears. I am one step closer to being home.

"Hello, you've reached the voicemail for Scott Sorenson. I'm sorry I've missed you. Please leave a message, and I'll return your call as soon as possible. Thank you."

I can barely wait for the beep before gushing out my ecstatic message.

"Scott! It's Georgia! You won't recognize this number — I'm borrowing a friend's phone. I'm in Bend. I've broken my ankle, and my Jeep has been vandalized. I've lost my cell phone, and I don't have any of your other numbers. I need your help. I need someone to come and pick me up and drive my Jeep back over the pass. I'm seeing an orthopedic surgeon tomorrow afternoon, so I guess we'll need to work around that...but please call me back on this number. Oh, hang on. I have to find it." I tuck the phone between my ear and shoulder and sort through the debris on the table. I locate Ben's business card and ramble off his name and cell number.

"And you can also call Ben's friend, Annie, at the Sisters' ranger station. I'm pretty sure Ben left you her number on your work voicemail. Please call me back as soon as you can. It's almost 4:00 p.m. and I'm leaving the hospital soon to find a hotel. I think that's everything. I miss you guys!" I end the call and then open up Google to scout a nearby hotel.

A quick search brings up a cheap place near me. I don't mind the quality. It's inexpensive, close to the hospital, and has what I need: a bed and a shower. I re-pack my bag and decide I'll worry about the hospital bills later; after I have access to my email again, and a clear head.

A Ford Explorer taxi ride to a local Wal-Mart and the assistance of a very helpful blue-vested employee leaves me with two filled prescriptions, a pair of pajamas, a handful of toiletries, and a new backpack. I am immensely grateful that the bear didn't obliterate my wallet. American Express to the rescue.

Another taxi up the street and I'm standing in front of the hotel lobby. The sliding glass doors open, and I crutch over to the front desk. Fifteen minutes later, I am leaning my weight against the entrance of room 334, pushing the heavy door open. It's dark and musty, like bottled up, stale air. I turn the lamp on next to the bed and crutch over to the window, open the blackout curtains, and peer through the thin, white privacy panels. The sun is setting, and the sky is turning cotton candy pink.

I yank the hotel comforter — a typical tan and gold-patterned monstrosity — off the bed, and drop my backpack onto the crisp, white sheets underneath. Using a crutch, I hop into the bathroom, swipe back the plastic shower curtain and turn on the water. I'm so anxious to take a shower that I'm almost giddy. I turn and flip the switch for the overhead fan and catch a glimpse of myself in the mirror. My shoulders fall. It's no wonder Ben left. My hair is a tangle of curls and frizz, somewhat restrained by the pitiful resemblance of a bun that's barely hanging on at the back of my neck. I can smell my body odor and instantly wonder if everyone else has smelled it too. I notice the dark circles under my eyes and my chapped and peeling lips. My teeth feel disgusting. I hop back out to the bed, grab the Wal-mart bag and make my way back to the bathroom.

The steam from the hot water begins to fill the bathroom, and I reach down to pull the lever on the top of the tap. A moment of silence envelops the room before the shower head hisses and spits and then bursts forth with a cascade of water. I slide the shower curtain closed again and sit down on the toilet lid. It takes me a long time to get undressed. Removing the splint is easy but pulling my tight fitting hiking pants over my broken ankle proves to be very challenging. I'm finally able to carefully step into the bathtub and grab onto the shiny metal bar along the wall, my wedding ring glinting up at me as tiny drops of water bead up on the thick band. I stare at it for a moment before grabbing hold of the band and sliding it off my finger, opening the curtain, and setting it on top of the toilet seat.

An hour later I am showered, cleaned up, and feeling enormously better. The Wal-Mart cotton shorts and t-shirt feel like silk pajamas after living in my hiking clothes for the last 24 hours. My hair is combed and lying wet against my shoulders, drying in soft waves. I replace my splint, take a pain pill and sit down on the bed, glancing at the clock on the bedside table. It's 5:49 p.m. I'm beginning to worry about Scott and Sylvia. It's Saturday night. Maybe they are out on a date?

I sigh and again make a vow to memorize all important phone numbers from here on out.

To distract myself, I gather up my filthy clothes and head to the bathroom sink to hand wash them with the complimentary shower gel on the counter. The water runs brown as I rinse the soapy bubbles from my pants and socks, wringing them dry with as much force as my exhausted arms can muster. I drape the wet clothes over the shower curtain rod and move the bathmat under my pants to catch any drips. With any luck, my clothes will be dry by the morning. Turing to leave, I catch sight of my ring on top of the toilet. Without hesitation, I grab it, lift the seat, and drop it directly into the water. I flush the toilet and drop the lid hard, wiping my hands against each other and turning back toward my bed.

Hopping back over to the bed, I collapse into the sheets; the crisp, cool material welcoming me with outstretched arms. The Vicodin is making me sleepy, and I feel my body beginning to let go. As I'm closing my eyes, an anxious thought suddenly occurs to me, and I reach over to the cell phone and check the battery. It's at 40%, and I don't have a charger. I decide to switch it off for the night to save the power, resolving to try and reach Scott again in the morning. Turning off the lamp next to my bed, I sink my head into the soft pillow and close my eyes.

I wonder what Ben is thinking about right now.

CHAPTER TWENTY-FOUR

GEORGIA

SOMETIME DURING THE NIGHT, I dream of Ben.

We're driving on a highway in his truck. It's daytime, but it's raining, and the light outside is dim. The windshield wipers beat fast against the incessant drops of rain, and it's difficult to see very far ahead on the road. I'm sitting in the center of the truck, pressed up against the side of him with my head resting on his shoulder. His flannel shirt is soft and warm, and I can smell the woodsy-pine scent of his skin — his right arm draped over me makes me feel safe and protected. I lift my head to look up at him; his beard is thick, and the soft dark hair curves upward toward his earlobes. I can't stop looking at him. I stare at his mouth — his upper lip slightly hidden by his mustache, his lower lip full, naked, and sexy.

I want to bite that lip.

He notices me staring at him and looks down at me.

"What?" He muses, the corners of his mouth turning upward into a seductive smile.

"Mmm, just thinking about those lips of yours," I tease.

He pulls me closer against his body and runs his fingers along the edge of my hip, pressing hard there, and then sliding his hand up along the length of my arm and shoulder. I lay my palm on his chest, feeling his heart beating through his shirt, the warmth of his body heating my skin. His shirt is unbuttoned below the neck, revealing his collarbone, raised and prominent under the small sprinkling of chest hair there. I touch a marbled button and slowly undo it; find the next one down, and unbutton it as well. I gradually slide my hand inside his shirt and across his muscular chest. Ben breathes in deeply, and I look up at him, watching his beautiful face as I slowly move my hand under the soft flannel.

He shifts in his seat.

The sound of the rain against the truck becomes stronger, the noise louder as we drive on. Ben focuses on the road and then looks back down at me, grinning. I sit up taller against him and bury my face into his neck, my hand still inside his shirt. My nose against his skin brings the delicious smell of him into my senses, and my heart skips all over the place. I open my mouth and press my lips against his throat, gently kissing the soft skin there before traveling up toward his earlobe, bringing my teeth against the small circle of skin, and biting down gently. Ben catches his breath, and a small moan escapes his mouth. With my mouth still circling his earlobe, I drop my hand lower inside his shirt, down the center of his stomach, my fingertips pressing at the top of his jeans. I feel the top of his belt buckle, and I move down from his ear, continuing to kiss his neck and trace circles against his skin with my tongue. Ben's breathing steadily intensifies.

Suddenly the truck decelerates and veers decidedly to the right. The smooth surface of the highway is instantly replaced by the loud sound of uneven gravel beneath us, bumpy and rough. My hand freezes and I catch my breath, looking out of the windshield, rigid in my seat. The wipers are still beating fast against the onslaught of rain. We come to a halt on the side of the road, the blinker clicking repeatedly — *tic tac, tic tac, tic tac*. I look up at him in question.

Ben throws the truck into park, rips off his seatbelt and turns his body toward mine.

"You are driving me crazy," he whispers, his dark eyes barreling into mine.

In one fluid movement, he's against me, his mouth pressing down hard against my lips, his arms wrapped around me, holding me prisoner against him. I lift my chin and kiss him back forcefully, opening my mouth against his lips. He groans and thrusts his tongue into my mouth. My mind goes wild, and I lose all control of my senses. He pushes me back against the seat, my head cushioned by our jackets bunched in the corner, and I bring my legs up and open on either side of his hips. I can feel his groin pressing down hard against my thighs, his belt buckle riding against my zipper. I can't stop pulling him toward me.

He stops kissing me for a moment and pulls back from my face. His cheeks are flush under the edges of his beard, his lower lip has swollen into a deep shade of red, and he's breathing hard.

My hands tangle up in his shirt as I search his face. His pupils are fully dilated, and he's staring at me as if he could devour me whole.

He exudes pure, absolute lust.

"I want you, Georgia," he breathes. "I want you right now."

My eyes spring open as I gasp for air. My heart is racing in my chest, and I can't seem to swallow. It takes me a moment to orient myself to the unfamiliar hotel room — I am lying on my back, a pillow across my chest, my arms wrapped tightly around it. I close my eyes again and will myself back to sleep, desperate to return to the sweetness of the dream. I roll over and hug my pillow, trying to savor every memory of his kisses, but am immediately brought into acute wakefulness by the pain in my ankle. I flip forcefully onto my back again in retreat from the stabs of pain; the dream turning wispy and fading from my consciousness. I stare up at the ceiling in frustration and grab the pillow, bringing it down hard against my face and groaning into it. Apparently, my unconscious mind has feelings for Ben that I haven't yet realized. I consider this for a moment and decide I'm not sure what to think about anything anymore.

Instead, I decide to focus on more tangible thoughts and sit up in bed and reach over to the lamp. The blackout curtains are still drawn, and the room is dark. I switch on the lamp and pick up the phone, pressing the power button and waiting while it restarts. The screen comes to life, and the small square labeled *phone* displays the number 2 inside a small red circle.

I scramble up to a sitting position, my focus suddenly razor-sharp.

The recent phone calls tab reveals Scott's cell phone number, and I breathe a huge sigh of relief. I look at the next missed call; it's a number I don't recognize, but the location says *Sisters, Oregon*. Ignoring that for a moment, I quickly push the voicemail tab and bring the phone to my ear. The message begins to play, and the sound of Sylvia's voice brings tears to my eyes.

"Gia! Oh my goodness, I hope this message reaches you. It's me!" she says. I can tell she's starting to cry. "We've been so worried about you!" Her voice is cracking, and tears begin to well in my eyes. "What the heck is going on over there? We were so worried — we called the police in Bend! Call me as soon as you get this message, okay. I don't want to hang up, but I want you to call. So...okay, bye. I love you!" I look at the time on the phone — it's just after 6 a.m. I press the callback button on the phone and hold it to my ear as it begins to ring. Before I hear a second ring, Sylvia answers the phone.

"Hello? Georgia? Are you there?"

"Sylvia! Yes, it's me, I'm here." We are both talking at the same time.

"Gia! Oh my goodness, are you okay, sweetie? We had to call the police! When I didn't hear from you after that call from the pass, I thought..." her voice cracks. "Well, I just thought the worst. I've been so...I've been...So worried about..." She can't quite get the words out.

"I know, Sylv. I know. I'm so, so sorry. I shouldn't have done the stupid hike. I should have listened to you. It was a really dumb idea, and I'm so sorry to have caused you any worry." A huge lump forms in my throat, and I'm having trouble keeping my voice even.

"—And the police in Bend couldn't help us right away. They could only take our information, and then, then they called back and said a report of a vandalized vehicle had come in from the vicinity of where you were supposed to have been." She pauses for a moment. "And I thought, I immediately thought, *that's her Jeep!* And then I was sure something horrible had happened to you." Her voice is rising in pitch, and she sounds panicked. "And then Scott finally got your call, and we called you immediately."

"—Shhh, it's okay, Sylv," I cut her off. "I'm okay. I'm okay." I pause for a moment and then reconsider. "Actually I take that back. Are you sitting down?"

"Oh, God. I am now."

"I made it to the top of the butte, and I even took some great pictures, and then I ate a late breakfast up there sitting on the porch of this old cabin. I guess I must have dozed off because the next thing I knew I was waking up, hearing this noise, this sound like a rustling in the bushes..."

"What. Are you kidding me with this?"

"And I realized pretty quickly that a bear—"

"A *bear!*"

"— Was making its way down to where I was sitting on the cabin porch. I had food with me in my pack, and I think he, or she, probably smelled the food."

Sylvia sucks in a huge breath. "Oh my word, Georgia, how in the world did this happen? I can't believe it!"

"I don't know. It's just incredibly bad luck I guess. Anyway, I ended up falling through the porch of the cabin, and I broke my ankle. It could have been much worse had Ben not come along when he did..." I trail off, thinking momentarily about the luck I had somehow lost, and then found again. "Anyway, it's a long story, but I lost my phone up there. And then we tried to reach you, but I couldn't remember your number, and I couldn't call the house. Which reminds me," my voice is forceful, "we need to re-install that landline a.s.a.p! This is just stupid not having one."

"I couldn't agree more. I am in disbelief at this story, Gia!"

"I know. Me too."

"And you're in a hospital now?"

"No. I've been to the ER, and I'm in a hotel at the moment. My ankle is in a splint. I have to see an orthopedic surgeon to find out if I need surgery. Right now, I have crutches, a splint and pain medication...which reminds me, I need to eat something and take another pill."

"When do you see the surgeon?"

"This afternoon, actually. I think my appointment is at 3:30 p.m."

"But it's Sunday."

"I know. I guess they have weekend hours? I don't know. I'm just following instructions."

"Well, we could come right now and bring you home. You could see a surgeon here tomorrow or the next day," she offers.

I consider what she says. I think about how nice it would be to sleep in my own bed, to have my own clothes, see my own doctor. I think about putting some distance between me, and whatever it is I feel for Ben.

"Yeah," I say, slowly. "I would like that. I've already reserved another night here though. I wasn't sure how soon I would be able to reach you. But I guess I can easily cancel that."

"Okay, and what about your Jeep then?"

"Oh. Yeah, I kind of forgot about that. My head's been spinning here." I rub my forehead. "I don't know Sylvia. I think Les Schwab was going to tow it down the mountain. I haven't talked to them yet. And this phone battery is nearly dead, actually," I say. A small panic rises in my chest. "Before I lose you completely: I'm at the Sleep Inn in Bend. It's close to St. Charles Medical Center. Room 334."

"Okay. Got it. Let me talk to Scott, and I'll call you back, okay?"

"Okay."

"I will see you soon, sis. I'm *so* glad you're okay!"

"Me too." It's the understatement of the year.

We hang up, and I look at the battery life again: 35%.

My stomach grumbles loudly as a hunger pang rings through my body. I set the phone down and turn the power off, deciding to take a shower first, and then sort out food and wait to hear from Sylvia. I consider taking another Vicodin pill but decide instead to see if I can do with just Ibuprofen. I'm tired of feeling so out of it. I'm tired of feeling so sleepy all the time.

I slide out of bed and test a slight amount of weight on my foot on the industrial grey carpet. My mother's warning about going barefoot on hotel room floors echoes in my mind. *Well, when you have a broken ankle all bets are off, Mom.* But as soon as I attempt a moderate amount of weight, a bullet of pain shoots up both sides of my calf. I suck in air through my already clenched teeth and pull my leg up sharply. Exhaling more evenly, I reach over, pick up my crutch and hobble over to the bathroom.

After a quick shower, I dress in my clean hiking clothes. My pants and shirt are stiff as boards, but at least they don't smell awful any longer. I use the courtesy blow dryer and my Wal-Mart round brush to tame my naturally wavy hair into something smoother — I'd like to look less like a wildebeest at breakfast.

I brush my teeth again, leave my toiletry items and pajamas in the bathroom, grab my backpack, and crutch to the elevator, reveling in the fact that I will soon see my sister.

CHAPTER TWENTY-FIVE

GEORGIA

MY TAXI DRIVER RECOMMENDS A local spot for the 'best caramel apple French toast on the face of the earth'. I take the suggestion and soon find myself standing inside an old Victorian-style home on the west side of town; the aromas of fresh ground coffee and toasted sourdough bread fill the small dining room. My mouth begins to water as I imagine biting into the crunchy crust of buttered bread.

There is a family in line ahead of me. The mom is dressed in what looks like an outfit straight out of a yoga magazine — long sleeved Lululemon heather gray shirt, tight-fitting black Capri pants with reflective striping along the calves, sporty Nike's, and a cross body bag that's draped from shoulder to hip. I make a mental note to try and find the pants on-line. I glance behind me and am surprised to find a ferocious line spilling out onto the sidewalk. I'm thankful I arrived early.

The hostess shows me to a small table by a window that overlooks the front of the restaurant. The small patio and garden area is spotted with metal tables and chairs, and a few blooming purple iris spill out over the pathways that wind through the setting. I lean my crutches against the window, slide across the smooth seat of the chair, and open the menu the young woman hands me. She pours me a cup of steaming hot coffee, and I warm my hands around the mug. A moment later a waitress appears, and I order the French toast.

"Perfect choice. It's my favorite," she says, winking at me.

As I relax at my table, I consider what's next: I need to call and cancel my appointment with the surgeon, and I need to call Les Schwab to find out about my Jeep. Sylvia is supposed to be calling me back, and then I can work out what time I should check out of the hotel. On my way out of town, I need to drop Ben's phone at the ranger station. No sense in paying postage when we're going right by it. At the thought of this, a small hope that I might see him blooms in my stomach.

I reach over into my backpack, pull out his phone and lay it on the table beside me. Should I turn it back on? I don't want to drain the battery any further, but I want to be reachable when Sylvia calls back. I take another sip of coffee and stare at the phone, my fingers drumming on the table. Looking out of the window at the scenery beside me, I attempt to distract myself, but it's no use. I quickly reach over and grab the phone, press the power button firmly, and hold it tight as it turns on. As the screen comes to life, I see the reminder of the second missed call from last night: the unknown number in Sisters. There's no voicemail though, and I realize it's probably a personal call for Ben. A woman, perhaps. Maybe someone he's dating. Maybe someone he has a relationship with — someone that's not me. As I realize the likelihood of this possibility, I set the phone down away from me. Strangely enough, it begins to ring, and as I switch the ringer to off, I notice the display shows the Sisters' number calling again. Should I answer it? What if it's his girlfriend?

"What if it's Les Schwab," the more rational part of my brain interjects.

"Hello?" I say, almost whispering.

"Georgia? Is that you sweetheart? It's Annie. From the ranger station? You remember me don't you?" Annie's demanding, yet caring voice cracks over the connection.

"Yes, of course! Hi Annie!" I say, relieved. "How are you? Wait a minute, are you working on a Sunday?"

"Oh, bless your heart, never mind me, honey. During the fire season, we keep the station staffed seven days a week. But that's neither here nor there," she clucks. "Listen, sweetheart. I'm calling because Benjamin stopped by here yesterday afternoon and asked me to call you. Check up on you, see how you're doing, by God."

Ben asked her to check up on me?

"That was really very kind of him, Annie. I'm doing all right. At the moment, I'm waiting for breakfast. I'm starving." I laugh. "I saw the Emergency Room doctor yesterday, and it turns out I've broken my ankle in two places. I'm on crutches now. I'm supposed to see an orthopedic surgeon later this afternoon, but I've talked to my sister, and I think she's coming to get me today." I pause and then decide just to ask. "How's Ben doing?" I ask, hesitant to know the answer. I chew on my fingernail as an image of his shirt unbuttoned over his chest flashes through my mind.

I can hear some muffled noise in the background, but I can't hear Annie any longer.

"Annie? Are you still there?" I ask, my voice a little louder.

"Yes. Yes, I'm here, darlin'. Just trying to decide how to answer your question. The way I see it, life is too short to be cautious, and I'm too old to play games." She clears her throat. "See, the thing is, sweetheart, Benjamin is...well, he's been through a hell of a lot in his life, you see. I know 'cause I seen him go through it. We've been working together for some years now, and it just tears up my heart because he's such a special man. By God, Georgia, he reminds me so much of my Frank when he was younger," she says, nostalgia coating her voice. "Ah, never mind, I've probably said more than I should. I know Benjamin wouldn't like me talkin' about his private life like that. I just...I don't know, honey, you just strike me as someone different. For some God-only-knows-why reason, I just have a sense about you. I can feel it in my gut."

"I don't know what to say, Annie." I pick up my coffee cup and take a long sip. "Thank you very much for sharing that with me though. It means a lot. Ben really helped me out up there, you know? He saved my life. I don't know that I will ever be able to repay him for that." A small ache begins to bloom in my chest.

"Well, if I know Benjamin, and believe me I *do* know Benjamin, he won't have any part of you repaying him. He's happy to help. It's his nature. Ain't nothing going to drive that outta him..." She clears her throat again. "I just wanted to let you know that he's lived a real rough life these last years." She pauses and then begins again in earnest. "Now you listen to me, Georgia, darlin'. It ain't my business to get involved in other people's affairs, but I just can't hold this back any longer: if you think you might have some sorta *interest* in Benjamin, why, I just want you to know that, by God, you should definitely, one-hundred-percent, abso-spankin-lutely let him know. I have a sense about these things, and I'm sensing he has a good interest in you." I can feel Annie's smile across the connection.

"Thank you, Annie. I'm not really sure about anything right now, but this really means a great deal to me." I say.

"It's my pleasure; I just wanted to say my piece. Now, what's this about you leaving town today?"

"Well, that's my plan, anyway. My sister is supposed to call me back on this phone. Actually, I better go, Annie. This battery is nearly dead, and I don't have a charger. I don't want to miss Sylvia's call."

"Oh dear! Yes, of course. Alrighty then. Bye now, Georgia. Best wishes to you, sweetheart."

"Thank you, Annie. Thank you for everything."

I end the call and check the battery life: 25 percent left. Out of the corner of my eye, I see a server holding several large plates of hot food, balancing them on her forearms, walking my direction. She carefully makes her way to the table in front of me, depositing the plates of goodness in front of the expectant customers, their forks at the ready.

I put the phone down next to me just as another server approaches my table, a carafe of coffee in one hand, and a thick ceramic plate piled high with fluffy French toast in the other. She sets the steaming plate down in front of me, grabs a roll of silverware from her apron, and puts it beside the plate.

"Enjoy," she says, filling my coffee at the same time.

I don't even know if I form a coherent reply before diving into the miracle of breakfast that's before me.

I finish breakfast feeling twenty pounds heavier but incredibly satiated. It's still early enough in the morning that I'm not sure Les Schwab is even open yet. I decide to head outside to soak up the sunshine and try to clear my muddled mind.

In the small garden in front of the restaurant are the several small tables and chairs I saw from my window. As I crutch across the winding path through the overflowing flowers, I spot a few brightly-colored Adirondack chairs with footstools and child-size tables. Some of the tables have chess game boards painted on top, and a small basket near the path holds playing cards, coloring books, and a few other board games.

This is quickly becoming my new favorite place.

I find a small wooden table with two chairs and sit down,

leaning my crutches against the seat across from me. Staring out at the traffic on the busy street, it's easy to marvel at the number of cars and trucks driving by. The day is already warm and a pickup with two paddleboards strapped to the roof, fins pointing to the sky, whizzes by; echoes of radio music waft in the air behind it. A moment later, a white SUV rolls by, a tiny black and white English bulldog hangs its head out of the window, his ears pointed to the sky, his large eyes scanning the scenery. I miss my Jeep, and I miss snuggling with Guthrie, his paws pushed up against my side, his stinky breath filling the air.

I sit in the sun for about thirty more minutes before deciding 9 a.m. is probably opening time for Les Schwab. I open the phone and look up the number. The website display lists their phone number and also their store hours.

They're closed on Sunday.

I put the phone down in front of me and collapse my head into my arms on the table, stomping my good foot in frustration and groaning loudly. Why can't anything actually *work* for me?

After a moment, I raise my head and sigh. Reaching again for the phone, I re-dial Annie to see if maybe she knows something about my Jeep. The phone rings three or four times, and I'm half expecting a voicemail recording to pick up when the next ring is interrupted midway.

"Hello?" a man's voice answers.

I sit back against my chair, surprised. "Oh, I'm sorry, I think I must have dialed the wrong number," I quickly say and begin to take the phone away from my ear to hang up.

"Georgia? Is that you?" I recognize the voice and press the phone back to my ear.

"*Ben*?" I whisper.

"Hi there," he answers. "How are you feeling?" His voice gives me goosebumps.

"Uh, I'm okay I guess. I'm sorry, did I dial the station? I mean, you answered like I called a residence. Oh, before I forget, this phone—"

"—needs a charger, right?"

"Yes! I've been so worried about using it. I think it's almost dead now."

"I know. I'm sorry. I thought of that after I arrived back at the cabin and saw the charger sitting on the desk. That's why I stopped in here actually. I wanted to get it to you so you could use the phone. I swear, I just walked in to call you, and I recognized the caller ID, so, I just answered." He pauses for a moment. "So, how are you? What did the doctor say?"

"You were right. My ankle is broken. I'm supposed to see a surgeon here in Bend this afternoon, but I might need to cancel that depending on when Sylvia can get here. I heard from her, so that's good. She's talking to Scott, and then I think they are coming to get me today." I take a deep breath. "My only real problem right now is that I've just realized Les Schwab is closed today, so I don't have a way to get to my Jeep." I sigh and drop my chin onto the palm of my upturned hand.

"A surgeon? Are you in much pain? You know what, never mind. Can we meet somewhere? Actually, where are you right now? I'd like to talk to you, but I'm afraid that phone is going to die."

I sit up straight and swallow quickly.

"Uh, sure," I answer, and look around me for something that might orient him to my location. I don't see anything obvious. "Well, right this minute, I am sitting outside an old house in Bend that's been turned into a restaurant. It looks like a Victorian home. I can't remember what it's called, but the French toast was amazing." I twist my body around and look for menus on the tables next to me. "Uh, I think it's called..."

The phone gives a small *beep*, and all of the sudden silence fills my ear.

I rip the phone away and stare at the blank screen.

"Hello? Hello? Ben?"

The line is dead.

I slam the phone down on the table and look up at the sky. "Are you trying to completely destroy me here?"

I decide to hobble back inside and order the drink this place is apparently famous for: the Bloody Mary.

Holy hell, they weren't kidding. The Bloody Marys here are huge — 23 ounces — and *potent*. I am only halfway through the drink, sitting outside in the sunshine when I realize I am well on my way to a good buzz. I remind myself it's a good thing I only took Ibuprofen. Otherwise, I'd be passed out by now.

This drink has everything imaginable impaled on a skewer that's so tall, it looks like a small antenna sticking out of the glass. A grilled prawn, a cube of pepper jack cheese, several cured meats, and a freakin' sausage, all battling for space on the long, pointed stick that's swimming in the tangiest, most peppery vodka I've ever tasted. After a few minutes with this new best friend, my worries really don't seem that overwhelming: I'll make my way back to my hotel, and my sister will show up there sometime later. We'll head home, and she and Scott can drive back to get the Jeep sometime next week. No problemo. I can easily just kick back, relax and enjoy this gorgeous Sunday.

As I look around at my surroundings, I wonder why in the world I've never thought about moving here? The town is amazing; the people are friendly and active, the weather unbeatable, the opportunity for outdoor activity incredible...I'm pretty sure an appetite for antiques could easily be discovered. I could convince my boss to open a small, rustic shop in town, and then I could come and eat breakfast and drink Bloody Marys here every single day. Ok, well, every single Sunday, anyway. That reminds me, I need to call Ed as soon as I get home, and let him know I won't be in on Tuesday, and will probably need a few days off.

I slip further down into my chair and lean my head against the back, closing my eyes. The sunshine feels so nice on my face and neck, and I hear the wind blowing gently through the huge pine tree above me. It's so soothing, so peaceful. I feel almost no pain whatsoever.

"Wow." A deep voice booms over me. "I leave you alone for 24 hours, and you turn into a lush?"

CHAPTER TWENTY-SIX

GEORGIA

My eyes spring open, and I have to squint against the direct sunlight on my face. Bringing my hand to my forehead, I shield the blinding light and see Ben standing over me with his arms crossed casually over his chest, a crooked grin playing at his mouth. I suck in a small breath of surprise, and he chuckles, his smile growing larger. He's gorgeous in his civilian clothes: a pair of dark denim jeans that hang low on his hips, and a white short-sleeved, button-down Henley shirt that hugs his chest and outlines his biceps perfectly. To top it all off, he's wearing mirrored aviator sunglasses. I am literally stunned by his presence.

The most wonderful feeling of happiness fills my body, and a huge smile breaks out across my face. I don't even care that I'm showing so much emotion. I sit up quickly, stand on my good foot and reach up to him with my arms, wrapping them around his neck.

"Ben!" What are you doing here?" I ask, dropping my arms around his shoulders and breathing in his warm, woodsy-pine scent. Why does he smell so damn good?

I realize I am hanging on to him for longer than necessary, and I slowly disentangle myself from his torso, sitting down in my chair, slightly embarrassed.

"I knew where you were when you described the house. It's the best place in town for breakfast..." he trails off, glancing at my nearly finished, cauldron of alcohol sitting on the table, "...and the best place for Bloody Marys, which, it looks like you have already discovered for yourself." He chuckles deeply, and the sound is almost more than I can handle. I try to stay on track.

"But we only spoke...I don't know, maybe twenty minutes ago? How'd you get here so fast?"

"It was actually about forty minutes ago. How many of those have you had?" He smiles and then turns solemn. "Seriously though, have you taken any pain medication today?"

"No, actually I haven't. I did take three Ibuprofen though."

"And that's managing your pain well enough?"

"I'm in pain, there's no doubt about that, but it does seem to be helping. And besides," I continue, "this brace, and this drink, help a lot," I say.

He considers my answer for a moment before motioning to the chair my crutches are laying against. "Mind if I join you?"

I nod, and he sits down, pulling closer to the table.

"I brought you the charger for the phone." He uncurls the black cord from his hand and lays it on the table. "It's solar, or electrical, depending on what you need. Actually a pretty cool little device. Here, plug it in now while the sun's out." He hands me the charger, and I dutifully push it into the phone. I watch as the blank screen suddenly comes to life and displays a mostly empty battery with a lightning bolt pulsing through it.

"Wow, that's handy, huh? Thank you. And thank you for letting me use your phone. I told you I was able to reach my sister, and I spoke to Annie earlier this morning. She was so nice, just checking up on me. She mentioned you stopped in there yesterday and asked her to call." I reach both hands toward my enormous drink and take a long sip from the straw.

He drops his head forward slightly, his voice quieter, "Where did you end up staying last night?"

I grin and decide to be truthful. "At the Sleep Inn," I reply. "And guess what? I didn't get to sleep *in* at all. Maybe I should sue for false advertising." I raise my eyebrows at him.

Ben puckers his lips and whistles in approval. "That is one classy joint you picked!"

"Yeah, well, when you're marooned in an unfamiliar town and have to see a specialist the next day..."

He sits forward in his chair and takes off his sunglasses, setting them down on the table. I stare at his glasses. I don't trust myself to look into his eyes.

"About that...I want you to know I feel really awful, Georgia." His tone is serious, and I have no choice but to meet his gaze, which makes me swallow hard.

"I should have stayed with you at the hospital. I should have made sure you were okay."

"It's all right," I say. "I managed just fine, and besides, I've survived worse." I smile weakly. It was true; I had survived much, much worse. And while coming out of that dark time had given me courage, it was still hard to relive the memories, to reopen the wounds. Some things were just meant to be forgotten.

"I just want you to know that I didn't mean to abandon you. I just..." He stops talking and puts his hands on the table, lowering his gaze. "Georgia, this is difficult for me to explain." He raises his eyes and looks at me, and I feel stone sober.

"The thing is," he says, clearing his throat, "it's hard for me to get close to anyone. I don't actually even *want* to be close to anyone. That's why I took the job at the lookout cabin. I knew it would mean seclusion and solitary living. And up until this weekend, that system has worked out pretty well for me. I rarely interact with people outside of the ranger station, and those folks there...well, they know me well enough to give me a wide berth." He sighs and looks away. "But I also was raised to be polite and treat a person in need with respect. My mother would have been very disappointed with the way I left you at the hospital." He looks up at me again and trains his eyes on mine. "I'm sorry I left you there, Georgia. I should have waited to see if your sister was coming. I should never have left, and I've been thinking about it ever since I walked out of that place."

Despite my best efforts to control any outward displays of emotion, I can't help but reach over and place my hand on top of his and give a small squeeze.

"You don't need to apologize, Ben. If I hadn't done something completely irresponsible, it's quite possible our paths would never have crossed. I think it's probably safe to say that we both have some collateral damage in our pasts. Stuff that might still be affecting us now. Being thrown together like that, I don't know, it probably forced some old memories and feelings to surface," I say quietly. "Honestly though, please do not apologize. Like I told Annie, had it not been for you, well, I don't know what would've happened. I owe you a great deal of gratitude." I bring my hands back to my lap and look away. Why am I feeling so teary-eyed?

"Hey, you don't have anything to do for a while, right?" he says, smiling at me again, and I feel my spirits lift.

"Uh, no, my schedule seems to be open at the moment," I smile. "I'm just waiting for my sister to call. Oh wait, I do still need to figure out where my Jeep is and how I'm going to get it."

Ben ducks his head sheepishly, "Actually, that's kinda been taken care of."

"What do you mean?"

"I mean it's already been moved. It has new tires, and it's parked at my house in Sisters."

"But...how did that happen? I have the keys still." I am suddenly aware that my mouth is open.

"Well, after I left you yesterday I ran into the Les Schwab guy at the trailhead. He was just finishing up with your tires, and we discovered the key issue. I guess it's a good thing your window was shattered — I just opened the door and hot-wired the Jeep, and now it's at my house." His last words come out in one, quick, run-on sentence. "So, would you..."

I hold up my palms in front of my chest. "Hold on just a minute, buddy. Did you just say you *hot wired* my Jeep?" I ask, narrowing my eyes at him.

Ben tucks his lower lip into his teeth and bites down slowly. Holy shit.

"Uh, yeah...about that." He lets go of his lip and curves his mouth into a grin. My stomach suddenly feels like it's filled with feathers.

"It's a skill I picked up a long time ago. Don't worry. I never use my powers for evil."

I laugh at him and shake my head. "Thank you?"

Ben pushes his chair back, stands up, and offers me his hand.

"So, would you like to accept my offer of friendship, and allow me to show you around this little town, or should I leave you to drown your sorrows?"

"As long as I don't end up an accomplice to grand theft auto, I guess it sounds okay." I agree, and place my hand in Ben's as he helps me stand up.

I reach for my crutches and stow them safely into my armpits. I feel Ben staring at me.

"What?"

He has a somber expression on his face. "Nothing. I just wonder how bad that break is. Surgery could render you pretty immobile for several weeks, then physical therapy..." he trails off.

"I just hope it's something that can be braced and left to heal on its own."

I remember Dr. Flint's questions and comments.

"My ER doctor mentioned he knew you. I had the impression you two worked together or something.

Ben crosses his arms against his chest, and his eyes dart down, and to the side. A moment passes before he responds.

"I worked with St. Charles docs when I was a paramedic. Anyway, it was a long time ago now. Obviously, I don't work in that field any longer. I just keep my certification current in case I need it." He motions to my ankle. "My first aid kit is stocked with supplies. Vicodin is the strongest prescription I carry, and I keep the kit locked," he says.

Is he defensive? Before I can decide, he asks me a question.

"Was it Mark Flint you saw?"

I nod. "I think so. I only know his last name. He asked me if I was taking any medication and then had me identify the pills you gave me. He said he knew who you were, and mentioned your paramedic training."

"Yeah, he and I went to the same high school. Even dated the same girl — separately, of course."

Ben winks at me, but I can see a shadow cross his face as the smile fades unnaturally. When he begins again, his voice is quieter — dull. "Our paths crossed again a while back," he says. "Anyway, he's a good doc. I'm glad you were able to see him."

I decide to try and steer the subject in a different direction.

"So, do you know anything about the place he referred me to: High Desert Orthopedics?"

"Mmhm, I know the place. I had my shoulder looked at over there about five years ago. They have great staff. I think they keep pretty busy with the level of outdoor activity around here. Speaking of outdoor activity," he motions to the rear of the restaurant, "we should get going. What time is your appointment?"

"3:30, but Sylvia might be getting me before that. I don't know."

"All right," he says. "We won't go very far." He's walking beside me, and I'm glad he can't see the flush I feel at my neck.

We walk around the front of the house and toward the back parking lot. I scan the area quickly but don't see Ben's Forest Service truck anywhere. As we near the parked cars, I follow Ben onto the asphalt, wondering where he is leading me.

"I'm over there," he says, pointing toward the far corner of the lot, "that brown Scout."

I see the two-tone Ford, topless, parked in the shade of a towering pine tree. As we reach the vehicle, Ben sets my pack down in the back of the open-air truck and helps me into the passenger side. I buckle my lap seatbelt and hang my elbow out over the door. Ben hops in, flips the sun visor down, and catches the keys that fall into his hand. He turns toward me, one arm across the steering wheel, his mirrored sunglasses reflecting the sunshine back in my face. A wave of heat passes over my face, and I involuntarily swallow.

"All set then?"

I nod, and as we pull out of the parking lot and wait to turn left at the intersection, I lay my head back against the seat, sigh, and look up into the gorgeous blue sky — wondering how in the world I'm going to keep my feelings from turning into anything other than the platonic friendship he's asked for.

CHAPTER TWENTY-SEVEN

GEORGIA

WE LEAVE THE RESTAURANT AND make a quick stop at a local market. I wait in the truck while Ben runs inside for a few items, and use the opportunity to check the charging phone. Sylvia still hasn't called, but the battery life is at seventy-percent now. I decide if I haven't heard from her by the time we finish whatever it is we're doing, I'm going to call her instead.

Ben reappears a few minutes later carrying a brown paper grocery bag that looks heavy. As he nears the truck, I spot the familiar white and green twist-off top of a San Pellegrino bottle, peeking out from the top of the bag. How did he know I like that?

He hoists the bag over the side of the Scout and sets it down next to my backpack, reaching inside and rummaging around for something.

"Ugh, where'd they go?" he mumbles.

"Where'd what go?"

"Here they are." He hands me a pair of tortoiseshell, oversized sunglasses. "I thought you might need them for the drive.

I'm sure they aren't the best quality, but they are better than nothing."

I'm touched by his gesture, and I slide the glasses on, look over at him and give him my best Marilyn Monroe lip pout while pretending to pose for a camera. I can't hold the ridiculous position more than a second before I laugh — more at myself than anything else.

"Thank you very much, kind sir," I say, giggling.

Ben stares at me for a second too long before smiling and starting up the engine.

"At your service, m'lady."

He throws his arm behind the back of my seat and reverses the Scout.

We head out of town, driving for the most part, in silence. The noise from the traffic around us, and the Scout's heavy tires against the pavement keeps us from having any type of meaningful conversation. The retro AM/FM radio is playing music, but I can't make out the songs.

We drive uphill along a curving road, passing numerous bicyclists wearing tight, colorful jerseys and padded spandex; their shirts advertising local breweries and well-known sporting gear brands. All the riders have the same physical stance: head down, hands on the lowest handlebar, rounded back and pumping quadriceps. It looks like torture. I turn and make an unhappy face at Ben as we move into the oncoming lane to safely pass another cyclist trudging up the never-ending hill. He smiles back at me.

"Yeah, but the way back is all downhill...smooth sailing right to the front door of the brewery," he hollers.

I consider that idea. Maybe I could manage the strenuous climb knowing there was a worthwhile reward at the end. Possibly, but probably not. I'd done a spin class at my local gym before — my butt hurts again just thinking about it.

As we continue up the road, we pass a gorgeous golf course on the left. The entrance looks like something out of a Town and Country magazine. Pristine, groomed golf greens lie beyond an immaculate river rock wall that runs along the roadside. A gorgeous wooden plank bridge spans across a glistening river that winds its way through the course. Bright orange Canna are tucked into the landscape; the giant, angled, golden flowers piercing the air like spears, the tall green stems and low lying leaves anchoring them to the ground below colorful flags that ripple back and forth in the breeze, giving off an authoritative air to the entrance.

"That's beautiful!" I yell across to Ben, one hand holding my whipping hair against the back of my neck.

He nods in agreement.

Gradually we wind away from the homes and resorts, slowly climbing into the uninterrupted outdoors. I note signs indicating upcoming points of interest: mountains, lakes, and campgrounds. This scenic highway is an outdoor enthusiast's dream.

We round a long corner, and I see the peak of an impressive mountain in the distance. I point at it with a smile on my face and look at Ben.

"Mt. Bachelor," he yells above the road noise.

"It's amazing!"

Several mountains appear in front of us as we drive closer. It's the end of May, but the peaks are still covered in white. Outcroppings of rocks and low-lying shrubs are visible in the areas closer to the tree lines. The views of the pristine wilderness surrounding me are simply incredible, and I am stunned by the sheer beauty of the natural world unfolding before me.

We drive past the entrance to Mt. Bachelor, and I notice several cars and SUVs parked in the enormous lot. As we pass by,

I see the ski lifts are in operation up and down the front of the mountain.

"Do they still ski up there?" I yell, pointing to the lifts.

"Yeah, up above."

I want to ask more about the skiing, and the mountain, but it's so difficult to try and hold a conversation above all the noise. Instead, I turn my head and try to take in the sights around me.

We wind our way down the highway, past trailhead pullouts, and campground entrances. I notice parked Jeeps with loaded roof racks, and two-tone Subarus with mountain bikes hanging off the back, their owners removing the straps and ties, getting ready to spend a beautiful Sunday in the outdoors. I look down at my swollen, bandaged ankle and a feeling of annoyance runs through me. The reality of the sedentary life I am now assigned to feels like a sharp slap in the face. I try to ignore the feeling and instead, look out of the window as we pass by gorgeous forests of pine.

We crest a small hill and Ben begins to slow the Scout. My senses perk up, and I look around in anticipation of where we might stop. He downshifts and signals to turn left onto what appears to be a rutted, and significantly muddy, dirt road. We bounce down from the highway onto the road, slowing to a crawl through the deep ruts. Ben twists and turns the steering wheel, trying to avoid the worst sections of the road. It's bumpy, and I can hear the contents of the grocery bag jostling behind Ben's seat. I reach my arm behind him and grab a handful of the bag in my fingers, holding on tight. My other hand holds firmly to the handle above the glove compartment.

"Sorry about the road. It's still early enough in the season that the mud hasn't dried up yet."

Ben's voice is soft again, the noise from the pavement now gone. I look over at him. His dark hair is blown backward from the peak of his forehead, and his wavy curls seem unruly and uncooperative. I can see his eyes behind his sunglasses; he's staring intently at the road ahead. With each hard turn of the steering wheel, I notice his jaw flex beneath the stubble of his beard.

"No, the road's fine," I reply, intentionally distracting myself. "I'm just worried about the groceries you have here." I tip my head toward the bag I'm holding on to. "If that's Pellegrino, you might need to open it slowly. It's getting pretty shaken up."

Ben nods as he navigates the ruts in the road, pulling us farther and farther into the tall pine trees. We finally come to a clearing that's apparently used for parking and camping. The trees thin out into a small round area, and I notice remnants of fire rings and stump seats.

He steers the Scout over to a shady spot near a clump of smaller trees and shuts off the engine. I turn around and look behind us. I can see what looks like the entrance of a wide, bark-chipped path. A small wooden sign that looks like a trail marker stands guard.

I swivel back around in my seat to face Ben.

"Uh, you're not thinking of taking me on a hike are you?" I am completely serious.

He's leaning over the steering wheel with both arms. At my question, he tips his head sideways, rests his temple on his forearm, and aims a grin at me.

"No, Ben," I say. "There's no way I can navigate these ruts on crutches, and no way I want to risk causing further harm to myself, especially just *hours before* I see my potential surgeon."

He sits back in his seat and holds up his hands in a sign of surrender.

"Ok, ok, calm down. Do you think I would bring you all the way out here to put you in harm's way?" He begins to laugh, I assume, based on the look that crosses my face. "Well, I wouldn't. I just wanted to show you some truly beautiful scenery, and maybe have a nice lunch together. These are things friends do, right?"

I suppose he has a point.

"Fine. Just so long as I don't have to go very far. You wouldn't believe how sore my armpits are already."

I unbuckle my seatbelt and begin to reach for the handle.

"Hang on. I'll be right over."

He slides out of his seat, and I watch him carve his way around the back of the Scout. He opens the tailgate and rummages through the grocery bag, pulling out items and putting them in my backpack. When he finishes, he gives the tailgate a hard shove, latching it into place, and comes around to my door.

He opens the door for me and hands me the backpack. Then, instead of helping me steady myself with a crutch, he turns around and backs up into the open doorway. He holds his arms out from his sides and glances at me over his shoulder.

"Well, c'mon," he says.

I stay in my seat, not quite sure where he's going with this.

"Georgia. Give me your legs."

He's still standing with his back to me, and as he speaks, he begins to wiggle his arms. "This is a modern day, very efficient mode of transportation. You might have heard of it? It's called the piggy-back ride." He laughs at his own sarcasm.

I consider this for a moment.

"Um, all right," I concede.

I mean how far could we be going, anyway? I wiggle into the backpack straps, turn sideways and scoot to the edge of the bench seat. I carefully slip my right leg down and through the space between his torso and arm, and then slide down off the seat, simultaneously repeating the process with my left leg, and hooking my arms tightly around his neck. I nearly lose my balance but right myself again by bracing sharply against his throat. Ben chokes and erupts in a coughing fit and has to lean forward, with me on his back, to catch his breath again.

"Are you ok?" I ask, somewhat laughing.

He coughs a few more times before standing up, semi-straight, and answering in a very hoarse voice. "I'm good. Just, next time, if you feel yourself slipping, just wrap your legs around my waist and hang on to my shoulders instead, okay?"

Wrap my legs around your waist?

"Ok," I say, and immediately flush. I'm glad he can't see my face.

Once I am settled on his back, Ben begins to walk toward the trailhead. He hasn't gone very far, but already I feel like I weigh more than the mountains I see around us. I try to hold my body up, somehow I think this will reduce the amount of weight he's bearing, but this just makes Ben laugh, and he chides me for thinking he's weak.

The bark-chip trail turns to soft dirt, and the pine trees fall away to reveal an open field with tall grasses and beautiful lavender wildflowers artfully arranged alongside the trail. The air smells different here; no longer full of pine and juniper, this area smells grassy, wet, and warm. Around us, I can see at least four soaring, snow-capped mountains. Ben points them out and tells me their names: Bachelor, Broken Top, South Sister, Middle Sister...we are walking in a lush valley at the foot of these tremendous giants.

He walks a few steps farther on the trail, shifts me on his back, and then steps off the track to walk through the grasses. Before I can ask what he's doing, we come upon a small stream running through the valley. He approaches the edge of the water and carefully lets go of my left leg. I steady it on solid ground, and then he releases my right and turns around to face me, hands on his hips.

"I think we can stop here and have a bite to eat. I don't know about you, but I'm starving."

I slip the backpack off and hand it to Ben. As I sit down, the ground around me erupts in a profusion of erratic jumps. Small bits of dark green and black pounce into the open air. A multitude of tiny frogs leap to freedom, trying to escape my giant feet and legs, hopping to the safety of the grasses near the water's edge. There are so many of them it's like a swarm of crickets around me, and I recoil my legs and arms in alarm and let out a shriek of surprise.

The sound of Ben's deep belly laugh draws my immediate attention, and I turn to stare at him and feel my eyebrows furrowing together behind my oversized sunglasses.

"What's funny?" I demand.

Ben's arms lie across his chest as his upper body rocks gently back and forth, shaking with his laughter. His deep roar softens to a snicker as he pulls out a hand from under his arm and points his index finger at me.

"The look on your face...priceless."

He's still smiling as he walks over to where I am and sits down. This causes another battalion of frogs to leap into flight, which in turn, causes me to jerk my body stiffly backward, and Ben's laughter begins anew.

CHAPTER TWENTY-EIGHT

GEORGIA

AFTER OUR LIGHT PICNIC OF salami, cheese, some multi-grain crackers, sliced apple, and pear, Ben and I sit back and drink San Pellegrino from plastic cups in relative silence, taking in the views around us. The food was delicious, and I am perfectly satisfied.

I look out over the small stream in front of us — it's only about five feet across and looks as if it's about two feet deep. Tiny tadpoles and small frogs swim around the green globs of muck near the edges of the water, the tall grasses shading the fragile habitats. The light gurgle of the passing water is interrupted only by the occasional splash of a frog or bird that's exploring the area. No rocks or other hurdles stand in the way of the water's smooth path; it glides by unhurried in front of us. I raise my eyes to the meadow in the distance, and from there, look upward into the impossibly blue, cloudless sky.

I look over at Ben and smile.

"This place is absolutely beautiful. Thank you for bringing me here."

He takes a drink from his blue plastic cup and sets it down on the grass.

"It's my pleasure. It's a great place to spend a day off." He pauses and then points across the meadow in the distance. "Sometimes I'll see deer grazing over there. It's amazing to watch them...so unafraid and peaceful."

I consider this.

"How about bears?" I ask, cautiously.

He looks over at me and places his hand over mine, patting gently.

"No. I've never seen a bear here."

After a second he removes his hand and begins to pick up some of the small rocks scattered around us. He turns one over between his fingers and after a moment, tosses it into the stream. He looks over at me and then looks straight ahead. I can tell he is mulling something over.

"My ex-wife," he says, quietly. "She was having an affair with another teacher at school. It'd been going on for over a year, and I had no idea." His voice is almost too small to hear. "The unfaithfulness was hard enough to accept, but it was made worse by the fact that everyone seemed to know about it. Everyone but me, anyway." He picks up another rock, and this time he throws it hard across the meadow.

"I found them, *together*, in my campus office." He looks away towards the mountains, his thoughts clearly elsewhere, his voice drifting away. "I would have forgiven her, you know? I would have taken her back. But she told me she didn't love me anymore and wanted a divorce. She wasn't interested in salvaging anything. She was in love with him. She wanted to begin a new life. With him."

Ben is quiet for a long time.

Finally, he turns his head toward me — his sunglasses mirror my face before he pulls them off, dangling the stem from two fingers.

"When she said she didn't love me anymore...well, I'd rather have my arm cut off than feel that kind of pain again." He shakes his head and hangs his sunglasses at the *v* in his shirt.

I don't know what to say. How can I tell him I know how he feels without having it seem contrite? Sure, we have different circumstances, but we had both experienced significant loss. I recognize the anguish in his voice, and it takes me right back to a drawer full of pain that I try not to open very often.

He is close enough to me that I simply place my hand on his back and leave it there for a moment, both of us staring into the sunshine reflecting off the water, lost in our own memories.

My backpack begins to quietly ring.

Sylvia!

I twist around and reach for the bag, open up the pocket and fumble around for the phone. My fingers bump into my camera, and I make a mental note to take pictures here.

"Hello?" I say, pushing the phone close to my ear. I notice Ben pick up his cup and tip it backward into his mouth.

"Gia? Is that you? Damn, this is a bad connection," Sylvia mutters to herself.

"Hi, Sis! Yes, I'm here. Can you hear me?" I plug my left ear, trying to hear her better. She sounds a million miles away.

"Ok, yes, I can hear you."

Her voice sounds off. Flat. My internal alarms start going off. Something is wrong.

"I'm going to talk fast because I don't want to lose you, and I don't have a lot of time," she rattles. "Gia, I have terrible news. I can't come to get you today after all." She pauses and then lets out a huge sigh. When she speaks again her voice is trembling.

Oh no.

"It's Guthrie. He. He was hit by a car. Scott and I are on the way to the emergency clinic."

My hand flies to my open mouth.

"Georgia, he's in so much pain. It's horrible." Her voice breaks, and I can only hear her sobs.

"Oh my God, Sylvia, what happened?"

"He was in the yard chasing the ball...you know, we were just trying...we were letting him get his energy out...before we left for you." She is having a hard time getting the words out. She pauses, and I can hear her blowing her nose. "Oh, Georgia, if he doesn't make it. I can't...I just can't." I hear some static and muffled noises.

"Sylvia? Sylvia are you there?"

"Georgia? Hey, it's me. Sorry. She couldn't talk any longer. Your sister, well, you know how much she...well, you know what Guth means to us, to all of us," Scott says. "Listen, we are on the way to the emergency vet right now. I'm really sorry about leaving you stranded. You gonna be okay for another twenty-four hours, or should I send one of my law clerks to get you?"

I don't even consider. "No, no. I'll be fine. There's no need to send anyone. Please take care of Guthrie. And please keep me updated."

"I will. Bye, Georgia."

I hold the phone away from me, close the screen and look up toward the stream, marveling at how circumstances in life can change just so damn quickly.

"Is everything okay at home?"

"No. It's my sister's dog. They are taking him to the vets. He was just hit by a car. I don't know how serious it is, but my sister is really upset. That was my brother-in-law at the end there," I explain.

"Ah, man, I'm really sorry. Will they keep you posted?"

"Yeah, Scott said he would call when they know more." I look up at Ben. "They don't have any children — I mean they haven't so far, anyway — and this dog, this dog is like their baby. It will break my sister in half if they lose him." I have tears in my eyes, and I raise my sunglasses to wipe the corners of my eyes. "Jesus," I say, embarrassed. "All I seem to do is cry around you. What great company, huh?"

"Not a big deal at all. It tears me up too. I'm a big softie for animals. Let's hope the vet can fix him up."

I clear my throat, say a silent prayer for Guthrie, and put the phone away in the backpack. It's after lunchtime, and I'm beginning to feel tired from sitting in the sun for so long. Plus, I am back to square one, which makes me anxious. My Jeep is in Sisters. Sylvia can't come to get me today after all, which means I will be living out of a hotel room with exactly one thing to wear, and I still need to see the surgeon. Maybe I can reschedule it for tomorrow. As I think about these issues, Ben's voice interrupts my thoughts.

"So, Sylvia's not coming today then, right?"

I am wrapping up the leftover food and putting our garbage back into the pack.

"Uh, no," I say, busy with my hands. "Scott offered to have one of his law clerks come out, but I said no. I'm ok to spend another night here. In fact, I'm going to see if I can reset my appointment for sometime in the morning instead. I'm not sure I'm up for another doctor visit right now."

Ben is quiet for long enough that I stop picking things up and look over at him. He's sitting with his knees bent, his forearms draped across his kneecaps, and his fingers intertwined with one another. He seems to be staring out at the mountains, lost in thought.

I reach over and lay my hand on his shoulder, looking at him in question. He immediately turns toward me and gives me a weak smile.

"Sorry. Busy with my thoughts. Are you ready to leave then?" he asks, looking backward toward the trail.

"If you don't mind? I need to figure out my next step here. I need to buy something else to wear, and I need to call the surgeon... Anyway, yeah, I should probably get back if you don't mind giving me a ride to my hotel?"

"No problem. I need to get home anyway. Gotta get ready for work tomorrow." He scoops up his things and then stands, yawning and stretching his arms over his head. His shirt lifts slightly above his jeans, and I catch a flash of skin and dark hair along his lower abdomen. I let that image bounce around the inside of my brain for a moment before settling back down. I have a ton of things to figure out, I tell myself. And besides, I don't want to ruin my chance at friendship with Ben just because I am physically attracted to him.

He helps me stand and hands me my backpack. The hard edges of my camera bump against my leg, and I am reminded I want to take some photos here.

"Hang on just a minute? I just want to catch a few shots."

"Of course, take your time. There are numerous places up here to photograph." He sinks his hands into his pockets and begins to stroll away, giving me some space to shoot.

I remove the lens cap and bring the camera to my face. I snap several shots of the mountains at once and then grab a series of the crystal blue stream in front of me. I capture a few close-up shots of some of the jumping frogs and then find some perfect eye-level insect activity at the water's edge. I shoot everything near us, and then lower the camera, turning to put it away. I stop as I catch a glimpse of Ben in the distance. His back is to me — one leg is stretched slightly out and to the side, bent at the knee. I raise the camera again and focus the shot on him, the mountains a white blur in the background. The sun creates the perfect shadow casting around him, and the snowy peaks in the distance offset the green grass of the valley. I take a few more shots before contentedly lowering the camera, and putting it away.

"I think I'm all set," I call.

Ben walks back to where I'm standing, turns around and crouches down in front of me. I smile and laugh, and climb onto his back. As we stand up, he loses his balance again and stumbles backward, dropping my left foot. I nearly fall over trying to hop on one foot while he tries to steady me. We both land hard on our rears but we're laughing too hard to even care much about it. My sunglasses bump down my nose, and I push them up onto the top of my head.

I slap him on the shoulder, laughing, "See! I told you I was too heavy!"

Ben is belly laughing but trying to regain his composure. "Are you ok?" he asks, mid-laugh.

"Fine. Just a little embarrassed."

"Remind me not to feed you picnic food again."

"Very funny," I mock. "Seriously though, do you think you can carry me back?" I ask and then break out into soft giggles.

"Of course I can. It's no problem. Really," he says, chuckling. "You have to stop laughing. Here, this time, let's both stand and you give me your bad foot, and then just jump your other leg up, and I'll grab it, okay?"

Oh, that gorgeous grin again.

I looked at him skeptically. "Are you sure? That sounds like a plan that is destined for failure."

"It'll work. Just trust me."

He turns around and starts backing up toward me, arms at the ready by his side. I balance on my left leg and kick my right one up next to his side. He grabs my calf and holds it tightly against his body. I hop a little closer to him and put my hand between his neck and shoulder, squeezing hard to stabilize myself before I jump my left leg up. Ben winces and begins to laugh, lowering his shoulder and letting go of my leg.

"Jesus, lady! You're giving me the Vulcan nerve pinch!"

I gasp as he releases my foot.

"Ah ha! A fellow Trekkie! I knew there was a reason I'm so attracted to you," I say, a huge smile across my face. Ben freezes and then begins to slowly turn around. The weight of what I've just admitted hits me, and I stop smiling abruptly. I drop my head and nervously adjust my backpack on my shoulders, looking anywhere but at Ben. He's stopped laughing too, and from the corner of my eye, I see him take a step closer to me. I'm still staring at the ground, taking particular interest in the frogs near my feet when I feel Ben take my hand.

I look up at him, knowing I've just ruined everything.

"I'm sorry about that. What I meant was..."

All at once Ben's mouth is on mine. His hands hold my upper arms as his soft, full lips press against me, gently kissing my lower lip and then moving to my upper. His mouth is so warm, so strong. Is this really happening? And his scent...oh God, he smells so incredible. Before I can even fully register what is going on, he slowly releases my lips. I'm still in a daze, and it takes me a moment before I open my eyes to look at him. He lets me go and brings the back of his hand to his mouth, shyly looking at me from underneath his dark eyelashes. My heart suddenly realizes what's just happened, and begins to beat furiously in my chest.

"Georgia, I apologize. I didn't mean...it's just that...well, I've actually wanted to do that for —"

I don't even let him finish.

I reach for his neck and mouth at the same time, pulling him closer. I kiss him intently, taking in every sense of him. He responds immediately; his arms wrap around my waist, and he pulls me tight against his hips. My breasts press against his chest as he kisses me back, harder this time. I slide my hands up, across the top of his shoulders and into his hair. I can't get close enough to him. Ben opens his mouth against mine and softly slips the tip of his tongue inside. I inhale sharply as my heart practices acrobatics in my chest. He slowly traces a hand up and along the side of my torso, and a small noise escapes my mouth. I am beginning to feel weak. All too soon, he brings both hands to my face and runs his fingertips along my jawline, gently finishing the kiss.

I open my eyes — my head still tilted back — and look up at him. He smiles down at me and brings me into his chest, wrapping his arms around me. I close my eyes against him and circle my hands around his waist. We stand this way, silently connected, for a few moments. I never want this moment to end.

Ben clears his throat.

"So..."

"Yes, so..."

We both smile and softly laugh, unsure of where we stand with each other.

"I hope I didn't just overstep a boundary."

I look up at him and raise an eyebrow.

"What do you mean?" I ask.

"It's just that you said you've recently come out of a particularly hard situation, and I've been through a lot lately too. And I hope...I mean, I guess what I'm trying to say is, I didn't mean to just wreck our friendship." He slowly lets go of me and takes a cautious step backward.

"No. You didn't overstep at all," I say. "My past plays tricks on my mind sometimes, but I like to think I'm unaffected by it now – for the most part, anyway. I know he can't hurt me anymore. And besides," I grin at him, "I've been wanting you to kiss me for a time now," I admit. "Although, I was getting the feeling you just wanted to be friends. Did I misread you?" I ask.

"No, you didn't misread me, but obviously I misread myself," he says, tilting his head to the side. "And for that, I'm glad. All right," he says, his voice louder. "Let's get you back to the Scout, and I'll drive you to your hotel." He reaches for my hand and stoops to kiss the back of it, his eyebrows waggling up at me.

I'm already putty.

CHAPTER TWENTY-NINE

GEORGIA

ON THE WAY TO MY hotel, I call and reschedule my consultation, opting for the morning instead. I'm relieved to reset the meeting. I'm not sure I'm ready to hear I might need surgery.

It's still warm outside, and as we drive through town we pass several breweries and tap houses; their patios filled with lounging customers shaded by colorful market umbrellas, relaxing with pints of beer in the late afternoon while lazy dogs lie at their feet. A young couple raises their glasses to us as the Scout rumbles by, and Ben holds up a hand in reply. It feels like I'm watching a scene from a favorite movie, and as I take it all in, I can't help but smile with happiness. It feels very *right* to be here. To be here with Ben.

The hotel parking lot is almost full when we pull in. Commuter cars and sedans take up most of the spaces, with a few SUVs mixed in. Ben drops me off at the entrance, and I wait while he peruses the lot for an available spot. I'm watching him drive slowly up and down the lot when a loud noise on my right catches my attention. A black Ford pickup is driving by, very slowly. Its engine is loud and commanding, and the truck is raised up so high in the air, it virtually towers over all the other vehicles. I can't help but think it looks completely out of place in this business loop of town.

I begin to glance back to the Scout, but a loud noise and screeching tires make me turn quickly toward the direction of the pickup. It's turning left now onto the main road, the engine is thundering, and a cloud of blue-grey smoke is rolling out from the tires as the driver peels out across the pavement.

I shake my head and turn back toward the parking lot to see Ben walking up. He's wearing his sunglasses, spinning his keys absentmindedly in his hand, and smiling at me for all he's worth. A thrill of excitement slips down my spine.

"I'll help you up to your room," he says.

I don't argue.

We step into the elevator, and I lower my gaze to the floor as I hear the door close, reaching forward to push the button marked 3. The elevator begins its ascent, and I glance over at Ben. He's turned his body to face mine, and he's looking directly at me. I catch my breath and feel a sharp quickening of my pulse as I stare back at him. I feel a little lightheaded. He steps closer, takes my hand in his and begins to trace slow circles on my palm with his index finger. I am slowly melting. The thought occurs to me that we are going to my room...where there's a bed.

Suddenly I'm having trouble breathing evenly.

Ben takes another step closer, leans his head in toward mine and places his free hand just below my collarbone. He slides his fingertips along the side of my neck, and I can't help but close my eyes as his mouth runs the length of my jaw. He reaches my chin and my lips part slightly, my head tilting upward in anticipation of the kiss I am now practically begging for.

The elevator lurches to a halt, and my eyes spring open as the loud *ding* echoes inside the small space. We drop hands as I let out a deep breath and sink back down into the crutches at my armpits. Ben grins at me and chuckles as he turns to face the opening doors.

"Very funny," I say, dryly. "You did that on purpose, didn't you?"

I pull the side of my lip into my mouth and bite down as I follow Ben out of the elevator. As we enter the hallway, I turn and pause, handing him my backpack.

"Would you mind opening the front pocket and digging out the room key, please?" I'm reading the room numbers as we go by, wondering what will happen when we reach mine.

We come to my door, and I stop and look over to Ben. He raises his eyebrows and holds up the key card in front of his chest; a shy, sexy grin breaking out across his face. *Dear Lord, have mercy.* If I've ever needed willpower, this is the moment.

I take a deep breath, whisk the card out of his fingertips and turn to the door. The keypad light turns green, and I remove the card, pushing the door handle down and shoving my shoulder against it. Ben's hand comes up behind me, and he finishes opening the door.

It's dark inside, the blackout curtains are still drawn, and my eyes have difficulty adjusting. I run my hand alongside the wall for the light switch. I can feel Ben behind me.

"Where is that..."

My words fall away as I switch the light on. The room is in complete disarray. My bed sheets are ripped apart, and the blankets and pillows are flung across the room. One of the drawers in the side table is missing from the stand, and the other one hangs precariously from its housing. The chairs and small table near the window are turned upside down, lying partly against the wall.

"Don't go any farther, Georgia. We need to report this right away." Ben's voice is deep and commanding.

But I only vaguely seem to register his words as I cautiously enter the dark bathroom immediately to my right — my hand reaching for the switch on the inside wall.

"Georgia! Please. Don't go any farther," he insists. I flip the bathroom light on and turn my head back toward his voice at the same time.

He sees the mirror before I do.

Four Bend police officers arrive shortly after 5:00 p.m. Two officers talk with the front desk clerk and the hotel owner at a low table near the exit to the courtyard, while Ben and I sit with the other two officers on upholstered chairs that smell old and of mildew. We discuss everything leading up to the time I checked into the hotel — my hike, the bear encounter, my ankle injury, my Jeep being vandalized, the ER visit, and where we'd been for the last two and a half hours. The two officers take turns asking me questions, although the younger one, Officer Roth, seems to be the only one writing anything down.

"So, Ms. Marks, you don't have any friends or acquaintances here in Central Oregon?" Officer Roth asks, still looking down at his notepad.

"No," I shake my head. "None at all. I've only been here once or twice before this weekend, but that was a long time ago."

"All right." He jots a few notes on his pad. "What about enemies? You make anyone real angry lately?"

I shrug. "Um, no, not that I can think of. I barely interact with people. I work in an antiques shop in a tiny little tourist town. I really don't even know that many people."

"What about past lovers or boyfriends?" the older cop interjects, thrusting his chin at me and shifting his eyes toward Ben.

"What?" I say, not understanding him.

"You know, guys you've dated, or guys you've just...whatever." He gives me a knowing look.

"What about them?" I answer, defensively. He doesn't need to know I've barely dated since leaving Mike.

"Well, what I mean is, if there are a lot of them out there, and things between you didn't end well —" Another glance at Ben "— then those might be people we would want to talk to." He pauses and then adds, "Ma'am."

"Listen, Lieutenant..." I narrow my eyes at his badge, "...*Dick*erson. There hasn't been any kind of parade of men in my life if that's what you're asking. I was married for seven years to a police sergeant, who, by the way, turned out to be an egocentric, abusive, alcoholic ass." I let that sink in. "I divorced him about a year ago and after that, well, I dated a few men here and there but nothing serious and certainly no one that lived over here. The only people that even know I'm here are my sister and her husband. I don't really use social media and rarely post anything other than my lousy attempt at natural photography." I shoot him a pointed look. "I hate to disappoint you, but I'm a pretty boring girl." I close my jaw hard and can feel my TMJ muscles flexing. What a jerk.

Lieutenant Dickerson rubs his chin and stares at me a moment longer than he needs to.

"Ma'am, we're just trying to help determine who might have a reason to write the word *Bitch*," he pauses, no doubt for emphasis, "on your mirror. It's also unsettling that your Jeep was vandalized while you were..." he glances at Ben, "*hiking*." His innuendo isn't lost on me, and I'm instantly pissed. "If you would like us to do our best job here, we need to have as much information as possible, no matter how embarrassing that might be for you." He purses his lips together and raises his eyebrows slightly.

I am livid.

"If I have anything to be embarrassed about, it will be for the way I'm about to react to you right now!" I yell.

"Ok. All right. Hang on for just one second now." Ben puts his hand on my arm and holds his opposite palm at Lieutenant Dickerson. "She's answered your questions. She says she doesn't have any idea who it could be. No one but her sister and brother-in-law even knows she's here. I don't see any reason to continue unless there are new questions or other ways you can help."

Lieutenant Dickerson looks at Officer Roth, and a silent conversation ensues between them for a moment. Officer Roth flips his notebook closed and pulls out another one, this one bound in thick black vinyl. He begins quickly writing down information on a form inside the book. He reaches the bottom of the page, checks his watch and then signs the document. He slips his pen back into his shirt pocket and tears off the last page.

"Here is your copy of the police report, Ms. Marks. This here is the report number." He points his index finger to a large, eight-digit number at the top of the document. "And you can use this number to look up the status of your report at any time. Just go to the website you see on the back of my card." I turn his business card over in my hand. "I think we are done here and can get out of your hair. If you discover that something indeed was stolen, please let us know right away. And of course, if anything else unusual should occur, you can call our offices at any time. Otherwise, we can reach you at the cell phone number you provided?"

I nod.

We all rise at the same time, and I shake Officer Roth's hand. Lieutenant Dickerson doesn't acknowledge me at all, reaching instead for Ben's hand, mentioning how nice it was to meet him and thanking him for his work in the Forest Service. I want to vomit. Instead, I turn my back on Dickerson, crutch over to the front desk and sign my checkout paperwork. There is no way I'm staying here tonight.

The clerk apologizes profusely and assures me again he didn't see anything or anyone unusual. He credits my card for the charges and gives me a special fifty-percent off coupon to use on my next visit. I shove my wallet into my backpack and mumble my thanks, still ticked off.

"Ms. Marks," Officer Roth approaches the front desk. "You mentioned you have an appointment with the surgeon tomorrow?"

"Yeah."

"And when do you plan to leave town?"

I sigh. "I don't know yet. My sister was supposed to be here today but...well, her dog was hit by a car. So, I don't really know. I'm kinda waiting for her to call me back."

"I'm sorry to hear about her dog," he says. "And I'm sorry to request this, but we really need you to call us when you do leave town. Just the number on the business card. Ok?"

I look at him. Is he serious? I can tell he's not trying to be a jerk — he's just doing his job. I relax a bit and realize I am just upset by what's happened and also by Lieutenant Every-Woman-Is-A-Slut Dickerson's attitude.

"Yeah, that's no problem, Officer," I say. "And thank you for your help here. I really appreciate it. Please let me know if you discover anything."

He tips his hat at me. "Will do. Take care now."

I watch as Officer Roth and Lieutenant Dickerson regroup with the other two police officers in the center of the lobby. They have a small conversation and then leave the hotel, one of the officers speaking into the radio on his shoulder as they walk outside.

"I'm glad they're gone," I say to Ben, not looking at him, my eyes still trained on the officers as they cross the parking lot.

"Oh? Why's that?"

I shake my head silently in answer. I hated to say it, even think it, but I really didn't trust cops. Not since one had repeatedly tried to beat me to death.

Ben stands by my side as we watch the police cars leave the parking lot. When they're gone, he takes my hand, stands in front of me and clears his throat.

"So, this is going to sound very forward, but under the circumstances —" He grins shyly at me. "—Would you like to stay at my house tonight?"

I raise an eyebrow at him.

"I have a guest room, and I'm happy to let you borrow it. I'd just feel better about you staying someplace safe."

"I would too," I admit.

"Good. Then it's settled."

CHAPTER THIRTY

GEORGIA

WE MAKE A QUICK STOP at Market of Choice on the way out of Bend. I stay in the Scout while Ben runs in to pick up a few groceries for dinner. While he's gone, I try calling Sylvia's cell phone, but there's no answer. I leave a message telling her again how sorry I am about Guthrie and asking her to call me as soon as they hear anything. After I end the call, I send her a similar text message. The solar charger gave the cell phone a good boost at breakfast, but now the battery is dying again. I'll need to plug it in at Ben's house. *Ben's house.* I contemplate what kind of home he has, and the fact that I'll be in it. He mentioned he has a guest room; is his house large? What kind of personal taste does he have? I can already guess he's not a messy kind of guy, the small cabin is evidence of that, but still, all kinds of questions run through my head as I wait for him to come out of the store.

While I'm sitting in the Scout, I realize this is the second time today he's bought groceries in order for us to eat. I pull my wallet out of my backpack and fold up two twenty-dollar bills, look around the cab of the truck and, for lack of a better hiding place, I slide open the ashtray and slip the bills in on top of the single key that's lying there. Maybe he will find them one day. Then again, since he doesn't seem to smoke, he might never find them and never know I was trying to help. And who knows what the key is for. I quickly open the ashtray again, pull out the bills and put them back in my pack. I'll find another place to put them at his house. I have a feeling he isn't going to accept any money, and especially if I just hand it straight to him. I roll my eyes at my own indecisiveness.

About twenty minutes later, I see Ben emerge, carrying three, large brown bags. Suddenly I am starving. I watch him walk across the parking lot toward me, watch the way he carries himself, and the way he looks in those damn aviators at the end of a summer day. He sees me looking at him, and a million dollar ear-to-ear smile opens across his gorgeous face.

The drive back to Sisters is stunning as we chase the sun that's beginning to set behind the mountain range. The snowy peaks reflect the residual warm glow, turning the evening sky to a breathtaking combination of deep purple and dusty rose. The few clouds that are in the sky turn shades of gray and blue. The wind whips my hair around, and I begin to feel cold. The night air soaking up the dampness from the ground.

Ben glances over at me and reaches behind his seat on the floor. I follow his movement, seeing that he is bringing up a blanket and lean over to help him. He hands over a soft red and black Aztec print wool blanket. I twirl it behind me and over my shoulders, bringing it closed in front of me with my crossed arms. It's immediately warm, and I put my face into the fibers at my neck and take a deep breath. It smells like Ben: pine trees and warm earth.

"Little warmer now?" Ben hollers over the road noise and wind.

I nod, mouthing *thanks* across the way at him. I am in heaven — riding in an open top Scout next to probably the nicest, most caring, and sexiest man I've ever met — wrapped up in a fantastically warm blanket, and watching the sun set behind the Three Sisters mountains. I shake my head and close my eyes. *Is this even real?*

We pull into Sisters and slow to the 25 mph speed limit, passing the elementary school on the right. The chain link fence is decorated with colorful fish and art pieces clearly created by the children; it's a welcoming sight, and once again I'm struck by the charm of this small town.

Ben's headlights light up the road in front of us, while the sidewalk lamps and restaurants illuminate the rest of the tiny downtown. Even though it's near the end of May, every storefront has white twinkle lights in the windows, giving the entire main street a happy, spirited feel.

Ben makes a left turn in town and drives south down the pine-tree lined road. We continue for another ten miles or so, climbing significantly in elevation before turning onto a narrow, gated gravel path. Ben puts the Scout into park and reaches forward toward the ashtray. He slides it open and retrieves the key inside. My mouth drops open a little in disappointment and surprise. I cluck my tongue and chide myself for not trusting my instincts as Ben hops out of the Scout and unlocks the gate.

As we continue up the driveway, the headlights flash against the wooden fencing on either side of the narrow road. We slowly head uphill, and I realize after a moment that the wind has died down. I release the blanket clutched in front of me and let it rest gently on my shoulder, open in the front. Ben reaches over and takes my hand in his own.

"This is the beginning of my property here," he says, raising his first two fingers off the steering wheel and pointing. "I lease the pasture on the right to my friend Dustin and his family. They have horses but don't have enough space where they're at right now. The pasture on the left has my cattle on it. We might see some as we drive up to the house."

"How much space do you have here?"

It's hard to really get an idea of what I'm looking at. It's fully dark now, and the pasture on both sides is heavy with pine and juniper trees.

"Little under fifteen acres."

"Wow, really? How do you find time to take care of it all? Especially when you spend so much time on the butte."

"I live here all winter. But once I start back up at the tower, I have a guy — Matt, and he comes by every day during the week. He looks after the cattle, takes care of the pastures, checks around the house for any problems and takes care of my mail. He's been helping me ever since I finished building the place. Actually, he *helped* me finish the place. I guess it's been about seven years now. Ever since I stopped teaching..." His voice trails off, and I sense he doesn't want to talk much more about his teaching job.

"You built your house?" I say. "Wow. I'm impressed."

Ben shrugs. "Yeah. It wasn't that hard."

"I think a lot of people might disagree with you," I say, and smile at him.

We wind our way uphill alongside trees and pasture for what seems like half a mile. Finally, the drive opens up, the fencing splitting off at right angles in opposite directions. Up ahead I see a building to the left with a large, solitary light glowing near the roof.

"Is that your barn?" I ask, pointing through the windshield.

Ben nods. "I've got your Jeep in there for now. We can take a look tomorrow if you want."

"Sure. Sounds good."

A moment later he turns the Scout to the right.

"Up ahead, over there, is the house." He picks up our shared hands and points toward a few soft lights coming through the trees.

The Scout crunches along the gravel and pulls up to the house. Although it's dark, I can see from the reflection of his headlights that the exterior of the two-story house consists of wide planked, dark wood, with small, multi-paned windows decorating the outside, and a deep, shadowed porch wraps around the house. Ben pulls up in front of the attached garage, puts the Scout into park and hops out. He grabs the iron handle at the bottom of the garage door and hoists it up over his head, the Scout's headlights exposing his lower back and the top of his underwear. I tug on my lower lip with my teeth as I watch his hips rock forward to push the door the last little bit.

He turns around, dusts his hands off and climbs back into the truck.

"I've been meaning to get an automatic door opener installed for years. I just don't seem to ever get around to doing it," he says with a shrug as we drive into the garage.

"I don't really want to let go of this blanket," I say as Ben comes around to my side of the Scout.

"I know what you mean; it's one of my favorites. They're a good company too; for every blanket you buy, they donate one to a local homeless shelter."

"Wow, really?"

Ben helps take it off my shoulders and tosses it behind the seat.

"If it makes you feel any better, there are two more in the

house." He cracks a warm smile at me. "C'mon inside. I'd like you to meet Charlie."

Charlie?

I slowly cross the gravel driveway on my crutches while Ben walks beside me, my backpack on his shoulders and the grocery bags in his hands. We reach the front porch, and he sets the bags down to grab his keys from his pocket. The front door is the most beautiful door I've ever seen. It's enormous; at least twice the height of a standard door, and double the width as well. The front holds six framed panes of glass, through which I can see into the entryway — a dim light shining from somewhere inside. The bottom fourth of the door is solid wood with molding framing the wide rectangular shape. It reminds me of something I once saw in an antiques magazine at work.

Ben leans in to unlock the door and pushes it open as he motions for me to enter first. I take a few steps inside, hopping onto a slate floor entryway. Turning around, I see Ben come through the doorway behind me; keys in his mouth and groceries in his hands. He smiles around the keys and kicks the door shut behind him. At the sound of the heavy door closing, the deep bark of a dog echoes from inside the house, and I look at Ben with wide eyes.

"You have a *dog*?"

He laughs. "Mmmhmm, hend hure ee lums." He takes a step forward to a small table alongside the wall and drops the keys from his mouth just as a large brown and white dog comes running around the corner, barking madly, ears flopping.

"Charlie! Ah good boy, come here, buddy."

Ben sets the bags down and drops to his knees as the dog jumps into his lap and begins licking his face and turning sideways around and around again in Ben's lap. The dog notices me near the door, and his barking becomes significantly louder and quicker.

"Charlie, shhh. Charlie! Ok, stop. This is Georgia. She's nice, you'll love her," Ben says, walking over to me. Charlie is sniffing every inch of my legs and pants, circling around me again and again. I hold my hand down to his nose and let him smell me. His barking stops as he sniffs my hand wildly and then exhales a big breath of air through his nose, ending the whole production with a sloppy lick of my hand.

"A boxer?" I ask. Charlie is letting me pet him, his tail polishing the wood floor.

"He's a Boxer-Lab mix. I rescued him as a puppy from the shelter about five years ago." Ben smiles at Charlie as he speaks to me.

"Awe, what a good boy, Charlie." My voice rises higher, and he paces back and forth against my leg, letting me pet each side of him.

"Yep, he's my buddy. Hey, let's get you into a chair, and I can start unloading these groceries and get something for us to eat." He motions for me to follow him into the house. Charlie immediately leads the way for both of us, pausing and turning around to make sure we are following. My armpits are killing me from the crutches, and I am desperate to put my leg up.

The room ahead is dimly lit. I see an armchair and a reflection of a lamp in a window, but the rest of the house is dark. Ben walks ahead of me, disappearing around a corner for a moment, and suddenly the room is illuminated.

"There," he calls.

It's a gorgeous sight. Before me lies an enormous living room with huge paned windows that line the outer wall. I crutch into the center and look up at the vaulted ceiling above me; open beams stretch across the room from the kitchen all the way to the massive river rock fireplace on the left-hand side of the room. I feel my mouth drop open.

"You built this?" I whisper, still gawking.

"Yeah, but trust me, I had a lot of help."

The fireplace hearth stretches at least six feet across, and the solid wood mantle sticks out from the rock about a foot. An oversize, oil pastel scene of the mountains leans against the fireplace. The entire structure is composed of rounded, light and dark gray, smooth rock, and stretches vertically, all the way to the roofline. On the right-hand side of the hearth is a built-in firewood holder, filled with split logs and kindling piled on top.

I turn to take in the rest of the room. A deep brown, nail-studded leather sofa sits facing the fireplace with an end table on either side. Two leather armchairs, each with its own ottoman, balance out the room. Draped over one end of the couch is a blanket similar to the one in the Scout, only this one is a deep blue-grey print with light grey fringe hanging off the bottom. I head in that direction.

"Offer you something to drink?" Ben calls from the kitchen. Charlie trots into the room and follows me to the sofa.

I look over at Ben as I cross the room, careful not to catch my crutch in the fringe of the oversize rug.

"I would love a glass of water, please," I answer.

"See, told you I had another one," he says from the kitchen, pointing to the blanket.

I lie my crutches down on the rug as I sink into the couch, my head leaning back into the cushion, the soft blanket ensconcing me. Charlie hops up at the other end of the couch and lets out a sigh as he settles his head onto his paws. This behavior is so Guthrie, and I am immediately reminded I need to call Sylvia again.

"Here you go." Ben stands in front of me holding the glass. "I'll get that fire going too. I think it's going to be pretty chilly tonight."

I take a drink and shiver — I'm already cold.

"Yeah, I just can't seem to get warm. Must have been all that riding around with the top off."

"Do you want to take a shower?" he asks. Almost immediately he adds, "I mean, to warm up. I mean you can use my shower...er, alone." He drops his head and starts to laugh at himself, and I can't help but giggle.

"No, it's okay, I knew what you meant. That might actually help. I *am* really cold all of the sudden."

"Okay, sure, no problem. My room is just at the end of that hallway." He points across the room and around the right side. "And there's a bathroom just inside." He stands up straight again. "Let me make sure the lights are turned on, and you have clean towels." He comes over to me on the couch and helps me stand up. "Here, I can just...well, here's one crutch...I can just help you the rest of the way if you prefer?"

"That'd be great. My armpits are killing me."

I hop, and crutch, down the shadow-filled hallway, my arm wrapped around Ben's neck and shoulder. He flips on light switches as we come to them, and at the end of the hallway, we turn through double doors, into a dark room. He guides me into the room and to the left before stopping and fumbling around for a switch. The room suddenly fills with soft light from a bedside lamp.

His bed is a log-framed, king size bed with another one of my new favorite blankets laying across the top as a coverlet. This one is a simple southwestern design with a dull white fringe that dangles off the end of the bed. A smaller version of the living room fireplace stands across from the end of the bed.

"The bathroom is just through that door." He points across the room to an open door on the other side of the hearth. "There should be clean towels on the shower..." He crosses the room and switches on the light, poking his head around the corner of the door. "Yep. I think you'll be all set." He furrows his brow. "Uh, are you going to be okay, um, by yourself?" He holds up a palm. "Please don't take that the wrong way. It's just with your brace, and ankle and everything, the last thing I want is for you to hurt yourself further before you even get to the surgeon." His hands are on his hips now.

"I think I'll be fine. I just need to go slowly. Is it a step-in shower or a tub?" I ask as I pass by him and enter the bathroom, hopping with one crutch. I stop and stare in amazement. "Oh, my. Yeah, I think this will be ok," I joke, staring at the walk-in, polished black pebble shower, and massive, stainless steel showerhead placed directly over the center. There's even a teak bench built into the stone wall. It is the most beautiful shower I have ever seen. Charlie wanders in and stands next to me, tongue hanging out. It seems he is also admiring the scene.

"Ok, well...then I'll just be in the kitchen." He turns his attention to Charlie. "C'mon out boy." Charlie takes a step toward Ben but then stops and swings his head back toward me. "Charlie, come on," Ben persists. Charlie looks up at me – tongue and tail wagging.

"Go on," I say, smiling and raising my arm toward Ben. "Go on. Good boy."

Charlie saunters out reluctantly, and Ben shrugs at me.

"I'll leave one of these bedroom doors open. Just holler if you need anything."

As he backs out of the room, he stumbles over the edge of the rug. He catches himself dramatically, turns around and walks calmly out the door without another word.

I smirk and cover my mouth to stifle my laughter.

CHAPTER THIRTY-ONE

GEORGIA

CLOSING THE BATHROOM DOOR, I make my way to the inviting shower. I have to step fully inside to even reach the stainless steel faucet, and I turn it all the way to *Hot*. A downpour of water erupts from the showerhead, and I back out of the enclosure, letting it heat up.

Getting undressed and removing my brace takes some effort, and by the time I'm ready to get in, the steam is beginning to float out in cloudy puffs. I ease myself into the water and breathe a huge sigh of relief. The uneven, smooth rock floor of the shower massages my feet as I stand, my body slowly warming up in the water and steam. After several minutes I sit down and relax on the bench. The water cascades over my thighs and all the tension stored in my shoulders begins to mercifully release. I drop my head back against the wall and breathe deeply.

It's hard not to think about what's happened today, and the implications of the message on the mirror. I'm starting to feel like someone is trying to keep me here, or is trying to scare, or even actually harm me. These ideas seem so ludicrous though. Who would have any reason to hurt me? Who would even know me, and even more so, who would know that I'm here? Suddenly an image of my ex-husband's face comes to mind. *Mike?* Could he be the one behind the vandalism and the hotel room, break in? I know he's certainly capable of doing these things, there's no doubt about that, but we parted ways so long ago. I haven't seen or heard from him in several months, and last I heard he was still working in San Diego with the possibility of a baby on the way. The longer I consider him as the perpetrator, the more unrealistic it seems. I rub a knot at the top of my shoulder. No, it can't be Mike. The two incidents are probably purely coincidental, more likely the result of my bad luck than any purposeful action. Nevertheless, I decide to contact Lieutenant Dickerson in the morning and see if he can check on Mike's whereabouts this weekend.

Having put that issue aside – for the time being anyway – I'm able to relax even further, and I close my eyes under the spray of the water. The feeling of the water against my thighs begins to stir memories of kissing Ben earlier in the day. It's hard to believe it even happened. I touch my fingers to my lips and lightly press, smiling as I remember the feel of his mouth commanding my own. Had I ever been kissed like that before? And his beard...it was just rough enough to leave my face a little raw. I let my mind consider how that roughness would feel on other parts of my body. I imagine us kissing in the shower, *this* shower, both of us standing under the cascade of water, my head leaning back, chin raised to the water as he presses the small of my back with one hand and pulls my body into his own. His mouth travels down my chest and then over each of my breasts, gently sucking and pulling on my nipples until they stand erect in his mouth. With his other hand, he slowly moves *lower*.

I spread my legs apart. My hands run up and down the inside of my thighs as I think about him, my head still leaning back against the shower wall. My mouth opens as my breathing steadily increases – my hands continuing what my mind imagines. I envision Ben's body against mine in the shower, his hips pressing against me as he reaches for my leg and hitches it high on his hip. He plants his mouth hard against my lips, his tongue revealing his desire for me. He pushes himself against the inside of my thigh, allowing me to feel his immense erection. A moment later he pulls away from my mouth, searching my eyes for permission. I reach down between the both of us and take hold of him, leaving no doubt as to what I want. He closes his eyes, a small smile appearing on his lips as the water slides over his shoulders and back. In one fluid movement, he bends his knees, rocks his hips forward and thrusts into me.

I am so submerged in this imaginary scene I lose control of myself almost immediately, gasping in the water and steam as I slowly regain my bearings.

It's definitely going to be difficult to sit across from him at dinner tonight.

CHAPTER THIRTY-TWO

GEORGIA

FINISHING MY SHOWER, I TURN the faucet off and exit the bathroom wearing Ben's plush white bathrobe, and an oversize oatmeal towel twisted around my head. I glance at myself in the mirror. My cheeks are a deep red, and my pupils are dilated — all easily explainable from my shower. Not a bad look really, until I focus on the crutches under my armpits. Still, I grin at myself in the mirror, shyly embarrassed at the thoughts that crossed my mind in the shower. I cinch my bathrobe tighter around my waist and hobble into Ben's bedroom to find my backpack. I look around the floor but don't see it anywhere. Didn't I leave it in here?

The sound of canine nails on the wood floor outside the bedroom echoes down the hall, and I tilt my head toward the open door. A moment later Charlie comes bounding around the corner, my shoe in his mouth.

"Charlie! Char—lee! Get back here!" Ben's voice carries down the hall, and into the bedroom as he jogs through and crouches down, patting his thighs to get Charlie's attention. A white dishtowel is slung over his shoulder.

"Char..." He stops mid-sentence as his gaze slowly rises up the length of my robe. When his eyes meet mine, his mouth opens slightly, and he carefully stands to his full height.

"Oh. Sorry to barge in," he stammers. "Charlie had your shoe and I..." His voice trails off as he stands in the doorway, staring at me in his bathrobe. I feel my face turn even redder as my hand goes to the belt at my waist. I try to act nonchalant.

"Thank you, Charlie," I say, smiling and directing my eyes at Charlie — his tail wagging non-stop.

Charlie drops my shoe on the carpet and jumps up on the bed, looking back and forth between Ben and me. I step forward and sit down on the bed next to him, petting his head and rubbing the inside of his ear. He responds by rolling onto his back and showing me his belly, which makes me laugh out loud.

"Charlie, come on, get out of there. Give the poor girl some space."

"No, it's fine," I laugh. "He's so cute, how could I send him away?"

I can feel cooler air on my skin, and I turn away from Charlie, only to realize my robe has shifted and the majority of my leg is now exposed. I pull it closed and hesitantly glance up at Ben. He's staring at me intently. All trace of a smile has vanished from his face.

"What is it?"

I follow his eyes and look myself over to make sure I'm not embarrassing myself in some other obvious way. I don't see anything blatant, and I look back at him, my eyebrows knitted together.

"Oh, sorry," I say, understanding. "I borrowed your robe because I couldn't think about wearing those same clothes one more minute. As a matter of fact, if I could use your washing machine tonight that would be terrific."

"What? Oh, yeah. That's no problem," he says. "I can show

you where everything is after dinner. Which, by the way, is ready." He puts his hand to his chin and then points across the room. "If you don't mind, I'm just gonna grab something from there," he says, crossing the room and entering the walk-in closet. A moment later he comes out with clothing in his hands. "Here are some pajama pants and an old t-shirt you can wear if you want. They might be more comfortable than that," he says, nodding toward my robe. "Although if you want to wear that, that's absolutely fine with me too. Or not. Whatever you want. To wear, I mean." He coughs nervously. Is his faced flushed?

"Okay, thank you," I say, as he walks toward the door to leave. "Oh! Is my backpack out there? I need my comb."

A moment later he returns with my bag. He sets it down on the bed next to me and then turns for the door. The commotion causes Charlie to stand up and jump off the bed, exiting in a huff.

"Thank you," I call after him.

Ben hesitates in the doorway and then turns around.

"What's the matter?" I ask.

A shy grin is plastered on his face. He looks at the ceiling and shakes his head slightly. He won't meet my eyes.

"What's wrong?" I press.

He slowly lowers his eyes to mine and takes a deep breath.

"I'm gonna take a huge risk here when I say this...but here goes. Right now, looking at you, you're the most beautiful, most sexually appealing woman I've ever seen, and it's taking all my willpower not to pull you into my arms and open that robe right now." He crosses one arm in front of his chest, locking his hand into his armpit: a self-imposed physical restraint. "I've done nothing but think about how good it felt to kiss you today, and how much I want to do it again."

I swallow hard.

He takes another deep breath and glances down at the ground before looking up at me again from under his eyelashes.

"I need you to know something though: I don't want to trample any boundaries you might have, Georgia. I know what you've gone through this weekend, and I know a little about the hell you went through before, with Mike. I don't want to lose control of myself with you, and possibly ruin whatever it is we have now, because... well, because I'm beginning to really care about you and what happens to you. I don't think I could live with myself if I were to unknowingly exploit the small amount of trust you've placed in me." His voice deepens, and he runs his hand down the back of his neck. "No matter how goddamn gorgeous you look right now."

He clears his throat and turns to the door, "So, dinner..."

"Ben, wait," I say, urgently.

But then I don't know what to say. I'm caught in an emotional tension, somewhere between the beginnings of love — this can't be love already, can it? For this man I hardly know, and the raw desire to have his hands all over my body. I move myself closer to the edge of the bed and reach out for his free hand. He places his hand in mine, and I trace small circles across his knuckles with my thumb. I raise his fingers to my mouth and lazily plant soft kisses where I have drawn circles. Pulling my mouth away, I look up at him.

"I don't have any boundaries with you," I whisper.

I stare at him for a moment before continuing. "I know I've only known you for a few days, but in that short time, you've already shown me more kindness and consideration than in all my married years. I don't know...it's probably foolish of me to feel this way, but even through everything that's happened to me this weekend, somehow I just know, without a doubt, that I can trust you." I squeeze his hand and continue, "Look, things in my life might be in total chaos right now, and I might feel utterly lost, but when I'm with you...I don't know — everything just feels right. I may be lost, but at least I know I'm lost in the right direction."

I kiss his hand again softly and lay my cheek across the back of his hand. "Ben, right now you're all I need." I look up at his face. "You're all I want."

A tender smile forms on his lips as he stands over me. I take his hand and pull him closer in front of me, slowly guiding his hand to the side of my neck, his skin on my skin. I hold it there, my hand over his, as I turn and begin to kiss the inside of his palm, my eyes closing. My movements cause my robe to open again, just above my knees, and I can feel the air on my exposed skin. I turn my face to look up at him; his dark eyes are hooded, his breathing quickening. I take my hand away from his and stretch toward him to stroke the side of his beautiful face, continuing down the side of his throat and bringing my fingertips to rest at the base of his neck. He leans down toward me, my legs shift to allow him closer, and I feel the robe open almost completely. His eyes flicker down to my naked thighs, and a growl escapes from deep within his throat.

"You're not playing fair," he chastises, wagging his finger back and forth in front of me.

"But..."

His lips are on mine immediately. He kisses me with intensity; his mouth pressing down hard on mine, and the towel around my head unwinds and falls away. His hands are in my hair, and he's owning every inch he touches. He thrusts his tongue deep into my mouth, and I inhale sharply, willingly accepting him. My senses are filled with his masculine scent and the taste of his mouth as I pull him closer and closer.

His hips slowly nestle between my legs, pushing the remaining robe out of the way. I can feel his desire through the roughness of his jeans, and I can't help but push myself against his erection. I pull his hand from my hair and slowly guide it down my chest and underneath the fold of the bathrobe, across my bare skin. I place his hand on my warm breast, my nipple erect.

"Oh fuck," he moans into my mouth.

He cups my breast and rubs his thumb over my nipple, back and forth, so slowly and firmly I think I might scream out in pleasure. My breathing is so ragged that I have to pull away from his kiss and lean my head back for air. He uses this to his advantage and drops his mouth to my clavicle and begins kissing the small bones there, never releasing my nipple and breast from his hand. With his mouth, he moves the remainder of the robe away from my chest and brings his face above mine, hesitating for a moment. I reach for his face, running my fingertips over his jaw and beard and pull him intently downward. His mouth finds my breast and the heat from his tongue sears against my skin. The feeling is almost too much to bear, and I raise my hips in earnest reply. Ben pulls up from me, moves his hands underneath my rear and scoots me effortlessly backward across his bed, the robe flopping closed over my body again.

He stands up, crosses his arms in front of his waist, and slowly pulls his shirt up and over his defined chest. Shadows from the dim table lamp play across his smooth olive skin as he drops the clothing at his feet. A thin covering of dark hair outlines his tight abdominals, narrowing down to his belt line and below. I feel a small smile at the corner of my mouth, and I find I can't take my eyes off this unbelievable man slowly undressing in front of me.

His hands find the leather belt at his waist, and my eyes hungrily follow. He unhooks the notches and begins to pull the thick strap from his jeans, his eyes never moving from my face. He drops the belt to the floor and places his thumb and forefinger at the top button of his jeans. I bite the inside of my lower lip as he unbuttons his fly, and I catch a glimpse of his erection tenting out through his boxer briefs. He slides his jeans off his thighs and crawls across the bed to me, every muscle flexing as he moves.

"You are incredible," I whisper to him as he reaches my mouth once again. He kisses me softly, tenderly at first, teasing my lips with his beard, my hands running through his hair and down the back of his neck. He is a wall of warmth against my skin, and I just want more.

"Don't stop," I say, breathlessly. *Please do not stop.*

"So beautiful," he says, surveying my body beneath him, running his hand over the top of my robe from my chest to my hips. "I want you. I want all of you." He's staring at me, searching my eyes for any sign of hesitation.

"Please, Ben, right now," I beg.

He can't hold back any longer. In a rush, his hands are on me, reaching for the robe and tearing it open across my body. My arms are pinned inside the oversized sleeves, layers of fabric blocking my arms and hands from moving. Ben seizes this opportunity to kiss and tease my breasts and nipples, and I cry out and lift my chin in response to the desire that's filling my belly.

He moves his mouth lower across my body, his tongue tracing a pathway down the center of my stomach. With his free hand, he begins to stroke the inside of my thigh and gently pushes it open farther. I feel myself becoming completely exposed to him, and I want more. *So* much more. A moment later, his tongue and fingertips meet each other at the apex of my thighs, and I nearly explode with lust. I am wild with desire, panting with each flick of his tongue against me, his fingers teasing and sliding. I am calling his name, moaning as he plays, unable to keep my breath steady as a tremendous tension builds within me.

"If you don't stop...I'm going to..." I breathlessly warn him.

"You taste too fucking good to stop."

Another flick of his tongue followed by the thick pad of his thumb rubbing small circles against me sends me completely over the edge. My hips bridge against his mouth as my thighs shudder, and I scream out in sweet relief.

A few moments later, I open my eyes to see a hungry look on Ben's face. He caresses my hip and bites his teeth down gently on the raised bone there. He encircles my wrists and slowly pulls me up and over the top of him, carefully avoiding and protecting my ankle. His gaze travels leisurely over my semi-clothed body as I look down upon him.

"Shall we continue?" he asks, his voice deep and throaty, and I feel his groin shift underneath me. He reaches up to my face and runs his hand along the length of my jaw. He pauses at my mouth and then rubs his thumb across my lower lip. I part my lips and take his thumb in my mouth, closing my eyes and softly sucking.

"Christ. You're going to drive me wild with that mouth."

I smile and release his thumb, leaning down toward him. My exposed breasts press against his face as I slowly kiss his forehead. His hands grip my backside, his thumbs kneading into my soft flesh as he takes a nipple into his mouth and begins a gentle rhythm of soft biting and sucking. I am deliciously overwhelmed. I slide away from his chest, moving my hips back and down against him, over his underwear band and directly onto the head of his erect penis, still covered by the thin fabric of his briefs. I wiggle out of the robe altogether and toss it aside. Fully naked, I straddle Ben's pelvis and rub myself back and forth over his erection. He closes his eyes and tips his chin toward the ceiling, sinking his head back into the pillow. I lean over him and lay my bare chest against his abdomen, slowly licking and kissing, circling my tongue and hips in unison as I gradually work my way lower. When my mouth reaches the band of his underwear, I slide my hand inside, take hold of him at his base and release him directly into my waiting mouth.

He gasps and lifts his head off the bed, wild-eyed, mouth

open in ecstasy. His hips rise to meet my descending motion, his breath shuddering in waves. His hand raises and smoothes my hair that's cascading over the side of him. He gathers it in his palm and brings his hand to the side of my head, finding, and joining the steady rhythm I am using against him. He is extremely aroused, and I feel him grow even thicker in my mouth as I run my encircled fingers up and down the length of him.

"I need you to stop now," he says, breathless, eyes closed.

I slow and release him, coming to rest on top of his thighs.

"Or what?" I tease.

"Or *I* won't be able to stop."

I put my finger to my lips and look up toward the ceiling, pretending to give this idea deep consideration. Suddenly Ben takes hold of my upper arms and flips me onto my back. He's raised over me, his hair disheveled, an intense look in his eye.

"Hold that position," he commands.

I watch him walk across the room — his tight ass a sight to behold — and disappear into his closet. After a moment I can hear him frantically opening drawers and banging around. A few minutes later he reappears, slightly flustered, holding two silver foil packets.

"Two?" I say, bemused.

"Two," he nods, shyly. "It's been a while."

I sit up and reach my hand to him.

"Come over here," I say, beckoning him with my index finger.

He walks over to the edge of the bed, tosses the packets down and very slowly slides his briefs off. I catch my breath as his erection springs free, revealing the entire depth of his arousal. Fully naked, he leans toward me and kisses me deeply, his hands gently laying my body back down on the bed and securing my wrists above my head.

"Don't move your arms from that position," he instructs, bringing his hands down the sides of my neck and over the swell of my lifted breasts. He gently rolls my nipples between his thumbs and forefingers, and again, I gasp at the sensation. I want to touch his face, want to grab hold of the back of his neck and pull him closer to me. I move my arms down to reach for him, and he clucks his tongue at me and shakes his head. Rolling off to my side, he moves his hand to re-secure my arms above my head and leans his face down over me, kissing my mouth with a slow intensity. The feeling is overwhelming, and my back begins to arch, my hips rise in response to the rush of excitement developing deep within my belly. I can feel my orgasm building again.

Ben slides a hand between my breasts and then flattens it against my stomach, gliding down over my pelvic bone and cupping me. His fingers slip inside, and I beg – panting in whispers and moans – I beg for him. He quickly opens a foil packet and unrolls the condom over his length. I am desperate, impatient, as he takes hold and guides himself to me. Pressing hard between my legs, and then holding back. His breath is labored and erratic.

"Georgia," he mouths, the word a silent plea.

Before I can even reply, he thrusts himself fully into me. My eyes slowly close, my eyebrows pulling together, as I let this intensely satisfying sensation travel through my body. *Oh, God.* I am lost in him.

He lays his body against mine, and we move, desperate for one another, our hips fitting together in perfect design, achieving a rapid rhythm of push and pull, never breaking our union. I wind an arm around his neck, my hand twisting in his hair, as the other presses down his spine and over his thrusting ass. I never want this feeling to end.

"My God...you feel...so good," he says between staggered breaths.

My climax is building intensely, as are the sounds coming from my mouth.

Ben closes his eyes, clenches his jaw and moans as I push my hips against him. He increases the tempo of his movements, and as he draws back, I wrap my legs around his waist and simultaneously lose my mind. He moves faster, deeper, harder...and a second later I explode into orgasm. My thighs shudder violently, and I cry out Ben's name as my body becomes rigid. He groans loudly and a moment later finds his own release, shuddering over the top of me.

We lay entwined together afterward, our breathing steadying as our bodies slowly melt into each other. After some time, Ben rolls to my side and kisses me softly under my ear before coming up onto an elbow. I turn my head toward him, and he gently moves a lock of hair from my forehead — tucking it away safely behind my ear, and smoothing my skin with a fingertip. When our eyes meet, I smile and intertwine my hand with his. He leans down and kisses the back of my fingers, his lips resting an extra moment before he looks into my eyes.

Slowly and softly...he smiles.

CHAPTER THIRTY-THREE

GEORGIA

MORNING BRINGS THE SOFT SOUND of birdsong from somewhere in the distance. For the third time in three days I open my eyes to new surroundings, and it takes me a moment to remember where I actually am.

My cheek is resting on Ben's bicep. Our hands are joined together between our naked bodies. Even though it's a king-size bed, it feels like we are sandwiched together in a twin; legs and feet intertwined, bodies pushed tightly against one another. I'm hot, and I need to stretch. Rolling back toward my pillow, I slide my good foot backward across the bed and promptly meet a soft lump of resistance. I stop and then push against it again, trying to move whatever it is — probably a stray pillow — out of the way. Movement at my feet is not what I expect, and I lift my head quickly. Charlie exhales loudly and abruptly stands up. He looks over at me, perturbed, and brings his front paws forward and pushes his rear backward into the air, yawning as his tongue rolls out of his mouth. When he's finished, he jumps off the bed and trots lazily out of the room. I whisper goodbye to him and turn my head back toward the handsome man next to me. A quickening fills my stomach as I think about last night.

Ben's head is tilted toward me, and I use this quiet moment to study his flawless face, memorizing his features. His forehead is smooth and relaxed, the soft lines of expression barely visible under the mass of short, dark, disheveled hair, reminiscent of last night's pursuits. His thick eyebrows are unruly from sleep, and his lashes fan out from his lids, blanketing his eyes in rows of deep brown. I notice, perhaps for the first time, fine crow's feet at the corners of his eyes, the creases evidence of laughter...or pain. Flecks of gray at his temples and into his beard make me smile, and I want to run my fingers through his hair and bury my nose there, inhaling his welcoming, woodsy-spice scent.

But it's his lips that really liquefy me. I could stare at Ben's mouth forever. In profile, his mouth is alluring and sexy as hell – his lower lip thick and full – meeting the protrusion of his upper in a perfect union. I gaze at him and remember kissing those lips last night and how good it felt to have them on me. A small shiver runs down my spine.

I reach over and gingerly run the back of my fingers across his beard – thicker this morning – and down the side of his neck. I feel his pulse gently rising and falling under his stubble, and I sigh, letting myself imagine for a moment what it would be like to wake up like this every morning. It seems ludicrous to even think like this, and I chide myself for being silly. Sylvia's voice in my head reminds me I don't want to lose myself to any over-romanticized ideas. I need to think clearly and rationally.

Physical needs demand my attention, and I quietly push away the blankets and scoot over as quietly as possible. Sitting up on the edge of the bed, I marvel at how sore I am. I have forgotten this feeling altogether – it's been so long since I made love to anyone. Sure, I dated a couple of men after I filed for divorce but none of them ever produced much more in me than slight interest, and I'd never been one to sleep around. But now, looking down at my naked breasts, my nipples slightly swollen and deep red, I remember the feelings Ben aroused in me, and I can't deny my desire for him; the feeling between my legs aching even more.

I grab the crumpled robe from the end of the bed and throw it over my shoulders. The entrance to the bathroom is only a few feet away, so I hop over, as lightly as possible over the creaking wood floor, and grab onto the doorframe, pausing for a moment to look back at Ben. He's still asleep, lost in the realms of dreams and relaxation, so I quietly shut the door and turn on the shower. While the shower heats up, I use the restroom, wash my hands, and open the middle drawer of the long, double sink vanity to search for toothpaste. I find it and reach for Ben's toothbrush, suspended in the holder by the far sink. I hesitate for a moment before putting it into my mouth – would he be upset? I shrug and plunge it into my mouth, smiling to myself. Considering where his mouth had was last night, this hardly seems offensive.

I enter the shower and tilt my head back against the cascade of water, the steam making a cocoon around my body as the water sluices down my bare skin. I wash my hair with Ben's shampoo, the scent masculine and intoxicating, and use his chunky bar of soap, covering my body with suds and rinsing away the sweat from the night before. I tilt my head back in the shower and let the water fall over me again, closing my eyes against the sensation.

The feeling of a hand sliding around my waist jolts me upright, and my eyes spring open to see Ben standing before me. His hair is damp and tousled, his face shining with the sheen of water. He smiles down at me.

"Did you use my toothbrush, missy?" His forefinger lifts my chin.

I put my arms around his neck and press myself against him.

"Why don't you come down here and find out," I say, shifting my gaze from his smiling eyes down to his mouth.

His eyebrows raise and then lower a second later as he cups my chin and leans down to take my mouth with his. He tastes of mint and fresh air, and I breathe in as his kiss deepens and extends. He moves passionately against me, his mouth claiming mine, and I can feel his growing desire at my belly. Without hesitation, I balance on my stable foot, and carefully wrap my right thigh and leg around his hip, suspending my bad ankle behind him. With his strong hand holding the back of my head, he kisses me hard, running his other hand down my spine and over my bottom, grabbing hold of my lifted cheek. He cups the underside of my rear and squeezes hard. I moan into his mouth and suck on his tongue as he slowly works his hand along the lower contour of my rear, rubbing and massaging me as he inches closer between my legs. Moments later, I am bent over in front of him, one knee on the seat in the shower, hanging on as he takes me from behind.

Afterward, we stand together under the water, his arms wrapped around me, holding me tight to his chest. As we stand, leaning in toward one another, Ben strokes my wet hair and rests the side of his face against my forehead.

For some reason, this tenderness is so fulfilling that it makes me want to cry.

Ben moves like a professional in the kitchen, and I have to admit: I'm a little jealous.

He sets to work right away since we're both ravenous — having abandoned dinner the night before. He's chopping and dicing with a speed and accuracy I've only seen on episodes of *Chopped*. Green peppers, mushrooms, and tomatoes all lie in perfect rows on the cutting board, waiting to be used in the omelets he's preparing. He looks so handsome standing at the kitchen island, a dishtowel thrown over his shoulder, an apron slung loosely around his hips, and I can't help but admire him.

I am banished to a bar stool on the opposite side of the kitchen island, happily sipping my cup of coffee in one of Ben's flannel shirts and a pair of sweatpants. I swim in his clothes, but it doesn't bother me in the least. My clothes are being introduced to a real washing machine for the first time all weekend — and besides, Ben's shirt smells like him. The thought that it was recently on his body makes me feel like a teenager nursing a crush.

I offer to help him cook. "I can actually cook well," I explain, but he blatantly refuses my offer, citing reasons of the impending doctor appointment. At the mention of this, I suddenly realize I haven't heard anything more from Sylvia.

"Have you seen your phone lying around here?" I ask. "I just realized I haven't heard from my sister."

Ben grabs the towel from his shoulder and wipes his hands absentmindedly, looking around the kitchen counter to spot the phone.

"No, I haven't. Did you take it out of your backpack last night?"

"Oh shoot, no, I didn't. I was planning to charge it again when we arrived and then, for some reason..." I eye him playfully. "I became desperately distracted." He lifts his eyes from the cast iron pan he's carefully monitoring and smiles slyly at me.

I set my good foot down on the ground, pick up my crutches and turn toward the bedroom to grab the phone from my backpack.

"Do you have a phone charger in the bedroom?" I ask over my shoulder as I start down the hallway.

"Yeah, it's on the nightstand on the far side of the bed."

"I'm going to check on my clothes too. Don't eat without me!"

As I crutch past the back of the sofa, Charlie raises his head, sees me moving down the hallway, and leaps off the furniture, following me toward the bedroom.

I hear Ben's voice behind me. "Good boy, Charlie," he says, and my heart gives itself a tiny hug.

I find the phone inside my backpack, and even though I know it will be useless, I try to turn it on. Nothing happens, as expected, so I hop over to the nightstand, find the cord tucked near the base of the lamp and plug in the phone. I wait for half a second to confirm it's actually charging, and then head across the hall to check my laundry and toss the wet clothes into the dryer.

On my way back to the kitchen, I hear loud snapping and popping noises, and a moment later my nose detects the unmistakable scent of frying bacon. I nearly burst with happiness. I open my mouth to yell how much I love bacon, and then abruptly close it, my jaw snapping shut. Is that *singing?* I bring my crutches to a standstill and listen — my head turned slightly. There it is again: a few hums, a murmur and then a few words of an Aerosmith song.

I move my crutches with as much stealth as I'm able, and quietly creep down the hallway. From my vantage point, I see the barstools sitting at the outer edge of the island, and every few seconds Ben's hands cross into view. I can't yet see his face, but as I approach I hear the singing grow louder.

I come around the corner and stand still. Ben's back is to me in the center of the kitchen. He's leaning over the stove watching the bacon sputter, singing his heart out to the wooden spoon in his hand and slowly shuffling back and forth. He's a horrible dancer, and I have to slap my hand over my mouth to stifle my laughter as I watch him putting the moves on his cooking utensil. He's mid-chorus when he spins around, spoon raised high to his mouth, ready to really make the crowd go wild when he spots me and immediately chokes, launching into a coughing attack and throwing the spoon down on the counter as if it had jumped into his hand on its own volition.

I clap and yell, "Bravo!" in between laughs so large that my side actually hurts a little. After a few moments, and many sips of water to soothe his throat, Ben begins to laugh as well and finally, reluctantly, he bends at the waist for a quick bow.

"Never would've pegged you for an Aerosmith guy."

He looks at me sideways, and the corner of his mouth rises playfully.

"Ever hear *Love in an Elevator*?"

We both eat our breakfasts in record time. We don't speak much, our mouths constantly full of the delicious food he's made. Afterward, Ben gathers our plates and silverware and turns on the water at the sink.

"Oh no, you don't. You shopped, you cooked, so *I* get to clean." I'm smiling, but my tone is firm enough that he holds up his hands in surrender, and slowly backs out of the kitchen, eyes wide.

"I'll just go and gather everything I need for the cabin this week. Meet you back here in..." he checks his watch, "what time is your appointment again?"

"11:20," I say, leaning down to open the gleaming, stainless steel dishwasher.

"Okay," he says. "It's 9:30 now. We should leave here in about an hour then."

I nod and smile as he heads down the hallway. It's not lost on me how easy this feels — me in his kitchen, cleaning up after a shared meal, laughing and teasing one another — if I really think about it, I have to admit it's scary as hell. This is all so soon. I shouldn't be moving so quickly. I don't even know him, or he me, for that matter. And yet, I can't ignore the pounding in my heart when I look at him, the ache in my chest when he kisses me, or the undeniable physical attraction we share. I sigh and decide to focus on cleaning instead of analyzing.

It takes me longer to clean the kitchen than I'd like, but only being able to use one foot proves harder than I thought. After loading the dishwasher, scrubbing and seasoning the cast iron pots, and wiping down all of the counters, nearly an hour has passed. I dry my hands, push the hair out of my face, and head slowly back to the bedroom.

My dry clothes are folded, waiting at the end of the bed, and I smile at Ben's thoughtfulness. I'm still smiling as I crutch over to the nightstand and check the phone. A half-charged green battery icon appears, and I sit down on the bed to dial Sylvia. A moment later I hear the line begin to ring, and I say a small prayer, hoping Guthrie is okay.

"Hello?" Sylvia's voice is scratchy and distant.

"Sylvia? Is that you? It's me, hon. How are things?"

"Hi, Gia." She clears her throat away from the phone. "Sorry, sis, we got in really late last night, and I had a hard time sleeping. I'm sorry I didn't call."

"No worries. How's Guthrie? What happened?"

"He's at the clinic still. He had to have immediate surgery last night. His hind leg was broken, and his right hip was cracked. He had a lot of internal bleeding...the doctor wasn't sure he was going to make it. Still isn't." Her voice breaks and she begins to quietly cry. "Sorry...you know he's like my child. He was in so much pain. Every time I close my eyes I can hear his whimpering. If he doesn't make it, I don't know what I'm going to do."

My eyes fill with tears, and I tip my head up to hold them back.

"I'm so, so sorry, Sylv. My heart is breaking for you." I pause, trying to think of something positive. "At least he was able to make it through surgery, right? Let's just take it one step at a time. When will you know more?" I cough and wipe away the tears from my eyes with the sleeve of Ben's shirt.

"The doctor is supposed to call later this morning and let me know how he's doing. They have him sedated right now, so at least I know he's not in pain anymore. I just want to be there and see him, you know?" Her voice sounds very far away.

"Of course. I would feel the same way. I *do* feel the same way. I love that guy so much."

She doesn't reply.

"Hey, it's going to be okay. He's going to make it through this. I just know it. He's a young dog. He's strong and healthy...he's going to be fine." I try to sound reassuring.

I hear her sniff on the other end of the line.

"I really hope you're right, Georgia."

"Let's trust the professionals and just keep thinking positive thoughts, okay?"

"Ok..." She pauses and then begins again, her voice louder. "Shit, Gia! I totally forgot! Did you end up staying another night at the hotel? Did you see the doctor? How's your Jeep? Oh! I can send Scott to get you right away?"

Now it's my turn to pause. "Um, you know, it's all such a long, convoluted story that I don't even want to get into it right now. I'm fine. My Jeep is ok, I think. And I see the doctor shortly. In fact, I need to get going. We're leaving soon." Damn. I close my eyes and hunch my shoulders. Maybe she'll miss it?

"*We*?" Nope.

I'm quiet for a moment and then decide to play it casually, "Yeah, you know, um, Ben — the man who rescued me and helped me down the mountain after the bear encounter..."

"Bear *attack*," she corrects.

"Yes, *attack*. Anyway, he met me after breakfast yesterday and we...we kinda spent the day together."

"And apparently the night too." I can hear her smile, but I know she's being cautious.

"We can talk about all of that later," I push her off. "But, I don't know, Sylvia, there's something about him. I'm not sure what it is, or what to call it — this is all new for me. But my heart, it just feels really kinda *right*." I lower my voice and begin to whisper. "I'm getting butterflies just thinking about him."

"Oh, my. We will definitely need a bottle of wine and some girl time to discuss all of this."

"Yes, agreed. Ok, I have to go. Don't worry about coming to get me just yet. I will figure something out. Let me talk to you after I see the doctor, ok?" I shift on the bed. "I'm thinking about you and Guthrie."

"Thank you. I love you."

"Love you too. Call me on this number immediately if you hear anything more, okay?"

"Okay. And you call me when you hear from the doctor."

"I will."

I end the call and flip back to the main screen. A text message is waiting, and I assume it's just a late message from Sylvia. I open it with the intention of deleting it, but when I read the text, I immediately realize it's not meant for my eyes at all.

CHAPTER THIRTY-FOUR

GEORGIA

THE BACK OF MY JAW feels strangely electric as a wave of anxiety floods my bloodstream. My hands have lost circulation, and I feel light-headed. I blink several times. I have to read it again.

It would be a shame if something were to happen to her other ankle. Or to you. Walk away — I know about Charlotte.

The phone drops out of my hand, jerking the charger out of the wall as it falls to the floor. I sit on the edge of the bed and stare at the phone in disbelief. My arms wrap around my stomach, and I sit there, hugging myself. What the *hell*? Who is this from, and who is Charlotte?

I am torn and confused. Part of me wants to buy a bus ticket out of Bend immediately, and part of me wants to take the phone to Ben and demand answers, or drive straight to the police department for protection. As these thoughts swirl in my head, everything seems to settle down to this: I feel completely helpless, paralyzed with fear by the fact that a psychopath is clearly following me, and is now threatening Ben.

I can't move, and I am suddenly freezing. My teeth begin to actually chatter. Where is Ben? I slowly stand up – my knees feel like the blood has drained from them – and look out of the windows in the bedroom. I see the side of the barn and the back pasture but don't see any sign of him. I pick up my crutch and hop around the side of the bed toward the doorway.

"Almost ready?"

I shriek and lose my balance, nearly falling backward.

"Whoa! Georgia, are you okay?" He reaches his hands toward mine to help keep me from falling, but I instinctively recoil my arms. I am near tears, my blood thunderous in my body.

"What is it? Did you talk to Sylvia? Is her dog okay?" He moves toward me – his arms open and intending to wrap around me. I don't know what to do so I let him pull me close, let him comfort me. My facade shatters, and I immediately break down into tears and bury my face in his lightweight jacket.

"Hey now, shhh, it's okay. I'm sure everything is going to be all right." He smoothes the back of my hair and wraps his arms around me. For a split second, I felt completely safe and secure, and I want this feeling to last, so badly that I can taste it in my mouth. Ben makes me feel wanted. He makes me feel protected and cared for, and that feeling is like a drug to me. A drug I can't get enough of.

I know about Charlotte. I swallow hard and pull out of the embrace, ducking my head to avoid eye contact and turning back toward the bed.

"I need to get dressed," I say, barely managing the words.

Ben stands still a second too long. He knows there's something wrong.

"Do you want to talk about anything?"

"No, I'm fine. I just want to get this over with. I'll be out in just a minute." I still can't look at him. I pick up my clothes and head to the bathroom. As I cross onto the cold tile floor, I grab the door and close it behind me.

I don't even look back.

We leave the house in relative silence. I can tell he thinks I'm upset from talking to Sylvia and the news of Guthrie — I had quickly mentioned he'd undergone surgery and wasn't out of the woods yet — but I can also tell he's preoccupied with getting to the cabin and starting his work week. At breakfast, we'd decided he would drop me off at the appointment while he checked in with the Forest Service in Bend. Something about going over current fire sightings, I think. I was barely listening at the time, and to be honest, despite the ache in my heart, I'm looking forward to being alone for a bit.

The Scout's top is on, and the back is loaded with supplies — his backpack is filled with food and clothing, the rifle, some miscellaneous tools. I sit in the center of the bench seat with the blanket over my shoulders and lap. Even though the sky is a perfect blue, the air crisp and clean, I cannot seem to get warm.

He lays his hand on my thigh as we drive away. It's so hard not to break down and tell him everything. Ask him all the questions that keep running through my head. I feel so disillusioned. And ashamed. Ashamed I have allowed myself to think I knew this man, that I could trust my own instincts, that he was someone different, someone I might have real feelings for — for the first time in a long time. Now I just feel incredibly stupid. I allowed a romantic day and physical passion the ability to completely turn off my common sense. And now look where I stood. Completely screwed. I can't drive, and even if I could, my vehicle is apparently back in Sisters — or so I'm told, anyway — at this man's house that I barely know, who apparently has something possibly dangerous in his past with a woman named Charlotte. And to top the whole damn thing off, I will likely need surgery on my stupid ankle. How is it I seem to always get myself into these situations?

I look out of the window at the juniper trees flashing by and remember the promises I made to myself over a year ago: no matter what, I would always remember my value as a person. I would never allow anyone to frighten me, harm me, or threaten me. My relationships would be honest and open, or there wouldn't be a relationship at all. Nothing was worth risking my life for again.

I shake my head and look down at my lap. How could I have been so blind, again? I didn't even know Ben. A weekend together, that's all. My oxytocin levels must have been off the charts to have let down my guard so fast, and I'm embarrassed to think how quickly I allowed myself to become intimate. How quickly I disregarded his concerns about crossing boundaries with me. *What a fool I was.* He probably made up the entire story about his wife cheating on him. Maybe he's never even been ma—

"You alright over there?"

His question brings my inner tirade to a screeching halt, and I flinch at the intrusion of his voice.

"Sorry, I didn't mean to scare you," he says with a small chuckle. We look at each other, and his smile fades. He raises his eyebrows in concern, his eyes darting between me, and the road ahead. There's no mistake: I see genuine concern on his face.

I look at my lap and fiddle with the fringe on the blanket.

"Yeah, I'm fine. Just lost in thought I guess."

He reaches his hand to mine and pulls it toward him, kissing each of my knuckles and then bringing it to rest on the side of his cheek. Tears well in my eyes as I watch him. This affection seems so real, so authentic. My stomach is flipping over on itself with feelings for him, and yet my brain is screaming at me to run as fast, and as far as I can. I bite back the words I want to say, the questions I want to ask. A thin smile crosses my lips instead, and I turn to look out of the window again.

We arrive at the address on my referral sheet from the emergency department. A sign on the outside of the building reads *The Center - Orthopedic and Neurosurgical Care and Research*. I see another sign, this one a type of flag, mounted high on a pole near the entrance, *The Center - Taking Care Since 1954*.

"This looks like the right place," I say, looking down at my paperwork and then back at the building.

Ben pulls the Scout up to the entrance, parks, and shuts off the engine. He turns toward me, one arm resting on the steering wheel, the other stretched across the back of my seat. He stares directly into my eyes and his eyebrows pull together, his teeth playing against his lower lip.

"Can I tell you something?" he asks. I swallow hard and reluctantly nod. "I can tell you're upset about something – maybe it's about your sister..." He pauses, then drops his gaze to the seat. "But if it's not. If you're having regrets about last night." He finds my eyes again. "I know we moved fast, and I just want you to know that I...I don't ever do that kind of thing."

I look at him and frown.

"What I mean is, I haven't been with anyone in a very long time. I don't do random encounters or one-night stands. Call me old-fashioned...I don't know. I guess I just don't want to become numb to real experiences." My heart wrenches as he reaches for, and holds onto, my hand. "So, if you're feeling like you want to wrap things up here...I mean, I can't stop you, but just know that last night — well this whole weekend really — it's meant a lot to me. It's actually meant more than a lot to me. I've begun to really care about you, and I haven't felt this way in a very long time." He looks out the front window and then back to me. Is he — are those tears in his eyes?

He clears his voice and inhales deeply. "Anyway, it's after 11:15, better get inside for your appointment. Here, I can help get you situated." He turns to exit the Scout.

I finally find my voice.

"No!" I say, a little too harshly. "I mean, no thanks." I smile gently at him. "I think I've got this. You go and take care of your work, and I'll meet you back here afterward. Right?"

He sits back in his seat, resigned, and nods.

"Yep. I'll be here," he says, smiling thinly at me. I hesitate and then lean toward him, my hand reaching for his face. He meets me, covers my hand with his own, and he kisses me tenderly, but with intent. My heart explodes in my chest and a thick lump forms in my throat. He pulls away and then softly touches his lips to my forehead, his thumb trailing after.

"I'll see you soon," I say and make my way inside.

CHAPTER THIRTY-FIVE

GEORGIA

"SO, GEORGIA, THERE ARE THREE bones that make up the ankle joint. Forgive me: you may have already been over this in the ED on Saturday, so bear with me here. Essentially you have the tibia here, the fibula, and then the talus. The lower part of the tibia and fibula is called the malleolus, and then here you have the outer malleolus, called the lateral, and the inner, called the medial. You with me so far?"

Dr. Tipman is pointing out the locations of the bones on my good ankle as I sit on the examination table, trying my best not to be anxious. He's a quick talker — as though he's had too much caffeine, but I nod and do my best to follow everything he's telling me.

"When a break occurs somewhere in these bones, it might be one bone, or it might be multiple bones. And when that happens you have what's referred to as an ankle fracture — a broken ankle. Now, depending on the severity and the location of the breakage, the fracture may need surgical intervention to re-stabilize the ankle and allow the bones to grow back together. In your case, it's your..."

He wheels across the room on his stool, grabs the chart resting on the counter, and scoots back to me, flipping through the pages, his pen following the lines as he scans the reports.

"...In your case, it's your tibia that's fractured, inside the medial malleolus right at the connection of the talus." He flips to a blue tab in the chart, pulls up the pages, and turns the chart to show me my own x-rays. "See, here is the tibia and it extends down here to what is commonly called the 'ankle', the malleolus, and right here, just before the connection of your foot, see that line, that's the fracture." I stare at the x-ray, fascinated by my own orthopedic structure, forgetting for a moment that it's actually *my* ankle that's broken.

"So, it sounds like you may have rolled your ankle inward, along something hard, when you fell through the porch, is that right?" He's reading earlier reports in my chart, deftly clicking the end of his pen in a rapid-fire cadence. Maybe he *has* had too much caffeine.

I clear my voice. "Um, yeah, I think so. It's kind of hard for me to remember exactly what happened now. I was really scared, and I think I was kind of out of it."

He nods and looks up at me, his eyes wide. "It says here you encountered a bear at the top of Black Butte? We have some random reports of bears on the outskirts of town here, but I don't think I've ever met anyone that's come as close as you have. That must have been extremely frightening."

"Yeah, it was. I try not to think about it too much." I pause and then ask the question I've wanted to ask since the moment I met him: "So, do you think I'm going to need surgery?"

"Well..." he draws the word out like he's getting ready to break into song. "It looks like your ankle is not misaligned. It looks to be stable, and the surrounding ligaments appear to be swollen, but not compromised. Because the fracture is so low in the foot, and because the break is relatively small, I would say you are not a candidate for surgical intervention at this time." I release the breath I've been holding and feel my shoulders relax.

"My recommendation is to treat you with an immobilizing splint, follow you with periodic x-rays during the healing process, and then transition you to a removable brace – similar to what you are wearing now. You can expect at least six weeks of initial recovery time, followed by a course of physical therapy exercises to rehabilitate the ankle. But based on your level of activity and physical condition, I really don't foresee any complications. The most important thing is to keep any weight off your ankle until we have the x-ray evidence that gives us the green light." He snaps my chart closed, and the pen clicking resumes. "I'm afraid driving is out of your foreseeable future, and you'll be using those crutches for at least another month, or you could rotate between those and the knee walker." He pulls out his prescription pad from his coat pocket. "I can write you a prescription for the knee walker, and if you decide you'd like to give it a try, then you'll have the paperwork all set. I should also point out that you might find you feel more comfortable wearing an ankle brace for even up to a year after you recover, especially if you plan to return to hiking or other outdoor activities."

It's a lot to take in, and I'm basically stunned into silence. I try and focus on the simple takeaways: no surgery, a brace, six weeks and physical therapy.

We discuss pain management and Dr. Tipman writes me a prescription for some anti-inflammatory medication should I need it, to reduce the swelling in my ankle, and also to help relax my muscles. I tell him I'm actually doing fine using Motrin and really don't have much pain unless I set my foot down or try to directly move my ankle.

After I explain I don't live here, he gives me a referral to an orthopedic specialist in Salem, who also has a satellite office in

Silverton. He advises me to call as soon as I am able to get home. "It could take a while to get you in," he says.

Dr. Tipman gives his pen a few more parting clicks and then slides it into his chest pocket with a final pat of his hand. "Do you have any questions about your injury or the treatment plan?"

"No, I think you've covered everything I had questions about. Thank you for your time. I'm sorry I can't continue my care here; you've been very helpful."

After I check out at the front desk — more bills I'm not sure how I will pay — I scan the parking lot but don't see any sign of the Scout. I'm actually relieved to have a few minutes to myself, and I look around for a quiet place to relax.

Sitting as far away from the reception desk as possible, I pull Ben's phone out of my backpack and locate the business card Officer Roth — the *nice* one — gave me, and dial the number. The line begins to ring, and I notice my hands are trembling.

"Bend Police Department, how may I direct your call?"

"Hello, I'm trying to reach Officer Roth please." I'm trying to keep my voice low.

"Thank you, one moment." I hear the clicking of a keyboard. "Ma'am, Officer Roth is out of the office at the moment. Is there someone else that can help you, or would you like his voice mail?"

I consider this for a second and decide to just bite the bullet.

"I guess I could also speak to Officer Dickerson if he's available?"

"Thank you, one moment." More keyboard clicks. "All right I'll connect you now."

I'm placed on hold, classical music drifting in and out of the connection.

"Yeah, Dickerson," he answers. It sounds like he's smoked a pack a day since he was seven years old.

"Good morning, Officer, my na — "

"— First off, it's Lieutenant, and second, it's after one o'clock. I'd say we're due for a 'good afternoon', eh?"

I can't tell if he's being sarcastic or not.

"Sorry, Lieutenant. My name is Georgia Marks. You interviewed me yesterday at the hotel I was stay— "

"— Yeah. I remember you." His tone is definitely clipped now. "Tall. Brunette. Crutches. Questionable incident in your hotel roo— "

"— Yeah, that's me." It's my turn to interrupt. "Anyway, Lieutenant, the reason I'm calling is that something else has developed, and I need your help."

The line is quiet for a moment. I hear a door close, and then the creaking of a chair.

"What *kind* of development?" he asks followed by a heavy sigh.

"Well, this morning when I checked the cell phone I'm borrowing, there was a text message. And the text message was threatening to the person that owns the phone. It was also threatening toward me."

"All right. Two things: one, who's cell phone is it, and two, what did the message say?"

"The phone belongs to— "

"—Let me guess: Mr. Smokey the Bear?" He guffaws at his own joke.

I'm silent for a moment as I consider just how fed up I am with this jerk.

"Excuse me, sir," I say, my voice sickening sweet. "I am so sorry. We seem to have started off on the wrong foot — probably due to my ignorance. Do you mind if we start again? May I ask your first name please?"

Dickerson clears his throat. "My first name? It's Lieutenant, but if you're nice, you can call me Robert."

"Okay, great. Thank you, Lieutenant. Now I feel better. Hey, since I've got you on the line now, and I would really hate to waste your time, I'll get straight to the point." The sappy kindness immediately evaporates from my voice as I force my words across the line.

"Here's what's going to happen, *Robert*. You're going to take down the information that I give you now because it's your job, and you're going to investigate it because the decent citizens of this town pay your shitty-ass salary." I stand to my feet, my finger pointing in front of me like an arrow. "And if you ever take that condescending tone with me again, I will come down there and report you to your Captain so goddamn fast it will make your head spin. So, cut the bullshit, stop treating me like an ignorant child, and do your fucking job, *Bob*!"

I sit back down hard in my chair, my chest heaving. My mouth is bone dry. I look around the room — it's empty, but I notice a woman at the front desk staring; she quickly turns away when our eyes meet.

I can hear heavy breathing on the other end of the line. A moment passes, and then Dickerson speaks.

"Ma'am, I apologize for behavior that might have been offensive to you." His words are knives directed right at my heart. I picture his teeth chipping and breaking as he forces himself to speak. "Please, do continue."

I release a deep sigh. "Thank you, Lieutenant. Now, as I was saying, the phone belongs to Ben Harrison, the US *Forest Service Technician* you met yesterday. He's letting me borrow it because mine was lost at the top of Black Butte. I read the message because I've been trying to communicate with my sister, and I just assumed it was her. I didn't even look at the number. I just read the text." I take a deep breath. "Anyway, the message was clearly intended for Mr. Harrison. It said, '*It would be a shame if something happened to her other ankle. Or to you. Walk away...*'". I pause, leaving out the end of the message. I'm not going to give this egomaniac the satisfaction of possibly having dirt on Ben.

"So clearly the person that broke into my hotel room is the same person that sent the text message and, I believe, the same person that slashed my tires and vandalized my Jeep. This person is following me around, and I'm starting to worry that something really bad is going to happen." I look over my shoulder out the waiting room windows, scanning the parking lot for Ben.

"All right, Ms. Marks, can you tell me the number the text came from?"

"I think so. One second." I fumble around the phone, switching between the phone screen and the text message screen and relay the number to him. "Can you look that up?" I ask.

Dickerson sighs. "Yep, I can do that. It will take a little bit of time, but I can do it. I wouldn't get too excited though. Anyone that wants to send Be...er, Mr. Harrison, an anonymous text message could do so by purchasing a pre-paid cell phone. In that case, I can trace where the phone was purchased, but that's about it."

"Ok, well if you can look into it, at least we can see if anything shows up." I hesitate, trying to decide if I want to stir this hornet's nest any further.

"All right, Ms. Marks, well, if there's..."

Oh, what the hell.

"Actually, Lieutenant, there is something else you should know, and something I would really appreciate you looking into for me." I take a deep breath as a wave of anxiety spreads through me like wildfire. "About a year ago, I divorced my husband. He was a police officer in San Diego — a sergeant — his name is Mike Rutherford. He was a severe alcoholic and a very controlling person. He became obsessed with me and turned extremely abusive. He didn't want the divorce and fought it every step of the way. In all honesty, it feels like I barely escaped from him." My anxiety is throttling my nervous system, and it becomes hard to continue the conversation.

"Anyway, listen, I know this sounds crazy, but it has occurred to me that it might be Mike that is behind all of this. With your connections maybe you could do some quiet checking around? Maybe see where he's been this weekend, or if he's even still with the police force? Maybe he's moved to Alaska or something." I stop talking and begin practicing my breathing techniques, taking a full breath through my nose, letting my diaphragm rise, and slowly releasing it out my mouth for a count of ten. I glance up at the front desk to look for a clock and simultaneously remember they never have clocks in these places.

"This definitely lends a new perspective. I'll check the telephone number and see what I can find out in regard to Mr. Rutherford. Will you be in town much longer? Can I reach you on this cell phone?"

I have to admit, he's being very professional.

"Yes. I think so. Actually, I'm not exactly sure." I glance out the windows again and see Ben coming across the parking lot toward the front door. "Uh...I think you can reach me on this phone still. Listen, I'm sorry, but I need to hang up. Let me know what you find out."

I click the phone off and slide it into my backpack just as Ben walks through the door and up to the front desk. My heart does a small somersault when I look at him. I raise myself out of the chair, throw my backpack over my shoulders, and begin to make my way toward him. A second later, he turns and sees me; his face breaking into a smile that reaches his eyes as he walks over to meet me.

"Can I take your pack?" He extends his hand and then looks

down at my foot. "New brace eh? So..." His eyebrows rise in anticipation. "Does this mean no surgery then?"

I shrug. "I guess not. I get to wear this brace for a while and then transfer to a boot I think. The doctor gave me the name of an orthopedic office in Silverton to follow up with...since I won't be here." I let that sit between us.

Ben stops walking. I stop a step ahead of him and turn around, looking at him with a frown.

"You ok?"

"Uh, yeah. I guess I just didn't realize..." he shakes his head. "When are you planning on leaving then?"

"I'm not totally sure yet. Guthrie just had surgery, and they aren't sure he's actually going to make it. I told Sylvia not to worry about sending Scott to get me; they've obviously got other things on their plate right now."

"So, no one is coming to get you?"

We start walking again and exit the offices into the sunny parking lot. I squint my eyes against the full sun as I search for the Scout, spotting it and heading that direction.

"No, no one's coming. Well, not really. Well, actually I don't know. Look, do you mind if we get something to eat?" I quickly change the subject. "I'll pay. I just need some food in my stomach. It's been a long morning."

"Yeah, I think that should be ok." He checks his watch.

"Sorry. I totally forgot it was Monday. You have to get up to the butte today. Never mind. If it's okay though, can you take me back to your house on the way? I'll just sort out my Jeep from there and talk to my sister again from your house phone." I reach out my hand to grab the door handle on the Scout and Ben places his hand over mine, moving his body very close. I look up at his face, confused.

He leans forward and kisses me hard, placing his hand at the small of my back and pulling me tight against his hips. I resist his kiss, pulling backward and stiffening my lips. He persists and kisses me deeper, rubbing the small of my back with his thumb. I'm quickly losing any fight left in me; the world around me seems to be on mute. I feel my shoulders relax and my lips begin to respond to his, following his mouth as we hold onto each other. I let go of a crutch, and it crashes to the ground, the sound reverberating in the hollow aluminum. Before I know it, I'm throwing my arm around his neck and tangling my fingers in his hair. He makes a sound at the back of his throat, and slowly slides his tongue into my mouth, pushing against me with his chest and bending me backward against his hands. I am filled with a sudden and intense desire for him.

"Hey, buddy, I got kids here!" A man yells from nearby. We break apart roughly, and both look to the right. A man with two children is pushing a woman in a wheelchair across the parking lot next to us. The kids are smiling and looking at us with interest. The man looks exasperated, and the woman in the wheelchair looks downright pissed. Ben and I are frozen like the sailor kissing his girlfriend in the famous photograph. He looks down at me and smiles and then calls over to the man.

"Sorry about that. What can I say? I think I'm falling for this woman!" My mouth pops open, and I stare at Ben, who is cracking his full voltage smile, shrugging at the stranger. He turns to look at me, and a look of fear replaces his bright smile. He slowly stands me up and holds the sides of my face in his hands.

"Um, I did not mean for that to come out of my mouth. Yet," he says, sheepishly. "I meant what I said — I'm not taking it back — I just didn't mean to talk about any of that so soon. I'm sorry if I've made you feel uncomfortable. Please don't feel like you need to say anything back, ok?"

He doesn't wait for an answer. Instead, he just pulls my face up to meet his and plants a chaste kiss on my forehead, and then on my lips. I am utterly speechless. Four hours ago I would have been ecstatic, but now? Now, I'm stunned and in shock. My heart is pole-vaulting out of my chest, but my brain is padlocking the door and grabbing the shotgun.

He chuckles as he helps me into the Scout and closes the door behind me. We drive out of the parking lot in an awkward silence and Ben turns the radio on softly.

"So...you don't have a confirmed ride out of here yet, right?" Is he purposefully trying to change the subject?

I shrug and look out the window. "No."

"And you don't have a way to get your Jeep home yet, correct?"

"Correct."

"And you don't have a place to stay tonight?"

I'm beginning to feel like real hell now.

"That is also true."

"Ok, so why don't you stay at my house again tonight. You can make any phone calls you need. I don't have to stay at the cabin tonight. I can finish the rest of this afternoon and evening up there, and if you still want to leave tomorrow and can't get a ride, I'll drive you home myself. Sound ok?" He looks at me, a big smile across his face. I consider his proposal for a moment as we drive along the highway and come up on top of the overpass – the Three Sisters Mountains take up the entire windshield view.

God, it is so beautiful here.

I look over at Ben. His kind eyes seem genuine.

"Alright," I finally agree.

"Good. Now, let's go get something to eat."

CHAPTER THIRTY-SIX

GEORGIA

AFTER A QUICK STOP IN Sisters for food, Ben drops me off at his house and helps me get settled on the couch with Charlie. He's in a rush — giving me a quick kiss goodbye before speeding out of the door. As much as I want to talk about the text message and who Charlotte is, I know he needs to get to work, and I actually need some time alone to think.

I can't seem to get past the idea that the Ben I know, albeit only for a very short amount of time, could be someone with a questionable background. He seems like such a good, kind-hearted person — a truly honorable man. Such rare qualities in people these days. Maybe he's just too good to be true. As soon as this thought crosses my mind, I chortle at myself. How arrogant I am. My own history is definitely not the typical story, so why should I be suspicious of him? Who am I to be judgmental? I'm surprised by how quickly some of my old feelings of insecurity and alarm bubbles up. Maybe my boundaries do need a closer look after all.

In all fairness, we've barely talked about our pasts with each other. We seemed to focus mainly on my injury at first, and then the physical attraction between us. There really hasn't been time for much else. Is it like this for others? Do people fall for each other so fast and so completely that they push aside all rational thought and just let their emotions lead the way? I don't know...I just don't know. I haven't had much experience in this field, and honestly, having never had a serious, healthy relationship, I'm not sure I'm the best judge of one. I lean back and wish for the millionth time that my mom was still alive.

As I recline on the couch with Charlie next to me, I realize I really don't know much about Ben at all; his childhood, his relationship with his parents, where he grew up...how did we skip all of these normal getting-to-know-you questions? And yet, would someone who's untrustworthy, someone with something to hide — leave me alone in his house? I look around the living room, focusing on the drawers, the cupboards, and the cabinets. I think about his bedroom closet and what might be inside. I think about the staircase near the entryway and begin to wonder what's up there. I haven't even seen the second floor; my crutches make stairs an impossibility.

Almost immediately I start feeling sick to my stomach at my desire to be so covert. The actions I am imagining carrying out are behaviors that Mike perfected during our marriage. He always searched through all of my belongings, my drawers, my clothing even. I eventually stopped using a cell phone password because he always accused me of trying to be secretive. Items in my purse were always out of order, and when I was out with girlfriends, Mike would text me non-stop. He even began texting my girlfriends' husbands to confirm everyone was where they said they would be. It was like living in a maximum-security prison with a life sentence.

My breath shudders as I notice my palms have begun to sweat.

I'm distracted from my thoughts when Charlie's ears perk up.

He shifts his position on the couch, and his head turns toward the front door behind us.

I welcome the interference. "Oh, hey, what's up, boy?" I say, turning my head to follow his.

Through the panes of the front door, the midday sun has cast a shadow over the front porch, making the entryway inside the house, dark. The driveway in front of the porch is brightly lit by the sunshine bouncing off the pine and juniper trees in the pasture beyond. Nothing looks out of place.

I glance back to Charlie; he's still watching the front door. After a moment, I shrug and turn back to face the large living room windows overlooking the pasture on the west side. I lean my head back against the couch cushion and stare at the ceiling, wondering how I could ever have been so wrong about someone like Mike. How could I ever have been so ignorant? And why did I continue to stay for so long? I know the answers, of course. I'd been over all of this before – in therapy and support groups, but sometimes, like now, no matter how much I try to reassure myself that I'm safe, that no one is going to wake me up in the middle of the night and hurt me, sometimes a large part of me believes I am just lying to myself, that I will never truly be free of Mike.

And clearly, someone *is* following me. I can't ignore or explain it away any longer.

All of a sudden, Charlie bolts off the couch, his back feet launching a throw pillow behind him and over the back of the couch as he runs to the front door, barking like mad.

"Charlie!" I yell and turn my head simultaneously to follow him.

There's no mistake: I hear footsteps on the wooden porch, but I don't see anyone through the panes of glass. The hair on Charlie's back is raised down the center of his spine, and he's barking so ferociously at the door that I can't hear anything anymore.

My heart is racing in my chest as I hold my breath. I am

frozen in place. Where's Ben's phone? Where's the house phone? My eyes dart around the living room and over into the kitchen. I don't see anything.

Suddenly I see a shadow cross the porch to the door. My throat is dry, and all I can hear is the whooshing of blood in my ears. Through the glass in the front door, I see the silhouette of what looks like a large man standing outside. My heart stops. I have no voice.

The man reaches toward the front door, his hand on the doorknob. I can't hear anything over Charlie's barking, but I do feel a sudden surge of adrenalin in my body, and I reach forward for my crutches as a possible means of defending myself against this intruder. The latch presses down, and the door begins to open. The man's foot comes through the door as I get to my feet, holding the narrow end of the crutch like a baseball bat, the larger end extending past my shoulder.

Charlie immediately stops barking and instead, begins to quickly wag his tail back and forth. The man reaches an arm inside and a large hand pets Charlie on the head and under the chin.

"Hey there, buddy. No need to bark like that at me. There ya go now. Ok, step back now and let me in."

The man's voice sounds scratchy and rough. I watch as he comes inside and shuts the door softly behind him. He has on a large cowboy hat, pulled low over his eyes and he's focused on Charlie, looking down, so I can't see his face. I remain standing behind the couch, my arms rigid.

The man finally stands up straight, raises his head and sees me standing in the living room. He jumps backward a step and yells something incomprehensible as he flinches, his arm flying up in front of his face and knocking his hat off the back of his head.

"Who the hell are you?" he yells.

I remain standing — my crutch cocked like a bat. The man's exaggerated movements startle Charlie, and he trots over and jumps up on the couch, standing next to me.

"Who the hell are *you?*" I say, eyes narrowed.

The man turns around slowly and picks up his hat from the floor, holding it over his chest.

"Ma'am, my name is Matt. I'm a friend of the owner." He removes his hat from his chest and stands with his feet slightly farther apart. "You best have an explanation as to how you got in here, else I'll be calling the police straight away," he says, pointing a bony finger at me.

I stand stock still, but begin to lower my crutch.

"My name is Georgia Marks. I'm a friend of Ben's..." I pause, recognition settling in. "Wait. Did you say your name is Matt? What are you doing here?" I ask, still suspicious.

"Yes, it's Matt. I've known Ben for many years now. I come by during the week and tend to the place while he's up on the butte. How do you know him?" He's still eyeing me with suspicion.

"He told me about you, Matt. I'm sorry." My shoulders relax, and I lower the crutch. "Ben and I met on Friday. I was hiking up there, on the butte, and a bear came along. There was a bit of an encounter. Anyway, Ben showed up and scared the bear off and now..." I raise my crutch to him. "Now, I've grown kinda reliant upon him." A thin smile crosses my lips. Charlie nudges my hand and pushes his body against my leg as I absentmindedly pet him.

Matt's posture relaxes, and he takes a few more steps toward me, stuffing a key into his pocket.

"It's nice to meet you, Ms. Marks. I do apologize if I frightened you, comin' in the door the way I did just now." His thumb hitches over his shoulder, pointing behind him. "I have a key to the house, and Mr. Harrison, well, he lets me take care of Charlie and the other animals here on the place. I was just comin' in to check on his food and water and turn lights on. Gets dark early over here and Mr. Harrison don't like to come home to a dark house..." He trails off, his gaze dropping down to the floor.

"It's nice to meet you as well, Matt." I begin to work my way around the couch toward him. "I'm sorry for my sluggishness here. I've just seen the doctor, and it appears I have a broken ankle." I manage out into the open floor space and put my crutches under my arms. "Pleased to meet you, sir." I extend my hand as I reach him. Matt shakes my hand with a strong grip.

"So, Ms. Marks..."

"Please call me Georgia." I smile at him, and he returns it, his face craggy and weathered.

"All right. Ms. Georgia. If you will be staying, I'll just leave the lights and Charlie in your care then. I have some work I need to do in the barn, so if you need anything, I'll be around for a while." He begins to turn toward the door.

"Uh, well, are you sure you can't stay for just a few minutes? I'd love some company for a bit. Could I offer you a cup of coffee? Tea maybe?" I motion to the kitchen, a smile on my face. I don't feel like being alone anymore, and Matt seems like a perfectly nice person to visit with.

Matt works his hands around the brim of his hat, and I can tell he's contemplating his reply.

"Well, I suppose that would be all right."

I smile at Matt, genuinely pleased he's decided to stay.

We make our way to the kitchen, and I bring out two cups, set up the coffee maker and take a seat next to Matt at the island while we wait. We sit in an awkward silence for a moment before I think of something to say.

"So Ben said you helped him build this house?" I ask, relieved to bring a subject to life.

"Yes, Ma'am." Matt's eyes brighten at the memory. "I use to live across the way, and when Mr. Harrison bought the property, he came to talk to me about fencing part of it off for pasture. He was real gentlemanly, and I immediately took a liking to him."

Matt's eyes are the lightest blue I've ever seen. As he speaks they seem to sparkle and dance at the memories he brings forth.

"After a few months, I realized he was the only one 'a doing any work over here so I came over and asked him if he'd like some help. Well, he was real proud, but he accepted my help with small projects, and after a bit, the small work led to bigger work, and before I knew it, I was working full time for Mr. Harrison. This was just grand for me 'cause I'm a retired contractor." His eyes lower for a moment. "Even though I don't wanna be. Anyway, I enjoyed the opportunity to work."

I nod, listening to his story and encouraging him to go on.

"About the time we finished building the house here, my wife...well, she passed away. Cancer. She didn't suffer much. By the time the doc found it, it was too far along. Anyway, after Mary passed, well, Mr. Harrison found he needed someone to help keep his animals and house cared for while he was on the butte. He asked me if I would do the job, and I was glad for it. We've been working together ever since." Matt's fingers interlace, and he rubs his thumbs together. "He's been an awful good friend to me, Ms. Georgia, an awful good friend."

"Yes, I can tell that's true, Matt." I lay my hand over his briefly. "I'm very sorry to hear about your wife."

The aroma of coffee fills the kitchen as the pot bubbles and sputters; the delicious black liquid begins to fill the carafe, fogging up the glass.

"Ben has been a good friend to me as well," I say. I look down at the counter in front of me. "He saved my life up there. When that bear came along...well, I don't know what I would have done if he hadn't shown up. And he's been helping me ever since. Did he tell you my Jeep was vandalized up there?" I raise my eyebrows at him.

"Yes ma'am, he did. Told me what happened and that I was to expect Les Schwab to be dropping it by. Asked me to have 'em put it in the barn." He shakes his head. "What a shame. Good looking rig, too."

"Yeah. I really love that Jeep." I rise out of my seat to get our coffees poured, continuing the conversation over my shoulder. "It was the first real purchase I made on my own after my divorce." I glance at Matt. "Cream? Sugar?" Even though I already know how he will answer.

"Black is fine, ma'am."

I pour our coffees and slide them gently across the counter, and then crutch back around and take my seat.

"If you don't mind me asking, how long were you and your wife married?" I hope I'm not offending him by my question.

"I don't mind at all. She's my favorite thing in the world to talk about." He grins at me. "Mary and I were married for fifty-five wonderful years. And I can say, without a doubt, those years were the best of my life." His watery eyes mist over, and for a moment I regret asking him about his wife. "She was the loveliest person I ever knew. Woulda given you anything you asked for. Always looking out for everyone else. Shoot, she was so busy carin' 'bout others she didn't realize she was even sick 'till it was too late. I do miss that woman somethin' fierce."

I smile at him, empathy flooding through me.

"A love like that is something to be cherished, indeed," I say.

Matt sips his coffee and looks at me intently.

"You mentioned you're divorced. I'm real sorry. If you don't mind me askin', how come that happened?"

I study him for a moment, considering his question. What did I have to hide?

"Well." I sigh. "Unfortunately, the man I married developed a problem with alcohol. A big problem. And when he was drinking, he became physically abusive and very controlling." I take a deep breath and let it out slowly. "After a while, I realized not only could I not help him, but I needed to help myself." I stare at the countertop. "I had to leave – escape, really. And once I was away from him, I finally realized what I'd been living with and worked up enough guts to file for divorce. It's been about a year now." I begin to chew on the side of my lip before shrugging and taking another sip of coffee.

"I am very sorry to hear that, Ms. Georgia. No one should live in that kinda fear."

We drink our coffees in silence for a moment. Only the sound of Charlie's nails against the plank wood floor can be heard as he walks toward the entryway and flops down in front of the door.

I turn toward Matt, appraising him.

"Matt, can I ask you a question?"

"Sure thing, Ms. Georgia," he replies, bringing the cup to his mouth.

I wasn't sure where to begin so I decide to just be blunt.

"Talking about fears has brought up something that's really been bothering me. You've known Ben a long time, right?"

"Yes, ma'am."

"Do you know anything about a woman named Charlotte?'

Matt's eyes widen, and his eyebrows push upward in surprise, his forehead breaking out in an accordion of wrinkles. Before he can answer, I interject, holding my hands out in front of me. "I don't need to know the details of anything. I just...well, someone sent me a strange message, saying they 'knew about Charlotte.' I was just wondering who she is, and why someone would bring her up," I explain.

Matt sets his coffee mug down on the counter and begins to push away from the island.

"Have you asked Mr. Harrison that question?" Matt sets his jaw, and I can tell I've definitely crossed the line. "Ma'am," he begins, picking up his hat and beginning to stand. "It's not my place to talk about Mr. Harrison's business. But I will say this: Benjamin Harrison is the kindest, most decent, trustworthy man I've ever know. I'd trust him with my life, and I know a lotta others that feel the same. He's been through a hellava lot these past few years. Taken a lot of flack from folks that didn't even know him. I'm not sure how you came to know about Charlotte, but I can tell you this: Ben didn't hurt that girl, no matter what folks might gossip 'bout."

He stands up from his chair. "Thank you kindly for the coffee, Ms. Georgia. I need to get to work, so I think I'll be off." He gives me a slight bow and begins to turn away. I can hear Charlie scramble to his feet around the corner.

"One second, please," I hurriedly say. What does he mean *Ben didn't hurt that girl*? What, like *hurt her* hurt her. Like a broken heart, or hurt her like friggin' killed her? I might have phrased my question impolitely, but now I'm *really* wondering who Charlotte is.

Matt turns back to face me, and I snap out of my thoughts. "Please forgive me," I say. "I was out of line asking you about Ben like that. I am truly sorry. I've been under a lot of stress these last few days, and when that strange message came through, well, I just didn't know what to think. I'm sorry if I've made you uncomfortable. It's my fault completely." I stand up and move toward him. "Here, let me walk you to the door at least."

Matt stands still for a moment and appraises me. "Thank you." He sighs. "I'm sorry if I was harsh. It's just I don't like nobody talking bad 'bout Mr. Harrison. I know him like most don't, and I can assure you, he's a good man."

"I believe you, Matt. I happen to think he's a good man too. I just think someone isn't too happy that he and I are friends." I pause and rub the side of my temple. "Thank you for sharing some coffee with me. I really enjoyed getting to know you, and I hope we can visit together another time. Maybe when Ben is here?" I stick my hand out to him. He grabs it up in his leathery palm and shakes it strongly before walking to the door. I follow behind him, the clunk...clunk...clunk of my crutches echoes around us.

"I'd be honored to visit with you and Mr. Harrison." He moves to open the door, and then turns back, staring at me intently. "I've know him a long time, and I can say this without a doubt: Ben would never lay a hand on you, or any other woman. He's pure gentleman through and through. Like Mary woulda said, *if he gives you his heart, you can count on it every day 'a your life.*"

For some reason, this sentiment fills me with guilt, and a ball begins to form in my stomach. I've been so dumb. I should have just told Ben about the text right away.

I nod in reply, the sting of tears sits behind my eyes, and I don't want to break down.

I smile and wave at Matt as he steps off the porch and wanders in a slow gait toward the barn. Charlie follows him halfway down the driveway, then stops to scratch behind his ear.

"C'mon, Charlie," I call, slapping my hands against my thighs.

Charlie's ears perk up, and he jumps to his feet, trotting back to me with his tongue hanging out.

CHAPTER THIRTY-SEVEN

GEORGIA

AFTER MATT LEAVES, I SETTLE in on the couch with Ben's cell phone and a book about cabins from the coffee table. Knowing someone is around on the property helps ease my anxiety about whomever it is that's following me, and I try to relax for a little while. Charlie relaxes too. He jumps up on the far end of the couch, turns around a few times, and sniffs the leather before curling up. It's not long before his soft snores fill the room.

I thumb through the glossy pages of the book, flipping through the gorgeous scenes of cabin interiors and exteriors. The displays on the pages are inviting and seductive; page after page of beautiful kitchens, living rooms, fireplaces, and front doors. Much of what I see in the book is reflected in Ben's home, and I wonder if he bought it for inspiration.

My head sinks farther into the soft throw pillows; my eyes becoming heavy. Charlie's soft snoring is hypnotizing, and I let the book fall open across my chest as I tell myself I'm only going to rest my eyes for a moment.

The ringtone of Ben's cell phone breaks through the solitude, and I sit up violently — the book falling off my chest and thudding to the floor as I reach for the phone on the coffee table.

"Hello?" My voice is scratchy and faint.

"Yeah, Ms. Marks? This is Dickerson, Bend P.D."

I clear my throat and rub my eyes, "Yes, I'm here."

"I have some information for you if you have a moment." His voice booms over the connection, and I have to hold the phone away from my ear.

"Yes, Lieutenant, please go ahead."

"All right, so I had Officer Roth check the telephone number on that text message. It's registered to a solicitation database — a company that sells computer antivirus software. They've been in business for a while." I hear the sound of rustling papers. "Looks like they are based out of California — the San Jose area."

"But the number was a local prefix, correct?"

"Yeah, local prefix, but that's how a lot of these solicitors get folks to actually answer the phone — they use a local number. At first look, most people think it's a friend, or a nearby relative calling since it's familiar."

"So is there any way to go further with that? Would it be possible to find out who sent the text?"

"Mmm, probably not but I'm gonna have Roth see if he can find out anything more just in case. In my opinion, whoever sent the text probably knew someone at the company — or paid a random employee there — to send it. Does Mr...uh, one minute, uh, here it is. Does Mr. Harrison know anyone from that prefix?"

"No," I quickly lie, closing my eyes against the guilt. *He's never even seen the text.*

"All right." He clears his throat, "I also checked on your ex-husband, and according to the San Diego P.D., he's still on the force down there. Had a promotion. Doing well with the team. HR says he's been on duty all weekend, so I think it's pretty safe to say he's not the guy here."

I sigh and crinkle my forehead. I was so sure it was him. The cellphone stalking fits his pattern so well, and vandalism is something he's definitely not above. Combine that with the slander on the mirror, and it's a dead ringer for Mike.

Except that it's not him. And if it's not, then I really have no idea at all who it could be.

"Okay," I sigh. "Back to square one then, I guess. Thank you for the call. I really appreciate your work on this. I'm still in town, so if you or Officer Roth need to reach me, I am still available on this number."

"Will do. You have a nice evening now, Ma'am."

I set the phone down on the coffee table and note the time: 6:05 p.m. I wonder what time Ben will be back and what he has in the fridge that I can possibly prepare for us. I scoot Charlie off the end of the couch just as the phone rings again. Glancing at the caller ID, I answer right away.

"Sylvia! How are you? How's Guthrie?"

"Hey, Georgia," she says, her voice flat. "He's not doing well.

"Oh no, what happened?"

"He vomited during the surgery and basically sucked food and fluid into his lungs. He's being treated for *aspiration pneumonia.* The doctor says it can be life-threatening. He says we should..." She's silent for a moment. When she speaks again, I can tell she's breaking down. "The doctor says we need to be prepared. If he survives, we are most likely looking at intensive care for several days, beyond the extent of his injuries."

I make up my mind in a heartbeat.

"I'm coming home, Sylvia. I'm coming home as fast I can get out of here, okay? I don't know how yet, but I'm coming. You go — be with Guthrie and Scott, and I'll call you when I'm on the road."

I'm already standing up and preparing to gather my things. "I love you, and I'll see you soon."

"I love you too, Gia." Her voice is barely audible.

I hang up the phone, drop it onto the couch and set off for the bedroom to gather my things.

"Lu-cy, I'm ho-ome."

"Back here," I call. I want to laugh at his impersonation, but I'm too focused on getting to Sylvia.

I look up from packing my things as Ben walks through the doorway, the huge grin on his face changing to concern immediately.

"Hey, everything okay?"

He puts a hand on my shoulder and looks into my eyes. He's carrying his radio and a binder full of paperwork.

"No, not really," I say. "I just got off the phone with my sister. It's her dog again. He's developed something serious, a pneumonia something or other – I'm not exactly sure what – but the vet says they need to be prepared."

"Prepared for what?"

I stop packing and stare at him for a second. A moment later his face drops. I nod and then focus on my backpack in front of me.

"I need to be with her. I know it sounds ridiculous, it's only a dog after all, but he's a lot more than that to her, and I know she needs me."

I look up at Ben, and my eyes fill with tears. I'm embarrassed, but I can't help it.

"Sorry. I know this is silly, but I need to go."

Ben gathers me in his arms and pulls me against his chest, rubbing my back and whispering into my hair.

"It's going to be okay, Georgia. If you need to get to the valley right away, I can take you." He pulls away, holding my shoulders and looking down at me intently. “Let me make a quick phone call to Annie, and pack a few things, okay?”

I nod, and he brings me close again for a second; kissing the top of my head before leaving to find the phone. I gather my backpack and join him in the kitchen, watching and listening to him talk to Annie, as they make plans for the cabin for the next few days. He hangs up and turns to me.

“That’s settled. Now I just need to talk to the guy that helps me out here,” he says, looking over his shoulder.

“You mean Matt? We met earlier. He’s really nice. Although he scared the crap out of me.”

“He did? Probably my fault. I forgot to tell you he would be by today.”

He pulls his baseball cap down farther and heads toward the front door. Charlie follows behind him, his tail wagging back and forth.

“I’ll be back in a second then. Would you mind grabbing some food we can take with us? There should be stuff in the fridge and pantry,” he calls from the entryway.

I gather some apples and bananas and grab a bag of crackers and a box of chips, as well as a collapsible cooler. Everything goes into the cooler, and I toss in some freezer packs on top, zip it shut and sling it over my shoulder. I’m at the entryway when Ben comes back inside.

“Here, let me help you with that,” he says, reaching for the bags on my body.

“Thanks. Are you ready?”

“Yep. All set to go. Matt is going to take care of the house and cattle for me, and Annie has a replacement to cover the cabin for the next two days.” He tucks a stray curl of hair behind my ear and places his hand alongside my cheek. “It’s going to be okay. We’ll get you home quickly.”

I smile hesitantly at him and whisper my thanks. He leans down and kisses me softly on the lips and then helps me outside.

When we reach the Scout in the driveway, I lay my crutches across the back floor, and Ben tucks our bags and the cooler behind the seat.

"Did you bring the cell phone?" he asks.

"Yeah. It's in my pack. I should probably keep that up front with me though just in case she calls again."

He hands me the phone as well as the blanket, even though the evening is still warm from the sunny day. I scoot along the bench seat, so I can be next to him as we drive. I want to be close to him. As close as I can get.

Traffic is light as we drive along the highway, the soft hum of the radio playing in the background. Neither of us speaks. I feel like we are each in a comfortable silence. I've decided I'm not that concerned about who Charlotte is compared to how much I care about Ben. More than one person has willingly vouched for his character — people that don't know me and don't seem to have any reason to lie. My gut is telling me Ben is someone I should be running toward, not away from, and right now I feel safe. In fact, I'm a little glad we're leaving. It feels good to put some distance between me, and the strange events that have occurred here.

As we pass by Suttle Lake, I peer out of Ben's side of the Scout. The gorgeous blue water shimmers against the fading light. A few boats and canoes head toward shorelines, and the lights from the lodges cast soft glows, flickering through the trees. As we climb higher, I see small ribbons of smoke wafting up into the air as evening campfires begin.

We begin to climb in elevation, making our way to the summit of the pass. As we round a sharp corner, we meet a line of cars coming in our direction — all of them following behind a slow-moving RV. My eyes carelessly drift past each vehicle, and then suddenly I see it. I whip my head around to look behind us as the white Jeep idles by. I grab hold of Ben's forearm and squeeze tightly.

"My Jeep! It's still in your barn!"

He smiles down at me, placing his hand over mine.

"I know. It's okay, baby. We'll figure out a way to get it back to you."

I just stare at him. How does he have this ability to put my mind at ease so instantaneously? A moment later, I relax my grip on his arm, and he takes my hand in his, slowly moving his thumb against my palm. I pull our joined hands to my mouth and kiss his knuckles one by one. He keeps his eyes on the road, but I see a small smile appear on his lips; it begins to curve upward toward his earlobe, his handsome beard standing at attention as his face moves with the smile.

"I am so lucky to know you," I say. Nothing else seems to matter anymore. Not his past or how I'm going to get my Jeep home, or my ankle, or my recovery...none of it. Sitting in this vehicle next to this incredible man that's holding my hand as he drives me through the mountains...this is what matters.

I squeeze his hand and rest my head on his shoulder. A moment later I feel him press a kiss into my hair and I smile to myself, the gentle rocking of the Scout lulling me into total relaxation. I silently mull over the words that have been dancing around the edges of my heart for the last twenty-four hours:

I think I'm falling in love.

CHAPTER THIRTY-EIGHT

GEORGIA

IT'S WELL AFTER 8 P.M. when Ben wakes me up for directions. I sit up straight, pull the blanket off my body, and blink several times as I look around.

We're just passing the Oregon Garden outside of Silverton. The large, carved wooden sign is visible under the soft glow of the architectural lights above it.

"Just keep going straight until you get to the first intersection," I say, stifling a yawn. I'm still tired. The Ibuprofen I'm taking seems to make me sleepy all the time.

Not surprisingly, Silverton has little traffic this time of night, and we drive right to Sylvia and Scott's house. I realize I've forgotten to let her know I was on my way as we pull up to an empty driveway and a dark house. I find my keys in my backpack and reach for my crutches. Ben comes around and helps me down from the Scout, the cooler bag over his shoulder and his heavy flannel shirt hanging over his forearm.

He follows me as I make my way to the front of the house, holding open the farmhouse screen door as I put my key in the deadbolt and push the door open. I flip the light switch, and the overhead light illuminates the small entryway.

"The kitchen is just through there," I say, pointing across the living room to our left. "If you want to put the cooler down? I'm just going to use the restroom, and I'll be right back." I turn on lamps, balancing my crutches under my armpits, as I go through the house and down the narrow hallway to the bathroom.

A moment later I meet Ben in the living room. He's seated by the fireplace, looking through a photo album my sister keeps near the hearth.

"These are really great photographs," he says. "I recognize some of these places."

"Thank you." I feel a small flush creep up my cheeks.

"Did you take these?"

"Um, yeah...they aren't very good though. It's just something I play around with. Sylvia likes to keep them all in one place."

"Did you have formal training? I mean, it's only my non-professional opinion, but these pictures are really amazing." Ben flips backward through the album. "Like this one..." He holds up the album showing me a recent photo I took in the Columbia Gorge, Multnomah Falls in the background.

"Thank you. I had a great hike that day," I say and then quickly take a breath. "So, can I offer you something to drink? Are you hungry at all?"

He puts the album down and walks over to me, sliding his hands around my waist. His touch makes my knees feel more than a little bit weak. How does he have this crazy effect on me?

"Are you trying to change the subject?" he asks, seductively looking at me from under his eyelashes. My stomach is full of butterflies, and I really want to kiss him.

"No, not at all," I say, my gaze drifting to his lower lip.

He leans in and kisses me lazily before pulling away to look me square in the face.

"Ok...maybe a little bit. Yes." I smirk back at him and slide my hand behind his neck as I pull him back to me. He kisses me again, this time longer and deeper. I feel his breath against my upper lip as he tugs at my mouth. He slides his lips along the curve of my jaw and bites softly at my earlobe; a wave of goosebumps ripples down my arms.

"So do we have the house to ourselves?" he murmurs, sliding both hands down the sides of my hips. My breath hitches in my throat.

"Mmm hmm."

My chin tips toward the ceiling, my eyes close, and my mind is clearing all conscious thought. He catches my mouth roughly with his as he wraps his arms around my waist and lifts me off the ground, holding me against his body and kissing me as he walks into the kitchen. When we reach the counter, he sets me down and presses me against it. I feel the cool tile against the small of my back, his arms encircle me in a strong embrace, and the smell of his warm skin envelops me. I return his kiss forcefully; it feels so good to be close to him again, so perfectly right.

The kitchen is dark, illuminated only by the soft glow of the living room lamps. Ben's face is a shadow in front of me, his body moving against mine in the dark. He breaks from my mouth and runs his lips along the length of my neck, nipping gently as he makes his way to my shoulder. With one hand, he unbuttons his own flannel shirt that I'm wearing over the top of my hiking clothes and pushes the soft fabric over my shoulder. He presses his mouth to the exposed skin at my collarbone and slides his tongue to my shoulder, his beard providing friction along the way, while his hand reaches under my shirt and cups my breast. He runs his thumb over the top of my nipple and slides his hand down the length of my torso, wrapping around to the small of my back and firmly pulling me toward the warmth between his legs. I lean my head back, exposing my throat to his mouth as my breath gathers in ragged gasps. He breaks contact for a split second, and I watch as he pulls a foil packet from the front pocket of his jeans. He tosses it on the counter beside me and gives me his full attention once more, replacing one hand at my back to hold me in place while his other moves down my torso, this time around to the front of my leggings. He guides his fingers under my waistband and firmly pushes my pants downward. Still kissing me slow and deep, he repeats this movement on the other side, and soon my leggings are stretched horizontally across my upper thighs. My fingers seek out the button fly on his jeans, and I hurriedly begin to pull it open while he slides the back of his hand up the inside of my thigh, stopping at the thin fabric of my underwear. He pauses and presses the heel of his hand flat against the skin just below my belly, his other hand bracing me from behind. My breathing intensifies as his fingertips slowly begin to inch downward beneath the lace of my underwear. I feel his hand behind me grip my rear as he pulls me toward his reaching hand, and I moan softly into his mouth as he intertwines his tongue with mine and simultaneously pushes his fingers inside. I let my weight drop against him, panting in his mouth as he brings my pulse higher.

"More," I breathlessly beg.

In one fluid movement, he withdraws his hand from my underwear, rips the thin fabric down to the level of my leggings and lifts me up onto the counter — the tile a shock to my bare skin. I lean back on my elbows, raise my hips and let him continue to remove my clothing. I watch as he shoves his jeans down, his tight-fitting boxer briefs stalling around his protruding erection. I sit up, reach inside his fly and free him from his shorts, as I situate my ankle alongside his hip and hitch it behind his back, pulling him closer to me as my hips rock forward, and up. Ben lowers himself before me and kisses each knee softly before pulling away and glancing up at me. His wicked smile makes my heart skip a beat before he lowers his head again, kissing and softly biting his way down from my knee and up the inside of my thigh. His beard rubs against my smooth skin as he uses his tongue to find his way higher. I am squirming on the countertop, unable to withstand the anticipation. When he reaches his target, the sensation is too great, and I cry out in pleasure, my head dropping backward. He gently pushes my legs farther apart with his hands as his tongue works relentlessly. My hips rise to meet his mouth, and he moans loudly as he continues to lick and suck in my most sensitive region. I can't take any more, and my thighs begin to shake uncontrollably, my breathing wild and loud.

"Ah, please!" I shout, my heart racing.

"Please what?" His calm voice is husky and deep.

"Please make love to me," I whisper fiercely.

I open my eyes as he quickly pulls away, slips off his briefs and stands before me. The dim light from the living room touches the edges of his muscles, showcasing every aspect of his beautiful form. He draws closer, and I touch his skin, trailing my finger down through the hair below his belly, following the contours of his hip and along his pelvis. I want him desperately, and he knows it. He's enjoying this. He's resting his hands on my thighs, his thumbs working in slow circles as he watches me, a seductive, dangerous smile on his lips. I hold his gaze as I travel my hand lower down his body, slowly encircling my fingers around him and taking hold. His lips part slightly, and his breathing increases steadily. He is looking at me intensely now, and he gradually lowers his head down toward my mouth. I'm waiting for him, and as his lips touch mine, I shift my weight on the counter, pushing myself closer. He is almost touching me, and I can feel the heat of him between my legs. He kisses me hard and fast, leaving me breathless as a deep ache spirals upward from my belly and travels through my body. I wrap my arms around his neck, and he pulls my hips up and off the counter, settling me down on the searing heat of his head. He holds me there, suspended for a moment, as he kisses me deeper, groaning into my mouth. I pull away and gasp for breath; the intensity between us increasing by the second. He sets me back down on the counter and grabs the condom packet, quickly ripping it open between his teeth, taking the latex and rolling it down his length. A second later he takes hold of my hips and lifts me up and onto his erection, groaning fiercely as he pushes himself fully into me.

It's too much for me, and a few minutes later I am screaming in ecstasy as I climax around him. I hold onto his neck as my hips rise with his powerful thrusts, his breath ragged as he continuously pushes and withdraws. A moment later he reaches his own orgasm, shouting against the side of my neck as his body quivers over me.

We both slowly melt into each other, relaxing and regaining our breath, and after a few minutes, Ben releases me. I run my fingers through his hair and over his broad shoulders, hugging him and resting my face against his skin.

When our pulses return to normal, he cups my bottom and walks with me, my naked legs still wrapped around his waist, out of the kitchen and down the hallway to my bedroom at the far end of the house. He gently lays me on top of my bed and releases me, his arms locked in extension on either side of me as he gazes down at me.

"I'm going to get our clothes from the kitchen. Don't go anywhere, okay?"

I can see him grinning at me in the soft light from the hallway, and I lazily smile at him. My heart is so full of love that my eyes begin to sting, and I know tears aren't far away.

A moment later he returns, his pants unbuttoned and hanging open at his waist, his shirt slung over his naked shoulder, the small bundle of my clothing in his outstretched hand.

"Where would you like these?"

I sit up and hold my hand up to stop him. "I'd like to never see those clothes again," I joke as he tosses the clothing on the floor.

Ten minutes later I am wearing a clean tank top and a pair of grey yoga pants as we lie together in my bed, my head tucked safely and securely in the crook of Ben's arm. We're both exhausted, and it's not long before I hear soft snoring as his chest rises and falls against me.

It's the most wonderful sound I've ever heard.

The next morning I wake to the sound of the garbage truck banging the trashcans around outside, and I open my eyes to the soft morning light filtering through the window. Ben's face is turned away from me. I smile tenderly as I recall the night before, nestling my face against his chest and closing my eyes in peace as his torso softly rises and falls with each breath.

Remembering why I came home early, I lift my head and listen for any sound of Sylvia or Scott in the house. I can't hear any movement or sounds of people; the house is silent. I wonder if Sylvia has tried to call Ben's cell phone, and as I lie in bed, I try to remember where I put my backpack when we came into the house. I sit up and quietly scoot over toward the edge of the bed, preparing to slip out without disturbing Ben. A slight movement behind me tells me I'm too late, and a moment later a warm hand slides over the edge of my hip and lightly presses into my skin. A soft kiss to my exposed shoulder blade follows, and I reach behind me and slide my palm along his cheek, holding his face for a moment.

"Good morning," he says, nuzzling the back of my neck with his nose, his beard tickling my skin.

"Mmm, I'm beginning to feel very spoiled, waking up to you every morning."

"I'm okay with that." He nips at my earlobe and whispers into my ear, "If you become too self-indulgent though, I'll have to discipline you." He slides the hand on my hip lower and pats me firmly. I'm immediately aroused, and I lean back against him and guide his hand around to the front of my pants.

Holding him exactly where I want him.

"So, where is everyone?" Ben asks as I finish cracking the eggs into the pan on the stove.

I shrug. "I'm not sure. That reminds me though: will you take a look in the living room and see if you can find my backpack and your phone? I'm wondering if Sylvia has tried to call that number."

He walks through the doorway and disappears into the living room, leaving me to finish making our breakfast. I push the bread down in the toaster and wipe my hands on the towel near the stove, glancing at the eggs to make sure they aren't sticking. I decide to see if Sylvia has any basil in the refrigerator and turn to rummage through it. I am bent over, opening up one of the lower drawers of the fridge when I hear Ben's voice behind me.

"When were you going to tell me about these messages, Georgia?"

I shut the drawer and slowly straighten up, my hand resting on the open refrigerator door. I turn to face him.

"What do you mean?" I whisper.

"What do I mean?" he repeats back, louder. "I mean I pick up my phone, open it up, and there are three text messages." He holds the phone out in front of him, the screen facing me. "One of these is from Sylvia, and the other two are from someone I don't know, but obviously *should*!" His face looks hard, and I notice his jaw clench.

"The other *two*?"

He ignores my question, flips the phone back around toward himself, and begins reading.

"'*It would be a shame if something were to happen to her other ankle...or to you.*'" He looks up from the phone to my face — shock and disbelief written all over him. He takes a deep breath and continues, "'*You think you can keep her safe? Think again, Harrison.*'"

My stomach falls as I hear this new threat, and tightness begins to cinch my lungs.

"Do you know who this is?" he asks. It's a question, but it feels like an accusation.

"Do *I*? No! Do you? It's your phone, do you recognize the number?"

He's pacing back and forth now. "Of course I don't! Why didn't you tell me about this? This first message was almost two days ago! You've been in danger, and I didn't even know. I've left you alone for Christ's sake!" he says, slamming his hand down on the countertop, and I flinch. "Georgia," his voice is lower now. "Georgia, don't you see? You could have been hurt, and it would have been my fault. Why didn't you tell me?"

I slam the refrigerator door and turn to face him, my arms crossed against my chest.

"Oh, I don't know, Ben. I guess I've had a lot on my mind! Let's see: a broken ankle, a vandalized Jeep, a trashed hotel room, falling in love with you, my sister's dog is nearly killed, and then I get a threatening text on your cell phone! Oh, and let's not forget I was almost eaten by a wild animal! I guess I've just been a little distracted."

"You could have at least told me about it! I could have unknowingly put you in a very dangerous situ— Wait. Did you just say you're falling in love with me?" In a flash, his face changes from angry to soft and boyish. He sets the phone on the counter and takes a few steps toward me, his eyes bright.

"That's what I said." I'm still pissed, my arms crossed in front of me.

He reaches for my shoulders and holds me. He's staring at me, but I drop my gaze to the floor.

"Georgia," he whispers, "don't you realize? I care very much about what happens to you. If you are in danger, I want...I NEED to know."

I step out of his embrace and raise my eyes from the ground to look directly at him.

"Who's Charlotte?"

CHAPTER THIRTY-NINE

GEORGIA

BEN'S BODY STIFFENS AS HE stares at me, all traces of happiness vanishing from his face. He drops his hands from me and takes a step back. He won't look at me.

"Ben?"

When he answers, his voice is so faint I can barely hear him. "She...she was someone I couldn't protect."

"What? What do you mean? Look, the same person that knows about my injury knows about you and Charlotte."

He silently shakes his head.

"Who is she?"

All of the sudden I smell something burning, and whip my head around to the stove behind me. Wisps of smoke curl up from the edges of the pan of eggs I have completely forgotten about.

"Shit!" I yell and pull the pan off the burner, fanning the smoke away and shutting the heat off.

"Here..." Ben mumbles as he reaches for the window, opening it wide. The cool morning air rushes in and stirs the smoke-filled room. I grab the dishtowel hanging off the oven handle and begin fanning the air toward the window. Just then the cell phone begins to ring. We both freeze in our places and look toward it. He reaches for it and glances at the screen before bringing it immediately to his ear.

"Yeah," he says, matter-of-factly into the phone. "Hi, yes, this is Ben," his tone softens noticeably, "Yes, it's nice to talk to you too. Yes, she's right here. Just a moment." He hands the phone to me. "It's your sister."

"Hello? Where are you? Is Guth okay?" I ask, watching Ben walk out of the kitchen.

"Hi, sis. I'm at Scott's parents' house. He's doing a little better. He's still got fluid in his lungs, and he's being treated with antibiotics, but he's awake, and he's comfortable. The doctor says he's making progress. Are you at home?"

"Yeah, we got in around 9:30 last night."

"How'd you get the Jeep back?"

It's hard to talk to her right now with my mind focused on Ben and Charlotte. I want to get off the phone with her, but I don't want to be insensitive either. "The Jeep is still in Sisters...at Ben's house. He drove me here last night. Did you guys spend the night there?"

"Ben drove you home?" I can tell from her voice that she's grinning. "Anyway, no, Scott and I were at the hospital until about 8:30, and then we just grabbed burgers and stayed at his parents'. It was easier since they live so much closer."

"Are you coming home or going back to the hospital?"

"I'm still here, but I'm going into the office in a minute though. I plan to check back at the hospital after work. You wanna meet up there?"

"Definitely. Just give me a call..." I glance toward the hallway for a sign of Ben. "Maybe call the house? I think I'll be here all day."

"Okay, hon. So glad you're home." She pauses and then

quietly adds, "Thanks so much for coming. It really means the world to me."

I smile into the phone. "No problem at all. Keeping my fingers crossed for Guth. Talk to you soon."

I hold onto the phone for a moment after we hang up, staring down at it in my palm. I set it aside on the counter and grab my other crutch, making my way into the living room.

Ben is standing near the fireplace, looking out of the window. I can't see his face. As I enter the room, he turns toward me.

"Okay if we talk?" I ask.

He stares at me. After a moment he nods and sits down on the footstool. I take a seat next to him on the hearth and suck in a huge breath.

"I need to know who Charlotte is and what happened between you two. I know it's none of my business, but based on the crazy things that have happened over the past four days, I think it's best if I have all the information."

I look at him, waiting for his response. He's staring at the floor, his forearms resting across the tops of his knees. He glances sideways at me — anguish painted across his face. He inhales deeply and then begins.

"While I was teaching at the college, I had a student in one of my classes — Charlotte. I was also her academic advisor." Ben pauses and swallows hard. "After some time working with her, I learned she came from a horrible situation at home. She'd been sexually abused for most of her childhood and had been moved into foster care sometime during her sixth-grade year. Fortunately, by the time she entered middle school, an alert teacher saw potential in her and channeled her into the right classes — kind of took her under her wing, so to speak. Incredibly, she graduated with a high GPA and was able to secure a scholarship to COCC. I became her advisor when she entered the Forest

Resource Technology program. She wanted her Associates' degree and had plans to go on to University after that."

I nod at him, listening and encouraging him to continue.

"She finished her first year in good standing, and then in her second year, she had some setbacks. I don't know if it was childhood issues that resurfaced or if it was a relationship that went bad...I don't know. All I know is she didn't finish her second year — she dropped out."

I notice Ben begin to rub his knuckles and fidget with his fingers. I've never seen him act like this before.

"Go on," I say.

He glances up at me for a second and then focuses on his hands. "When school started again in the fall, she began showing up in my office during advising hours. At first, we just talked; I encouraged her to return to school, tried to get her interested in the program again. She never really talked about what had caused her to drop out; she said she just ran into some *issues*. I didn't think it was my place to ask for details." Ben takes a deep breath and grips the back of his neck. He looks up at me and begins to chew on the side of his lip.

"What is it?" I ask softly. He's quiet for a long moment.

"This is really hard to verbalize," he finally says.

"Take your time. It's okay." I reach over and rest my hand on his knee for a moment. He looks at me sideways, staring into my eyes for a second, and then focuses on the room behind me as he starts to speak again.

"About the time Charlotte showed up again, I found out my wife was having the affair. I don't know exactly how it all happened, but shortly after she said she wanted a divorce, well, Charlotte and I began an intimate relationship."

He won't look at me. He just keeps staring straight ahead. His voice is so quiet that I can barely hear him. He looks so ashamed and embarrassed.

"She was twenty years old. We dated for about six months. She told me she loved me, but I could never reciprocate the feeling. I just couldn't do it. My heart was broken. My wife was in love with another man. I think I was just numb. I don't know? Maybe it was the rebound, maybe it was her age — maybe it was that I really had no idea what was going on with me emotionally. Whatever the reason, I just couldn't give her the kind of commitment she wanted — the kind she needed."

"She began accusing me of wanting to get back together with my wife, which I'm sure was true, I just couldn't admit it. She started picking fights and doing really odd things: showing up at my campus office drunk, making big scenes in front of faculty and students. She even began leaving odd messages on my phone, and then when we would go out together, she would cry a lot and scream at me about how much she loved me and how I couldn't love her back. It started to cause a real problem at work, and I knew I had to end it. I was already taking a huge risk by having a relationship with a former student, let alone one that was clearly becoming very unstable."

Ben suddenly stands up and walks over to the window, his back to me. He stands there for a moment, his hands in his pockets, unmoving. And then he drops his head forward. When he speaks again, I don't even recognize his voice.

"I ended the relationship. I ended it, and it destroyed her." His voice cracks and his shoulders fold forward. I hurriedly get up and crutch my way over to him.

"Ben," I say, gently pressing my hand in the center of his back, "Ben, it's not your fault. She clearly wasn't well."

He turns suddenly to face me, his eyes red, tears pooling at the corners of his lashes.

"That's just it. It *was* my fault!"

"No, Ben, you didn't do anything to her, you — "

"— She took her own life, Georgia! She killed herself. She overdosed on pain medication and alcohol, and she fucking died."

I stare at him, speechless and stunned.

"Oh my God," I whisper.

"She used meds I had in my kit," he says. "I did it. I killed that girl. And Mark Flint, the doctor you saw in the hospital? He was the doc on call that night. He took her in and pronounced her. I killed her, and Mark knows it."

"No. You can't think that way. You didn't kill her, Ben. It was a horrible accident."

I'm insistent, but I can tell he's not hearing me. I shake my head at the floor and then look back up at him. One arm is crossed solidly against his chest, and his other hand curls against his mouth; his body is armor against these memories — memories I've demanded he talk about. I feel sick to my stomach.

He drops his gaze to the ground and begins to whisper something. I have to step closer to hear him.

"I'm sorry?"

He throws his arms down at his side and looks me straight in the eye.

"She was pregnant!" he says so loudly it makes me jump.

The tears that he's held in check suddenly drop like cement blocks across his cheeks. I don't know what to say. I stand in silence, my hand across my mouth in horror. Anger and sadness radiate so passionately from his eyes. I feel it burning my face.

"The baby...*my* baby..." He turns back to the window, the glare of the sun reflecting off the saline in his eyes. "There was nothing they could do."

"Oh God." I sit down hard on the nearest chair and sink into it, my head reeling and my stomach nauseous. I can't think straight. Nothing makes sense, and worst of all, Ben has shut down. He won't look at me. He just stares out of the window. I can't stop replaying in my mind the words he's said. I can't grasp the hell he's been through, the pain he's experienced. But most of all, I can't ignore the fact that it's me that has brought this tragedy back to the surface for him. Through me, someone has found and exposed this raw nerve. I've forced him to excavate this terrible event all over again.

It's all my fault.

"I am so sorry, Ben," I whisper, imploring him to look at me. He won't. When he finally speaks again, his voice is terse, quick, and direct.

"So whoever it is that is sending these messages wants to make a point. It's someone that either knew her, was somehow involved with the school, or read the news here and has done some investigating. Either way, it's really fucking evil."

My mind is spinning.

"I had no idea. Please believe me, Ben, I would never have asked you to tell me. In fact, I wasn't even going to ask you...but then you saw the messages, and then...I just...I mean, the hotel room and the messages...I thought I needed to know what happened."

"Well, now you know," he says to the window.

I stand back up and reach out to him.

"Ben?"

He slowly turns his body toward mine and looks at me, despair clouds his features, and his dark eyes look black, filled with sadness and anger. The Ben I recognize is nowhere to be found. His glance travels past me and over the room, his eyes landing on the coffee table to my right. He reaches down and scoops his car keys off a magazine and heads toward the front door. He opens the door and is halfway through it before he stops and looks back over his shoulder.

"I need some air."

The screen door slams behind him and a moment later I hear the Scout start up and accelerate down the road. I sit, stunned, in the middle of the living room — unable to move from my chair. All sound slowly fades as my mind works to make sense of what's just happened.

Somewhere in the distance, I make out the slow *plip-plop, plip-plip plop,* of the kitchen faucet as it drips into the scorched pan.

<<<<>>>>

You have finished reading *LOST in the RIGHT DIRECTION*. I hope you have enjoyed Ben and Georgia's story so far. The sequel, *LOST and FOUND*, is releasing soon, so don't go away.

If you have a moment, please help other readers find this book by leaving an honest review online. Reviews are one of the most powerful ways to help authors reach new readers, and I would be so grateful if you would consider leaving a review at one or more of the following sites:

Amazon
Barnes and Noble
Goodreads
iBooks
Kobo

AFTERWORD

AUTHOR'S NOTES

The cabin shown on the cover of this novel is the actual structure that stood atop Black Butte from approximately 1979 until the time it was condemned and burned on November 29, 2016.

Although I hiked Black Butte several years before I began writing this novel, I unfortunately failed to take photographs of the cabin or the fire lookout tower at that time. I began writing this story in early November 2016, and it was always my intention to hike the butte again, take photographs of the cabin, and finalize the descriptive details of it as accurately as possible. Discovering the structure had been destroyed before I could see it again was a terrible surprise.

Fortunately, I discovered that a good friend had hiked the butte prior to the burning and had captured photographs of the cabin. It is with his express permission and generosity that this image appears on the cover. Thank you to Tom Hoffert for supplying this picture.

To the best of my ability, from both personal experience and extensive research of the area, nearly all locations in this novel are real and are described as accurately as possible. Characters in the novel (with the exception of Sylvia – see Acknowledgments) and the events that occur within, however, are complete works of fiction and are not based on real events or people, either living or deceased.

It may be of interest to know that the blankets referenced in Ben's vehicle and home are based on real products provided by the company Sackcloth and Ashes. Sackcloth and Ashes have an incredible mission: *"For every blanket you purchase, we give a blanket to your local homeless shelter."* I have personally purchased several of their blankets for myself – and as gifts – and can say without a doubt that they truly are wonderful products. For more information please visit www.sackclothandashes.com, or look for their stunning Instagram feed online.

And finally, for more information about visiting central Oregon please visit:

www.visitcentraloregon.com.

ALSO BY MEGAN CARR

Thank you for reading *LOST in the RIGHT DIRECTION*, the first book in my Pacific Northwest Love Story series.

Want to know when I release new books? The best way to find out about pre-sales, special early release pricing, and advanced reader copies, is by joining my *5-minute newsletter* email list. Every month you will receive news about novels I am working on as well as music, food, exercise, podcasts, and products I can't live without.

As a special thank you for trusting me with your email address, I will send you a free copy of the first chapter of *LOST and FOUND, A Pacific Northwest Love Story, Book Two.*

Here's how to sign up:

http://eepurl.com/deRUg1

ACKNOWLEDGMENTS

I am so thankful for the very special people in my life who helped me bring this story to life.

Thanks to my mother, Kathleen Cornell, who read my manuscripts faster than the speed of light and cheered me on from the very beginning. Thank you mom, for fostering my love of reading at a young age, and encouraging me to write this story even when I thought I could not.

I am so grateful for my "number one fan" and co-conspirator in all things books and movies: my mother-in-law, Carolyn Carr. Thank you for patiently reading every chapter as quickly as I could edit them, for proofreading, and for serving as a sounding board. Without your constant support throughout this process, I would never have made it this far.

My appreciation to my aunt, Nancy DiBella, who read my early manuscripts and provided invaluable support and encouragement. Thank you for your honesty, your willingness to give these books a try, and for your never-ending positivity in my life. Your devotion to Ben and Georgia's story has meant the absolute world to me.

To my first reader, my early-morning gym cohort, and the funniest lady around: Tracie Hall. I love you, girl. Thank you for making me — and countless others — smile every single day.

Without the professional editing services of Claire Allmendinger of Bare Naked Words, this story would most certainly be unreadable. Thank you, Claire, for your extra sharp eye, your knowledge of all things grammar, and your enviable English wit. One day I will make it across the pond and look you up.

No one has had more patience with me than my cover designer, Renee Barratt. Renee's attention to detail, organization, and ability to keep from strangling me after each requested change is a profound testament to her professionalism. Thank you for working late, night after night, to produce such a gorgeous cover.

My sister, Chelsea Lipson, and I joke about sharing the same brain. We finish each other's sentences and know what the other is thinking before a word is ever said. Although we often fought — as sisters growing up tend to do — we developed an unbreakable bond that has seen us through good times and bad. None of the characters in this book are based on real people...except Sylvia. Sylvia's personality is based on my sister Chelsea, and she's one of my favorites in the book. Thank you, Chelsea, for always being there. I love you to pieces.

And finally, to my husband Brian and our children, who buckled up and endured this rollercoaster ride with me. Thank you for accepting the theme park our house became during this process, and for your love and patience with me every single day. You are my world and I love each of you dearly.

ABOUT THE AUTHOR

Megan Carr is an emerging author of romance and romantic suspense. *LOST in the RIGHT DIRECTION* is Megan's debut novel.

facebook.com/megancarrauthor

twitter.com/megancarrauthor

instagram.com/megancarrauthor

Made in the USA
Las Vegas, NV
12 January 2023

65479407R00184